PRAISE FOR ˊ

'Ashenbrooke was a gripping   ˌı delved into the past of a small American   ̣ı by a dark and mysterious entity. Recommende   ̣vers of horror novels which focus on psychological aspe ̣ ̣s of the genre, along with some occasional gore.' - BookishBeyond.com

'A smart and beautifully written ghost story. I loved it.'

'It had a 'stranger things' vibe. Highly recommend.'

'The story in itself is enthralling, but I would say the real merit of this book is its ability to touch subconscious dreamlike states and bring our own ghosts for a visit.'

'The literate person's supernatural novel.'

'I didn't want to put this book down. The story has lots of twists and turns which kept me hooked. Light hearted moments mixed with a deep understanding of human nature, which unexpectedly struck me. There are not many books I would want to re-read, but this is one of them!'

'Beautifully written, probably the Quentin Tarantino of ghost stories.'

ASHENBROOKE

Robin Styles

ISBN: 9798799587758

PROLOGUE: AWAKENING

As I cross the cobbled square leaves fly up behind me, whipped into the air as my feet fall. I imagine that to the old men who populate the benches of the square it must appear that I have a red and yellow slipstream behind me as the leaves intermingle in my wake; the sort of slipstream a superhero might have in an eighties movie when he had to run really fast to save an old lady from getting hit by a bus. I like that these men might have this impression of me and so I run faster, stir up more leaves, and begin to zig-zag as I pass the clock tower, swirling the leaves in ever more exciting patterns.

- I am late old men. There is crime to stop, innocent people to save, wrongs to right!
- There is no reason to rush. You cannot change things. But you can sit here. Enjoy the falling of the autumn leaves. There is comfort in watching time pass.
- No, I still understand urgency! I must put the world to rights – I must hurry!
- Ah, the folly of youth.

...and I'm already past them, huddled together around their chess sets. Their long campaigns last months, years even. And whilst they fight, drink their coffee, and shoot the breeze, they keep an ever watchful eye on us all from their vantage point here at the centre of Ashenbrooke. These men keep the scorebook of this town; who fought when, who lost, and who won. Between them they store the history of us all. And from time to time they crack open a volume, mull it over, voice their thoughts, and write comments in the margins.

I would be more surprised to see one of them missing from their sacred position here than I would to wake up and find the stone statues of old generals on horseback that border the square had all rode away in the night. As I run towards the gate in the eastern wall, I see my father's old friend Hank sitting at the table nearest the gate.

- Slow down Charlie! You'll break a leg!
- Just try and stop me!
- Don't tempt me son!

...and I'm already past him, through the gate, down the steps, and running down the tree lined path towards the library. I am fast, I am on point. There is air in my feet and breath in my lungs. Damn, I just cannot be stopped today. I see the Library through the trees; a formidable old building. Red Brick. Ivy creeping along the sides. Without a doubt it is a building that looks the part.

I run up the path, hands in my pocket, fumbling with my pass. I take it out, swipe and the doors open. I made it. I'm here. I'm fine.

- You're late Charlie!

He is not wrong but I find Mr Brayman's exclamation an unhealthy dose of reality so early in the morning. Once inside I remove my coat, pull my name badge from my bag and find my keys, whilst also attempting to concoct a suitable excuse for my boss.

- I'm really sorry Mr B but it's that damn clock. It has me all turned around. It's been broken for months now and nobody can even be bothered to fix it. And I have a pretty great internal sense of time but I'm serious; If you walk home after work and the clock tower says its 6pm and then you get in and the news says its 7pm but your watch says 6.30pm it's bound to have repercussions. It leads to problems, one of which is tardiness. It's a civic matter really, I was even thinking of starting a petition...

Is he buying it? He might be buying it...Mr Brayman is a fair man, a man of values, he'll appreciate this.

- I'm going to stop you right there Charlie. Because there is only one clock that matters and that is the clock right behind the reception desk over there. You see it? The one that says 10.15am. From now on that's your only clock. And you know that Saturday morning shift nobody wants this week? Guess what? You just earned it kiddo.

I retract my last statement. Mr Brayman is a dick.

He wanders off towards his office and I take my seat next to Susie at Reception.

- Clocks? You went with Clocks as an excuse? Why not stick with something simple, like you were late taking your brother to school? Or your boiler packed up?
- Because, Suze, they're too easy. I like a little inventiveness. And besides, I am worried about this clock thing. What has happened to this town? They can't even fix one clock?
- Every town has a broken clock or two Charles. It's the rules. They add character.
- Yeah, but most towns have ones that work too. I'm going to do something about it. And don't call me Charles.
- Well...Start your darn petition then. I'll sign it for one.
- Okay, well...maybe I will.
- Fine then.
- Fine.

She flicks an elastic band at me. I bat it out the air with a ruler.

- Have we even had one customer yet today?
- You know we haven't.

As you may have guessed, this is not the hardest job in the world. Suze and I man the reception desk here at Ashenbrooke Library and assist the seven or possibly eight customers to grace our building every day. There is really no reason for Mr Brayman to have us both working on the same day other than the fact that I think he just likes the company. That's the real reason I will now be working on a Saturday morning because I think he can hold this place down by himself. Mr Brayman, James to his friends, is one of the few men I know that I would use the word 'ruddy' to describe. His thick red hair and full beard, coupled with a taste for plaid shirts gives him an appearance of a man who should live in a cabin far away from the world. But instead, he has chosen this library as the setting for his solitude. Rather than chop wood in the open air, he devises filling systems for the ample collection of books this library has amassed over the years, he chats to the regulars, and he strolls the catacombs (the name given to the basement level of this building where books are stored like remnants of another age). As I'm sure the old men at the centre of town would be happy to inform you, in the year since his wife passed away Mr B has not often been seen far from this place.

It is strange but I have felt the pull of this place too; the quiet sense of permanence in the walls. It was designed by Teddy Ashenbrooke III and has the appearance of his own private study. Great oak bookcases line the walls from floor to ceiling, books huddling together on every shelf. I've often had the feeling that it is the combined strength of these books that really keeps the building standing, that all of the words in the vast ocean of books here have fused together over the years and formed a kind of web that holds the place together. I can't believe it has been just over a year since I returned from college and Mr B gave me this job...

Susie's elbow pokes me in the side suddenly, stirring me from my reverie.

- Don't look now but I think we have our first catch of the day.

I must admit that I was surprised as the front door opened and in strode the polished shoes and tailored suit of Maximillian Shurdach. Usually an aloof and quiet man, Max can often be seen sitting in the square at a table by himself reading a book with a coffee by his side. As always he is impeccably dressed but today Max looks anxious and harried. He is at the desk as soon as he is through the door. Suze is first off the mark.

- Hi Max...

- I need to find a book.

- Well, you're off to a good start, what with...
- Look, please. I need to find it right now.
- Um...sure. Do you know the Title or Author?
- I, I don't know the title... It's by Carl Jung. It's a book about dreams.
- Oh, that sounds cool. Well, I'm sure we've got something around here. I mean, the collection is pretty varied so we have a little something about everything. There's a heck of a lot of books here, you know? Let me take a look...okay, dreams, what sparked this interest anyhow?
- What does it matter? Can you help me or not?
Suze, whilst a helpful person by nature, is apt to snap on occasion and so to spare Max an assault by the 3 elastic bands sitting next to her right hand I decide to step in. Besides, I'm curious now.
- I can help you Max, we have a whole section on dream theory and the unconscious down in the catacombs. It's something I studied a little in college actually. I can take you down.

We make our way down the long spiral staircase to the basement. Whilst Teddy Ashenbrooke's design for this library has given us a sumptuous setting for study – all leather sofas and writing desks – it has not actually provided much space for the keeping of books. And this is why the catacombs were built in the basement. Now, Catacombs may give the impression of abandonment, rows upon rows of books covered in cobwebs and never visited. This is only partly true. Whilst the basement does only see one or two visitors a week, since Mr B had become the manager the place had never looked so bright and well-maintained. Whilst I walked Max down to the section on dreams I was suddenly struck by an idea.
- Max, I feel you'll know the answer to this - do people still make petitions? I mean, you heard a lot about them in high school and they seemed to work well but what really happens? What do you do with one once you have all these signatures?
- Hmm?

- I mean, do I pin it to the Mayor's door? It just seems so 18th century...

- Charles, I don't know what you're talking about. Where is this book? I really haven't got much time.

- That's exactly what I'm talking about; time. It's all off in this town since the clocks starting running down. You must feel it. I want to start a petition to fix the clock tower...

- Charlie! Where are these books!?

Okay, perhaps I should drop this for now. I show Max to the section and he begins to rifle through the shelves furiously, dropping one book after another onto the floor.

- Max, I'd really appreciate it if you could keep those in order.

No reaction. He drops one here, then there. This is not good.

- I mean, I know you don't have a library card, and if this is how you're going to be treating the books then I really don't know if I can sign you up.

- Charlie, please! help me look.

We find it together at the end of a row. There's some new age books on dream catchers, then some classic Freud, and at the end of the row:

Dreams by C G Jung. ASH 154.63 JUN.

He snatches it from the shelf before I even have the time to move my arm. And he is off, marching back towards the staircase.

I chase after him.

- Seriously, Max, you need to sign up for a library card...

Dammit, he is faster than me and he is half running across the library as I reach the top of the stairs.

- Max!

For fucks sake.

- Max!

He bolts and runs straight for the front door, pulls it open and darts into the sunshine outside. Just as suddenly as he had arrived, he disappears once more from our quiet little world.

Susie looks at me and smiles.

- Mr B is gonna kick your ass. I guess you are working Sunday now too.

- Funny. You're so damn funny. Thanks for all your help by the way. You know, your legs do move.
- But only if I want them to.
- Dammit, I didn't even get his signature for my petition.

She broke into a huge grin.

- Well, I guess that was the excitement for the day...

She was not wrong. I spent the rest of the afternoon filing index cards.

As I head towards home, slowly crossing the square, I hear the town clock ring out. The sound is long, drawn out, each chime reverberating off the quiet buildings as the sun sets on our little town. I have heard towns described as sleepy and when I read that in a guide book somewhere it conjures up an image. There has to be afternoon sunshine, definitely a gentle breeze blowing across a lawn, ducks swimming in ever increasing arcs over the surface of a pond. I would be laying in the grass, the sun warming my face, with a book open on my chest as I drifted off, safe in the knowledge that if I did sleep, I would wake up to this same scene. Time wouldn't have passed and I would wake with so many hours left before the sun went down.

This is not how our town is sleepy. Our town is tired. Our town is an old man sitting in the square, his head slowly bobbing forward, drifting off whilst the sun sets.

- *Wake up old man, there is so much to do, you must set off home, you must fix things.*
- *I am happy here. And besides, I don't have the energy.*
- *You do. You can make it home. You can cook and set things right and you can sleep later. When it is time.*
- *But you don't know how good it feels as I sit here. My eyes closing, my head falling.*
- *Please don't give up yet.*
-

And he is gone just like that. To dream dark dreams with no discernible end. As I reach the bottom of the hill the clock tower gives out its long last cry. It chimes six times. I look at my watch. It is almost eight.

*

Max pored through the pages in search of something. He'd know it when he found it. A sign, a clue, the answer to the half formed question in his mind that had been tormenting him for weeks. And that's when the hand drawn map fell from between the pages of the book.

*

The leaves which have fallen from the elm trees are piled high and create an ever changing sea of reds, oranges and yellows that wash around my feet as I walk. I stop for a second at the foot of Elm Hill and turn back to look over the town. The sun has begun to set and in the tradition of great New England sunsets it looks as if the town is bathed in fire. Light glinting off the bell at the top of the clock tower glares dazzlingly. I can even make out the now crimson red bricks of the library and the dark trees that border the town rising high behind them. I can see people too, dark shadows moving around down there in the flames and I wonder where they are going and what deeds they have left to do before the light is gone.

I begin to trudge through the leaf sea, towards the formidable shadows that comprise my home. A large wooden structure that once crowned this hill like the beam of a lighthouse, it is now mostly dark, except for one low light shining out from the kitchen window. It is not long until I arrive at the door and as I fumble trying to take the keys from my pocket I suddenly lose my footing in the swirling leaf sea, slipping on the dark wet mud beneath. I manage to stay upright but I lose the keys and they fall below the surface of the leaves. Dammit, I can't see them anywhere. I rummage around in the dirt at the bottom of the sea and whilst I am stuck here, just on the threshold of home, the wind whips up suddenly, whisking leaves up around me – in my face, in my hair. The wet muddy flesh of one leaf sticks to my face. I know that I have to be quick now.

I feel the cold sinking in. It's funny, that's how it is here in the fall. The sun goes down and the temperature plummets. I bat away the leaves as they swirl around me in little whirlwinds and I see it, a slight gleam of silver under the leaves. I reach down, hook it up and the key is in the door in one deft motion. I turn the latch, push open the door and in a split second the cold world is behind me and I stand in the bright wooden living room of our house. My brother sits in front of the television, PlayStation controller in hand.

I walk over and prod him in the side with my foot. He squirms away, never taking his eyes from the screen.
- Hey Bobcat, what did you make us for dinner?
- Yeah, right. You know it's your turn.
Damn, he's right. It's Tuesday. I walk over to the cupboards and survey our depleted supplies. Would Salsa work as a pasta sauce? Rice. Peanut Butter. No bread.
- Thanks for picking up the shopping. How was School idiot?
- We mostly bunked off, went down to Fairview, scored some crack. You know, the usual.
He thinks he's funny.
- Oh little brother – Fairview? How many times have I told you that you need to drive out to Rush Valley to get the good stuff? In Fairview you're mostly getting baking powder.
- Thanks for the tip bro, I'll remember it for tomorrow.
- What are you playing anyway?
- New Burnout. You in?
- You know it. Pizza?
- Pizza.

I speed dial 3: pizza-a-go-go. Perhaps it gives you some sense of our priorities over the past two years when I tell you that in at second place is Ashenbrooke General, and cruising into first is Burt's Pakora. I really need to start cooking some real food but for some reason the cupboards are always bare. I hold the line and toy with the cupboard, careful not to dislodge the broken door that is wedged into the frame. I had noticed the house changing for a while now. At first it was the smallest things. My eyes would wander over this kitchen that I knew so well and I'd be struck by the sheer amount of dust coating everything. I mean my brother and I were perhaps not the cleanliest of people. We weren't expecting Town and Country magazine to be shooting its next spread here, but we looked after the place okay, and it should not be this dirty.

I sit down at the wooden table carved with grooves from endless summer afternoons. It's hard to pinpoint exactly how it is changing. When I think back 5 or 6 years, I have so many memories of this kitchen table at breakfast. I think my brother's record was 4 bowls of cheerios – even I was impressed. He had to lie down after that. But what strikes me most in these memories is how bright everything seemed. We had one of those metal toast holders and I swear the light that reflected off it was dazzling. The spoons, the counters. We didn't mind at the time but the light was really so loud. I suppose it woke us up and got us ready for the day. We'd do this every morning. Toast, Coffee, Cereal – a full continental spread. Our mother insisted that we never left for school on an empty stomach and believe me, that was never a problem.

What is different now is the quality of the light. Here, in the living room and kitchen it is still pretty bright. Dusty, but bright. We spend most of our time here in fact. But upstairs it is as if the light cannot quite reach the corners of the rooms. The darkness has set up home and no matter what type of light bulbs I try (and I've tried a few) nothing works. The only way I can really explain it is to say that there is a conflict in the house between what is still ours and what isn't. The parts we truly know are ours, and the peculiarities enforce our sense of ownership; we know, and we alone, which cupboard door would fall off if opened, which chair has lost its stuffing and is constructed to look real but would actually swallow anyone foolish enough to sit in it. These things make the place ours. But the darkness in the hallway on the second floor, the way shadows lay longer than they should on the carpet of our father's study; these things aren't.

Partly the decay is enchanting; the weathered walls give light to various airs and draughts that fill the rooms. Sitting in the downstairs bathtub, watching the steam circle in currents around the room, you can see through the cracks in the frosted window panes to the garden outside, where ivy has begun to creep into the room. The wooden window frames are now warped from the changing seasons and you can make out patterns in the frame; a well, a tower, a woodcutter chopping logs in the forest.

The phone line crackles in my ear.
- pizzagogocanitakeyourorder?
- yes, one extra large Hawaiian please.
- thisisrenyard?
- uh huh.
- betherein10.

After pizza comes movies, that was the order of things in this house. The three of us used to sit together down here when she could still make it downstairs. I remember watching the two of them sat together, the light show flicker on their faces in the darkness, curlicue flames cracking wood in the fireplace. Quite often on these nights she would fall asleep at some point in the middle of the movie and then wake at the end, foggy with sleep.
- *Good film, hey mum?*
- *Um, yes...wonderful.*
- *And I didn't expect the clown at the end.*
- *No, me neither.*

- *uh huh, yeah, there was no clown. Time for bed, yeah?*

Well, it was just the two of us now but you had to keep some traditions going. Besides, I was responsible for giving him a proper movie education now and so here we sit. The lights are down, the volume is way way up, the popcorn is popped, and some shit is about to go down at the Nakatomi plaza. It's one of the few movies I would happily watch a hundred times but by the time Bruce is bandaging up his feet in the bathroom I find my eyes feeling fuzzy around the edges. It's funny how you never realised how tired you are until you sit down and find the soothing sounds of Bruce Willis beating down German terrorists could really lull you to sleep...

*

The back door is jammed. And I need to get out. I mean, I really need to get out. I've just seen the blue fox running through my garden and that bastard is fast. And if I'm going to catch him I'm going to need A) to be faster than him, B) to be trickier than him, and C) doors that open.

I consider my situation. And I realise that my knowledge of foxes mostly comes from the Roald Dahl story 'The fantastic Mr Fox'. Now, what did that fox like? Cigars and poker if I'm not mistaken. Okay, my dad has a box of cigars hidden around here somewhere. I check the backs of cupboards, move aside bottles of port coated in dust. I must find them fast and in my hurry I knock over a bag of cous cous which scatters on the counters like the sound of hail striking the floor. The raining cous cous doesn't stop, it falls and falls, the small yellow dots covering my feet in yellow the way blossom falls from the trees in spring. And I find them! Yes! Okay. I reach far into the cupboards and retrieve the wooden box of cigars, the crest of my family etched into the top. I dust off the box and, setting it down on the surface, I open the lid. Inside are rows of cigars, this is perfect. But hold on, on the right hand side, poking from the top of one cigar is a gleam of metal. I pull it out and quickly begin to unroll it, tearing at the leaf until I find inside an old brass key. This is it, that little bastard is in trouble this time.

I hurry back to the bay window to look outside. I see the tangles of trees amongst the darkness. The moonlight is not too bad tonight, I can see outlines of shapes but still all the colours are greys. Except for one. I see the light blue swish of a tail down by the holly bush. I've got him! Tonight I've got him and I can't tell you how long I have searched. I run to the back door, find the lock and this new key fits like a dream. I pocket two cigars before I leave as I will need these when I meet him. And then I turn the key, pull back the door and step from one home to another.

The moonlight beats down on the garden and I can see everything. The dark tangled forms of the elms surround me and the smell is so sweet and strong, like perfume or aftershave applied too liberally. The slightly bitter tang masks something else but right now I don't have time to stop and work it out. It has just rained and has left puddles in random patterns all over the garden. Each puddle contains one slice of the reflected moonlight. I look out down the hill and it is clear where these light puddles are steering me. Down the hill, halfway between our house and the tall brick wall that fences our garden lies the well. The glowing silvery puddle lights lead up to it like the strip lights on a runway. And crouched by the well is the blue fox.

In every other aspect the blue fox looks like any other fox you would find wandering the streets of our town once we are all sleeping, scavenging for scraps of food. But the hue of his coat is peculiar. The colour is dark, like the parts of the puddles not illuminated by moonlight but also like the moonlight itself. His strange colouring is made all the more exasperating because it is the perfect camouflage at night and once you lose him in the bushes or in the long blue grass you will not find him again. Still, I have not been this close to him in a long time and so I break into a run. Tonight I will get this bastard.

Damn, I'm fast. I am running down the hill, jumping the tangled roots that line the path, breathing through lungs that just don't tire. As I reach the point where the tree line ends and the open *path to the well begins he sees me. And bolts. Damn. I breathe in deeply, taking in the aroma of the fresh rain mixed with the blossom on the grass and find a little more speed from somewhere. I am at the well as he is halfway to the wall. I've got him, there is nowhere to go, the wall is six foot tall and there is no way he is scaling that. I fight on, and now he is metres from me. I consider the best way to trap him and that is when I see where he is going; there is a small gap at the base of the wall where the rocks have crumbled away. Dammit, no! There is only one play left to me now, I'm gonna have to bring him down with a full leaping tackle. I sprint with all my reserves and leap as he darts for this gap in the wall. I come down hard and my hand closes around the soft wet fur of his tail. I've got him! But then he pulls hard, with energy I didn't know he'd have. I grab hold tight, my fingers trying to grip his fur and pull him back towards me. But it is a losing fight, the damp has made his fur slippery and as he pulls hard all I am left with is a hand full of dark blue hair as he disappears through the hole and out of sight once more.*

Aaaaaaaah! I can't believe he did it again. I roll onto my back and lay there amongst the blue grass and look up at the white moon. I pocket the blue fur that he left me. Those cigars will have to wait for another night I guess. Damn him! Still, it's not so bad out here right now. I breathe in the smell of the rain and listen to the quiet night air. It's peaceful here and I guess I'll get another chance – he is drawn to our house for some reason.

Just then I hear a snarl. Is it him? Maybe he hasn't left yet! I roll onto my front and crawl to the hole he leapt through. Whilst big enough for a fox to crawl through, it is still pretty small and whilst I pull closer to it, it only affords me a very limited view of what is outside our garden. I hear him snarling but I cannot see him anywhere, in fact all I can make out is a once polished Italian leather shoe laying in the tall grass, now caked in mud...

*

Bobby could feel his brother's presence like a fog in his own mind, an awareness of another's will watching something, enjoying something, anticipating the next scene. It felt substantial, like a weight on his thoughts. He could feel the attention, the wavering, and knew the moment that it was gone. He looked over and saw Charlie sleeping on the sofa, his head drifting back on the cushions. His attention was switched off, his mind resting. With Charlie asleep, he felt his own mind unfurl, put its feet up on the couch, spread out to the corners of the room. He rose from the sofa carefully, and tiptoed to the kitchen, where he could look out of the darkened kitchen window toward points of light in the distance, orange and purple against the night. At this time, in the depths of the night there were no colours discernible on the lawn, in the house merely shades of dark and lighter grey. He wandered through the darkness and felt her presence, just like Charlie's; another's thought at the edge of thought, another view of the room overlapping with his own, so that it was seen together; haunted, quiet, and still. He could relax again. They'd made an uneasy truce with the house but he felt best when he could just let it all go, could just sit here in the startling, strange, and ever present now, feeling her here with them in this quiet house. He heard her again, shuffling about in the rooms upstairs.

*

I feel a grip on my shoulder and I'm being shaken.
- Wake up.
What is going on? All I can think of is the sound of hard rain hitting the ground. The shaking continues. He is speaking softly but now I can feel the urgency in his grip. I open my eyes and the room is blurry but when I see the look on my brother's face I wake up and realise I am still on my sofa in the lounge. He looks scared. Just like when we used to share a room together. He would wake me up in the night, sure that there was something behind the curtain or in the cupboard. I found it annoying back then. And now, as my eyes are coming into focus and I feel sleep pass away, I find it annoying once more.

- What? What are you doing? What time is it?
- It's around 3. You fell asleep.

My mouth tastes like postage stamps and my back aches. I look around the room and see that he has turned off the TV, rolled out the sofa bed and turned on the lamp in the corner of the room. I seem to have just fallen asleep on the sofa and liberally spread popcorn over myself and the cushions. This is fine. I could go back to sleep now and all would be fine.

- Bobby, just go back to sleep. I need to sleep.
- I can't. I heard it again.
- You didn't. You didn't hear it again. It's just because it's late and dark. Go back to sleep.
- I did hear it. Get up.

He squeezes my shoulder and that does it, I can't get back to sleep now. I am tired and I half want to punch him but instead I get up and brush the popcorn from my clothes. I should brush my teeth anyhow.

- Okay, tell me what you heard.

I get up and wander to the kitchen sink as he tells me what has happened since I slept. I put the popcorn box away in the cupboard, next to a pack of cous cous and gaze out the bay window. Why does this feel familiar?

He tells me that he didn't want to wake me after the movie finished so he just got out the sofa bed like we sometimes do, turned out the lights and prepared to bunk down here. But about 10 minutes ago he woke up in the darkness to the creak of floorboards and the sound of crying from upstairs. He is an idiot. He thinks he's been hearing crying in our house on and off for a week now. I think he and his friends have watched one too many horror movies and I also think I need a decent night's sleep for once.

- Great. Look, we're not going upstairs okay? I am not running around our house in the middle of the night.
- Can't you hear it? Just listen.
- Okay, I'll listen.

I stop and listen to the house. It is 3 in the morning and it is just so quiet. I remember lying in bed at night when I was younger trying to isolate all the different sounds I could hear. The creaks and sighs of the house settling, the leaves of the trees as they blew in the breeze. Sometimes an owl would cry out late at night but really it was as close to silence as I'd ever heard. The only sounds I could hear now were my brother's breathing and mine. We stayed still for over a minute. Then it caught my ear. Soft but undeniably present. I could hear a sob. And I could hear the breaths between the sobs. It couldn't be anywhere but inside the house. Maybe he was right, maybe there was someone crying.

- You hear it don't you?
- Yeah. I hear it. But I don't think we should go up there. Not now.
- We have to.

I look at his face pleading with me.

-*Why do we have to go up there Bobby? Why can't we leave it alone?*
-*Because it might be her.*
-*You know it can't be her. Whatever is up there is not going to be her.*
-*It might be.*
-*I'm sorry Bobby, she's gone. You know she's gone.*
-*But maybe she isn't gone all the way.*
-*Bobby, you really want to do this tonight?*

I see his face, he believes it all, every bit. How can he? I get it I do but we watched her die. In pieces. In days. She isn't here. It's the memories. They live in the fucking woodwork of the place. Dinners at that table, her sitting, always sitting, on that bench in the garden. How could we not feel her? But it's not real, it's sense memory, it's reflexes. We expect to see her, and so we do. But she isn't here. It's just all the pieces of a life that was here. And now it's gone. But he's too young to know better. Too...something, too trusting? Too naïve? If wishing could make it so...But if that were true she'd have never left in the first place. All these pieces of a life that accumulate, filling up rooms and houses. Even the cups reminded me of her. Fuck it, we should get moving. Even now, I just can't say no to him.

- Okay. We're going but bring that with you, yeah?

I point over to the corner of the living room, where his baseball bat and glove lays. It's been a while since we've been down to the pitch but the bat has stayed there in the corner since we last went. I guess I thought it might come in handy to have a weapon lying around in case of uninvited house guests.

I root around in the cupboards looking for our flashlight. I'm not taking any chances tonight. I know how dark it can get up there and if we're really going looking we're going to need all the light we can get. Still, I have the strangest sense of déjà vu as I am rooting amongst the cupboards – I guess I haven't quite woken up yet and it is just my mind playing tricks on me. I find the red flashlight tucked away in one of the cupboards beneath the sink and I reach in to retrieve it. It has some heft, it will do just fine. I look over to my brother who is standing by the door to the corridor holding his bat to his chest, an expression of fear and excitement on his face. I cannot tell you the number of times I had to do this with him when he was younger. Our father always said the best way to conquer fear was to see for yourself that there was nothing to fear in the first place. I've always agreed with that statement and as I walk over to my brother now I remember all the times we would go hunting. There was the time he was convinced there was a zombie at the foot of the stairs, brought back to feast on our brains in the night. In the end it was just a dark sweater hung up on a coat rack next to some galoshes caked in mud. There was the looting pirate that turned out to be a hat, a shawl, and a walking stick. There were the ghosts that were merely curtains blowing in the wind.

*

Max reached the abandoned site. The rotted millwheel lay collapsed and the mist from the river obscured the fallen buildings. It was here, he could touch the rotten wood and almost feel the heat still in it. He stood and closed his eyes, listening for the faint sounds at the far reaches of perception. The music, the voices, muffled but there. He strolled through the remnants looking for it, unaware that there was a dark figure following behind him, fitting its footsteps to his.

We step out together from the lounge into the corridor that leads to the staircase. Because the bulbs had gone in the hall we would need to get to the second landing before we could turn the upstairs lights on. As we reach the staircase I look up into the blackness. The faint sound of sobbing seems to float towards us from somewhere up there. It comes and goes, so quiet. I turn on the flashlight and shine the beam upstairs but the old problem remains. The beam cannot break the darkness and so all that we achieve is a murky grey half-light to lead the way.
- Just stay close, okay?
- Okay.
And with that I place my foot on the first stair and we begin our ascent into the grey darkness.

We climb up into darkness, hopeful, stumbling, not sure what we'll find. The stairs curl around our house like a sleeping snake and as you ascend you are afforded a view of the next floor. We take each step slowly, the grey beam of my flashlight bobbing ahead of us in the murk. Bobby and I tended to sleep downstairs in the living room these days so it had been a while since I'd been upstairs. And I remembered why; it's incredible how safe keeping one door closed can make you feel. The rest of the house doesn't seem like ours anymore.

We need to get to the lights on the second floor and then it will be better. Everything is better in the light. We keep going, the flashlight revealing almost nothing. The grey carpet. A tennis ball on one of the stairs. The sobs were getting a little louder now. They sounded muffled as if someone was crying into a pillow but I still couldn't place where they came from. Damn, why was this staircase so long? I start taking the stairs two at a time, rushing towards the light switch at the top. Bobby tells me to slow down but I can't, suddenly I need to get there. I race ahead and finally we're here. I reach out, flick the switch...and nothing. I flick it back. Again. Again. Nothing. Fuck. Chills are rising up my back and it feels like the sobbing is right behind me now. There is something dark and moving to my left, something on my right. I start darting the flashlight around, trying to break the darkness.

Suddenly Bobby rushes past me and to my right. He is running into his old bedroom and before I know it light spills across the floor of the landing, the shadows stop moving and lay flat across the carpet of the landing. It's okay, there is nothing here. An empty landing, closed doors. Where before I saw shadows moving in the darkness and on the walls now it is just the quiet grey stillness of a house in the dead hours before dawn.
- Are you okay?
- Yeah, sorry. I don't know what happened. I don't like being up here.
I walk over to his room and step inside. The bunk beds we used to share as kids are still in there, and that stupid superman lamp looks at me with its idiotic grin, full of the irresponsible optimism of youth.

It is strange to be in my brother's room again. When I was ten I moved into my own room but Bobby insisted on keeping our bunk beds here. Our parents tried to convince him otherwise and we even went on a trip to Ikea to show him all the different new beds he could have, but he was having none of it. He said they were perfect because sometimes he wanted to sleep near the ceiling and sometimes he wanted to have a roof and sleep near the floor. It was great for his friends to stay round. He just loved the bunk beds. And it was a good call. Many nights our dad would get into the top bunk and start reading bobby stories only to fall asleep about four pages in. Bobby would sneak down to his own bunk and sleep. I always slept better in the presence of another; I guessed he felt the same.

I remember this one day I had been out in the yard with him trying to teach him how to climb the trees. If you had the skill you could jump from branch to branch and cross the whole back yard. It was my own city in the treetops and as he had reached the grand old age of five I thought it was time he was allowed admittance. So I was there, I'd helped him with a leg up to the first branch and was trying to spur him on to make the jump to the next. I think the exact words I used were 'come on, you can do it you little dipshit'. You know, helpful stuff. And to his credit he made the jump. He just wasn't so good at the staying on after the jump.

I saw his legs go out from under him and I already knew it would be bad. I couldn't reach him in time and he fell, head first, onto the hard winter soil. I heard the crack. And then the howling. He had a lump the size of an egg on his forehead and I remember creeping to his room later that night and seeing him asleep in the bottom bunk, our mother sitting in a chair next to the bed watching.

- Charlie. Seriously. Are you okay?
- Yeah, I'm fine. Really. I've just had enough of those fucking lights. We should move on shouldn't we? It's not coming from here.

We walk back out to the landing together but are careful to prop the door open. We head towards my father's study because although we both know where we have to go tonight we would like to kid ourselves for a little while longer. It is just a few steps and we are there and then the door is open. It is quiet. His lamp works too, a green desk lamp where he worked but now there are no papers here. It is still and his desk is empty. The books stare back at us from their shelves. The study is definitely uninviting but there is nothing here. And as we leave, we know we don't need to visit my bedroom either. We walk straight to the staircase that leads to the third floor. We both look up into the darkness and there is no denying that the soft sobbing sounds

24

are coming from the room where our mother used to sleep.

The three of us sit in her bedroom; Bobby perched on the edge of her bed and me sitting in one of dad's old armchairs. There was an old Jimmy Stewart movie playing on her little TV and her eyes were drifting closed as she watched it and we watched her. It had started towards the end of January. Later she started falling but at first she just seemed dizzy. We would be in a cafe in town and when we had finished our coffees - a skinny decaf soya latte for her, a black coffee for me. The doctors liked to tell her things she couldn't have. Caffeine was one of the big no nos. She would stand but she'd take an extra moment. I could see her white knuckles gripping the chair as she stood and I realised then it was getting hard for her again. To be out, to have the energy for everyone. It was the third time it was back and I could see she was tired. More tired this time.

That January I could tell she wasn't feeling herself because she'd stop talking to everyone we met. Goddamn, our mum could talk. I don't think we ever took a taxi without knowing the driver's life story by the end. It would drive me nuts. We would go on holiday and she would spend half the morning talking to the owners about when they bought the place, her holidays as a child. It was impossible to get anywhere fast. But this started to stop. People in the street would say hi to her and she'd be pleasant but her attention was elsewhere. It was only later I realised it was taking all her energy just to stand and be out with me.

The falling began in February. I was walking up the stairs when I heard the thump. I ran to her room and she was laying by her bed. She had fallen getting out and hit her head against the chair by the bed. I got her back in bed and we called for the doctor. He insisted on tending to her alone and when he came downstairs I knew from his eyes. That fucker has already given up. He told me three months. We could hope for three months. Sometimes she cried. And sometimes she accepted it. And sometimes she threw mugs at the walls and later she didn't have the strength to.

And so we'd spent the time like this, when we weren't at school we were with her. Watching movies was all she could manage, the pain was too much for her to concentrate on books and so we sat together, sometimes we talked and sometimes bobby and I would play games whilst she slept. When I took her to the bathroom all her weight would be on my arm and that weight was nothing, was feathers, it felt as if she was leaving us day by day and one day she would weigh nothing, would be air.

And now here we stood in the darkness looking up towards her room, where the slow steady sobs of our mother could be heard just as real as they had ever been.

Bobby took the first step. I looked back towards the dull light which still poured from my father's study. I didn't want to go up there but her sobs called to me. Her sobs? Why do I think they are her sobs? He thinks she is still here but she is gone. She died. I can still see her face in the morning, waxen and fixed, a slight grimace on her lips. She was taken and we buried her and they are not her sobs. The only thing I can hear right now is a stranger crying. A stranger in my fucking house. I follow him.

We take the stairs slowly and I feel myself once more gliding up this staircase. Before I know it we are there, standing at the last door in the house we keep closed. The house is still and the hollow echoes of those sad sobs bounce back to us from the wooden stairs beneath our feet. I knew what we would see on the other side and it made my heart skip a beat. They'd wanted us to clean that room, to box her things away. To empty it of her and label those boxes and put each one in its new place. In its safe place. In its light, clean safe place. They'd ask, each day, if we'd done it yet. But fuck them, we wanted something of her here (Is she still here?) We'd wanted to keep that room, cluttered with books, cups, photos, pillows, our old art projects, wind chimes, magazines and morphine (Is she still here?). That room that was her. A life had been here and fuck them for wanting to take that away. For wanting to put it in a box and leave it somewhere where it made them feel safe.

Bobby's touch on my arm brings me back and I realise my

hand is still on the cool metal of the door handle. I liked to know that room was there but I didn't like to see it that often. But it's time. The sobs were hushed now and as I looked at him it could have been years ago.

I turn the key and push the door away from us. He is on my left and will see in first. My heart stops as I see his face turn white. A small sound escapes him, a soft sound, like air escaping. There she is (she is not there) silhouetted against the window pane, her body withered, almost translucent against the indigo starlight.

No...Her nightdress hangs from the clothes rail near the window. The window is half open as she always kept it and the cold breeze ruffles the folds of her dress in the moonlight.

We both stand looking at her room. It is still now. And it is hard to hear one single sound except our breath and the whistle of the wind creeping in.

-I'm sorry Bobby. It was the wind. Just like before.

-It was not. We did not leave her dress like that, her window open.

-Are you sure? When was the last time you were here?

-I don't know.

-It could have been any of them, rooting through. Her friends, you know what they're like. They left it like this.

-No, it was her. This place is still her. She is here.

-She's gone.

- Stop fucking kidding yourself. We heard her cry.

-Did we? Did we? We are tired. And we want it. We want it so bad. We keep this place like this, frozen. Look at it. It looks like she has stepped out to the bathroom. Like she'll be back in a minute. But she won't.

-

-You don't think I want it too? For it to be some kind of mistake? Or worse, a big fucking joke. I want them to be hiding in that closet, ready to jump out. They'll step out with huge smiles on their face. We got you! Didn't we have you fooled? You were totally *fooled! And they'd show us how they faked it all. Did you see how we faked cancer? Faked death? Damn, we are good at this. And to see the looks on your faces, it makes it all worth it!*

    -You're an ass.

    -But they won't, because the biggest fucking joke of it all is that it all happened. And they're dead. And we're here.

    -

    -

We stand looking at that room for I don't know how long and then suddenly I walk to the window and close it, lay her nightdress down on her bed and we leave. I lock her room and we head back downstairs in silence, the still shadows watching us as we go back down, down to our room. Once back in the living room, we lock the door to the hallway, turn on the lamp and return to our camp beds. In some strange way it feels safe again. She's stopped crying and all I can hear is my brother's steady breathing and then the occasional trill as the birds wake up.

*

Max ran as far and as fast as he could, until his heart beat filled his ears, and his left leg gave, and he went down, his shoe catching on tangled roots, wrenching his ankle round in its socket. He crawled, dragging himself along through the mud, his world a mixture of his racing heart and the ragged breath raging above him.

PART I: THE ATALONGA

Deep into that darkness peering, long I stood
there, wondering, dreaming,
Doubting, dreaming dreams no mortal ever dared to dream before;
But the silence was unbroken, and the stillness gave no token,
And the only word there spoken was the whispered word, "Lenore?"
This I whispered, and an echo murmured back the word "Lenore!" –
Merely this and nothing more.

- From the original manuscript of Edgar Allan Poe's
'The Raven', courtesy of the Teddy Ashenbrooke
Collection, Ashenbrooke Library, MS POE 172.11s

We are thus driven to admit that in the dream
we knew and remembered something which was
beyond the reach of our waking memory.

- Sigmund Freud's 'The Interpretation of
Dreams', ASH 150.1592 FRE

DOWN BY THE RIVER

Sheriff Michael Sullivan did not wake up to the trilling of his phone by the bedside table, he woke up almost 15 seconds later with the receiver in his hand and Carter on the other side of the line.

- Sir, are you there?
- Uh-huh.
- Sir, you need to get down here. I'm out at the Atalonga River.
- Uh-uh.
- Seriously, you need to get here faster than slow.
- ...
- Did you hear me?
- Uh-huh, river. I don't want to go fishing.
- No, we're not fishing. There's a body here.
- Carter, if this is a joke, can we skip to the part where it's funny?
- It's not a joke.
- ...
- Its Max Shurdach. He's dead.
- I'm on my way.

Mike found a fresh shirt in the closet, badge and cards on the table in the living room, keys in the kitchen. On any other day there would be time for coffee. There would be time for percolating and music and papers. There were routines to be observed, routines that would usher in the beginning of a new day; that would welcome it and bring good luck. These rituals were like an orchestra tuning their instruments, preparing for the coming symphony. Everything had its rhythm and everything had its place. A call like that was a cymbal crashing at the beginning of the first act. It wasn't right. There was a time and a place for cymbals and there was a time and a place for phone calls and neither was at five in the morning. As for bodies by the Atalonga, they'd never quite fit in...like the cowbell. Oh well, time to roll into the storm. Mike grabbed his jacket and a CD from the top of the stack. Agents of Fortune, Blue Oyster Cult. It seems today was destined to start with a cowbell.

He'd parked over on Levinson and started down the hill in the soft grey haze of morning. Once he'd made it down the hill to his car, he turned back to look at the Saratoga apartment block he had called home for the last year; light spilled from just a few windows. Most of the residents wouldn't be up at this hour but the few who were had begun their morning routines. The light from televisions cast out into the still dark morning; blue, green, blue, red, blue, and green as the pictures changed. To Mike the chorus of light and dark and colour was like lights on an old switchboard, a Technicolor code just waiting to be cracked.

He sped away from the Saratoga Apartments and along Levinson towards the outskirts of the town. The haze began to lift even in the short time he was driving, and the windows of the highest buildings began to glow bronze as the sun rose. The earliest residents of the town were up already, walking their dogs or taking tai chi classes in the park. The latest residents of the town were stumbling home, bleary eyed, with their heads full of the crystal clear chirping of the birds in the trees. He envied them both in their own way, it must feel good to greet the day that way; to rise when the sun does. It must feel even better to be stumbling towards sleep, safe in the knowledge that the day, and the town, had started again and would continue without you, while you rested, that there were so many quiet bright hours left until the sun went down...The car swerved slightly and he jolted awake, steadying it. Coffee. Coffee would have to happen and soon. It was time to wake up. He fed the CD into the player and listened to that cowbell kick in. He gunned the accelerator. *All our times have come...*

As Mike made his slow descent towards the river the clouds did not drift and the shafts of sunlight stood perfectly still, each illuminating a footprint hastily made. The slight chill in the air meant that winter would be here before long but just now it was as if time itself hung as delicately as the leaves on the branches of the trees. He headed towards Carter and the prone figure by the lake, careful not to disturb the trail of footprints. As he approached a leaf detached itself from one of the huge elms towering overhead and descended, in ever increasing arcs until it landed on a muddy, torn shoe, discarded by the side of the river. A few feet from the shoe lay Max Shurdach's body, just as muddied and just as torn. It was difficult to tell how much was mud and how much was blood at this stage; he was caked, from head to foot. The only colour left was his pale blue eyes, distant and sad. One leg, the shoeless one, was shredded; matted chunks of trouser and flesh ground together.

- You find him like this, Carter?
- He was facedown, I rolled him to see if he still had a heartbeat. But I haven't touched him since.
- Good. That's good. Let's close his eyes, okay?
Carter knelt and brushed the eyelids closed.
- Have we taken any photos yet?
- Not yet, Sir. I came straight here when I got the call, I thought it was a crank. I didn't think to bring one.
- Sure, sure.
- Lewis and Potemko are on their way from the station.
- Call them, tell them to bring one. We'll leave him till then.
Whilst Carter went back to her car to radio the others, Mike paced the scene. The path of footprints seemed to lead back along the river all the way to the woods. He had run for a long time. Those pointed shoes had given the indentations an unusual shape but from the angle he could see Max had been setting quite a pace. Besides those prints there appeared to be nothing, no set of footprints leading away, and no knives, scythes, or whatever could have done that to his leg. Just a

path and a crumpled body at the end of it like a dirty full stop. He stood, gazing down at what was left of the body as Carter returned.

- They'll be here in 5.

- Good.

The silence crept back in. Apart from the murmuring of the river and the solitary call of a cuckoo from the woods, there was almost no sound out here.

- You think it was a bear? There's been rumours. Hikers going missing in the mountains up river. We haven't had one around here but it could be...

- The mess sure looks like a bear could have done it but wouldn't there be some sign of it? There's nothing but...

A phone rang out loudly making them both jump. Mike mouthed the word sorry, took it from his pocket, and answered.

- Mike. Get up.

- Sorry?

- Get up. Now. Your alarm is waking up the whole neighbourhood.

- ...Emily?

- Yes. This is your loving neighbour Emily. Now get the hell up.

A cog turned and clicked into place. Shit. He had left in such a rush this morning and now his alarm clock had gone off.

- Oh, shit. Sorry. I'm not there.

- So, you're not being woken up by the incredibly loud and annoying alarm that is currently blaring from your apartment. May I congratulate you on your excellent choice? Now, how the hell do I turn it off?

- There's a key. I taped it to the back of that painting in the hall between our apartments. Let yourself in and just pull the plug. It's by my bed.

- Okay. And Mike?

- Yeah?

- Next time you don't make it home, don't set the alarm okay?

- I...that's not...

The line went dead.

- That your lady?
- Not my lady, just a pissed off neighbour. This is exactly what happens when you mess with the rhythm.
- Huh?
- Nothing.

The station wagon rolled up minutes later and Potemko shot straight out.
- Boss, we were already en route but I stopped to pick up a Kodak on the way.
- You bought a disposable camera?
- Yeah. What can I say? I've got ingenuity.
- That's one word for it.
- You want me to get snapping? I'll get one of you kneeling next to the body.
- It's not...These aren't holiday photos. Just take some of the body, the footprints and the scene. Not the scenery. The scene.
- I get it's not a holiday. I mean, he's having a pretty bad time if it is. I've got twenty four shots though. We could do a couple for posterity. Maybe you and Carter investigating the scene. Lewis with the evidence kit?
- Okay, look, Potemko, we've got to get this done. I want twenty professional shots of the body and the scene. We'll do a couple for fun. Then we all get him in the wagon and back to the Station House. Deal?
- Deal.

*

- Okay, Lewis, you set up the board. Find a nicer photo of Shurdach than the ones we took today. We are going to run this in teams. Carter and Potemko, I want you on the bear angle. Contact the local counties, the rangers, local law enforcement agencies, I want to know patterns of local bear movements, whether this was a one off, or whether we need to warn the town. Lewis, you're with me. I want to know why Max was way out by the Atalonga by himself. I want to know *if* Max was way out by the Atalonga by himself. There were no signs of anyone

34

else with him but we are taking nothing for granted at this stage. We are going to piece together his last 48 hours. Potemko, your first priority is developing those photos. Lewis, put together his last movements. Carter, you're in charge of the house. I'm off to see the Doc. If you get any phone calls from the local press let them know we'll be having a meeting here at five.

And with that the sheriff shot out of the squad room, jumped in his car and headed across town to the courthouse morgue. Suspicious deaths were rare in Ashenbrooke but when they did crop up it was Marty Harrison that got called in to perform the autopsy. The senior medical examiner in town, Harrison would pack up his equipment and bring everything over to the small badly lit basement room beneath the courthouse. Mike guessed that Harrison was in his late fifties, but his thick white hair and olive complexion gave him the ageless quality of a Hollywood leading man. Mike guessed he'd mostly be cast as the put-upon father these days, but there could still be a few romantic leads out there for him. As Mike descended the stairs he saw the doc standing over the mangled body of Max Shurdach, shaking his head. He looked up at the approach of footsteps, and whistled before he spoke.

- Phew, first actually suspicious death here in about twenty years I'd say.
- What makes you think it's suspicious?
- Well, I don't think he passed away peacefully in his sleep, did he?
- Maybe he did. It could have been narcolepsy. A nice moonlit stroll down by the river then bang, he falls asleep, drowns and something chews on him. Case closed.
- Now that, Mike, is why they pay you the big bucks.
- It's all in a day's work. So, assuming for a second there was some foul play involved here, what can you tell me?
- Okay, these are just my preliminary thoughts mind you, you'll need to come see me tomorrow when the full autopsy is complete...but the victim has several bite marks on the legs and on the face. It would appear on first inspection that these were

received before the point of death.

- So, he was chased and then brought down?
- That would be my theory, yes. This bite here ripped through the tendon. That would have been bloody and that would have brought him down fast.
- Can you tell what type of animal?
- I'm not sure yet. Maybe a racoon?
- A racoon?
- They can be pretty fierce when startled.
- You're honestly telling me this is death by racoon disturbance?
- No. I mean I don't know. In truth the damage is more consistent with a bear attack. I'll have a better idea of the animal tomorrow. But that's one interesting thing, none of these wounds would have killed him. Can you guess what did?
- Hypothermia? It's got to get pretty cold out there at night.
- That would have been my first thought too. A combination of the cold, the shock, and the blood loss.
- But?
- But all signs point to a massive heart attack.
- The sort of massive heart attack that could happen naturally as part of our simple sleepwalking theory?
- Only if he was having some damn scary dreams.
- Hmm...So you're telling me it was the stress of the attack that killed him?
- Yes, not surprising really, considering the situation. Look, that's all I can tell you for now. I'll finish up here this afternoon and take any samples I need back to the hospital. Come visit me tomorrow afternoon for the full results.
- Will do. And thanks for your help with this, I appreciate it.
- You're welcome. I always thought he was a nice fellow, respectful. Not a good way to go.

Ashenbrooke's police station was not the busiest of places and so it happened that the small room which was used for occasional press briefings was usually lent out to a number of support groups and clubs in the evenings. Which meant that they would need to wrap up the press conference by six in order that the quilting society could get in and set up. Seeing as there were only two representatives from the press seated in the room at five when Mike arrived, he doubted this would be too difficult a task. As he stepped up to the podium at the front of the room, he could see Mary from the Ashenbrooke messenger and Bill from the gazette. Before he could speak, Mary began:

- Is it true what we've heard? That Max is dead?

- I'm afraid so; Max Shurdach was discovered dead at the Atalonga River at around 5am this morning by a local hiker. Our working theory is that he was a victim of a bear attack. However, we are awaiting the autopsy report, to confirm.

Bill's face flushed red and he sat forward:

- I've been saying for years we need a proper solution to the bear problem. They're migrating further south every year and we will only see more of these deaths. Have we heard from Saratoga about dangerous bears in the area?

- We will be liaising with departments in the tri-town area to establish the location of bears in the area, and will be issuing the necessary warnings as we see fit.

- What was he doing all the way out there by himself?

- I'm afraid we don't know as yet Mary. And that is my first concern; we need to establish that he was on his own, and that we shouldn't be looking for any more victims in the first instance. If you would both be so kind as to include the following statement in your articles, I would be most grateful. We are requesting information from the town about Mr Shurdach's last known whereabouts. We wish to speak to anyone who spoke to Max on Monday or Tuesday. Anyone with information can call the station house.

- And when will the funeral be?

- His daughter gets in to town tomorrow and will be making arrangements.

- I didn't know he had a daughter. Where is she from?

- She's flying in from Seattle. She's a lawyer up there. Okay, that's all for now. You know the number, do call the station any time if

you have any further questions.
- Okay. You staying for quilting tonight Mike?
- No, I've got a few things to finish up and then I really need to get home. Got a big day tomorrow. But tell Helen I said Hi.

As Mike pulled into his parking spot he saw that the blue and green lights of the apartment block had shifted into a new pattern as some of the inhabitants had left for the night and others were relaxing in front of their televisions. If you looked hard enough, these patterns showed up all over the town, and if you looked even harder they could tell you something. He wondered what patterns he has missed today already and whether he'd be able to see them tomorrow. The key was to focus on the details now, and the big picture later. And the most pressing detail right now was to leave the car, get some sleep, and let his mind unravel the threads of the day before picking them up again tomorrow. He took the bottle of red wine he'd picked up on the way home and headed towards his apartment. Once he was in the corridor he noticed that the painting in the hallway between his apartment and Emily's had shifted a few degrees to the left. It was only eight so he knocked on the door opposite his own. 30 seconds later he heard the snapping of locks and Emily appeared in the doorway.
- Well, if it isn't the stop out – you just getting home now Mike?
- Emily, it's not...
- Hey, don't worry. I just need my beauty sleep is all so how about you don't set that incredibly loud alarm of yours for a little while? There's nothing wrong with a nice quiet radio alarm.
- Okay, deal. Look, this morning I was out on a call, there was a bear attack out by the Atalonga. I got you this as a peace offering.
- Well, if you're going to bring me wine for the trouble then maybe the alarm wasn't all bad. I'm just cooking actually, there is more than enough for two and that Rioja will go very nicely with gnocchi. You should join me.
- You sure?
- I insist. Come in. You look like you could use some food.

Emily gestured to a seat at the kitchen table and turned back to the stovetop, stirring swiftly. She fetched two glasses from the top cupboard, uncorked the bottle, and poured.

- So, Mike, you have to tell me. Should I be worried about bears? Should I be on the lookout?

- I don't think so, not unless they are lured downtown by the affordable housing and great take outs.

Mike sat gazing out the window as she set down two plates. They clinked glasses and the muted streetlight bounced off the cutlery, giving a soft glow to the dinner table.

  - Well, that is good to know, I won't be keeping my eyes peeled for bears in trench coats and dark glasses then.

- Good. But do report them if you see them. And besides, technically you're in the safest possible place to be in this town.

- Well, that rather depends on whether the Sheriff is home or not, doesn't it?

- Touché. But you know, if the bears ever do break into town and try to hunt you down, you know where that key is now. I've got a pistol hidden in a box in the wardrobe. And I keep the cupboards well stocked with honey, so you can use that to distract them for a while whilst you get hold of me.

- That's good to know. I make a mean honey flapjack so maybe that will keep them happy for a while.

- Hey, if you want to practice them, I'm happy to be quality control, just to make sure the recipe is good enough to keep them distracted for long enough.

- We'll see. If you keep bringing the red wine, you may have yourself a deal.

- And speaking of which, this is really great by the way.

- Thanks, it's one of my 4 dishes I do very well.

- I'm impressed, that's 3 more than I do very well.

- And what would your one dish be?

- Risotto. Mystery risotto based on what I have in the fridge.

- Hey, I approve of any dish that requires a bottle of wine to be opened in the process of cooking.

- Me too, I think that's why I never got round to learning another. That and the hours I work...and I always seem to live near great take away places.
- Mr Wonton is not a great take away place. I wouldn't have thought it was possible to get fortune cookies wrong until I went there. They taste like burnt ham.
- Yeah, that is an achievement. But Burt's Pakorah, that place is fantastic.
- Fair point, that one's good.
Mike and Emily sat talking until the traffic in the street below had ceased, the second bottle of red was half empty, the gnocchi was all gone, and the assorted noise from the other apartments had ceased. Mike stifled a yawn and looked at his watch. 12.30am.
- I'm sorry Em, it's the day, not the company. I think I'd better hit the hay. But I have to say, this has been a welcome ending to an unusual day.
- Let's hope it doesn't take another maiming before we do it again.
- It won't.
She walked him to the door and waved goodbye as he walked the 7 or 8 steps across the hallway.
- Sleep well Mike.
- You too Em.

Mike stumbled into his own apartment, the full weight of his tiredness descending once he'd closed the door. He saw the mess from this morning and didn't even try to tidy up. He merely ran through his routine by reflex, brushing his teeth whilst undressing and trying not to spill any toothpaste on the floor. He climbed into his bed, drew the covers up and fell back onto his pillow. He was just beginning to reflect on what a strange day it had been and to think that sometimes it was good to mess with the rhythm, when he descended into the warm grey darkness of sleep.

THE OWNERSHIP OF TREES

The early October sunlight fell through the branches of the large elm trees in dappled patterns, turning the yard into a patchwork quilt of gold and shadow; burnished greens nestled against gold, blues against muddy browns. The overarching branches of the elm trees formed a protective canopy over portions of the lawn, keeping them hidden in moving shadows. Bobby sat on the back stoop holding a mug as its steam circled in rising currents into the air.

The Trees (In Chorus): We own these moments Bobby. All of this. The golden light stroking our branches. The still warm quiet of the morning. It's beautiful. I wish we could stay here, the leaves washing against our trunks. This shouldn't have to end. Ever.
Bobby: I used to own you. You were ours and when I touched your bark I knew it.
The Trees: But we're wild now. We'll fill this yard with roots and take it back for ourselves.
Bobby: I miss it.
The Trees: You can sit with us. But we'll never be yours again.

He did sit there, watching them; how unruly they'd become. Their branches were wild, dancing like fools. Well, at least it was quiet and the sun was warm. Sometimes the nights were easier to forget, sometimes they weren't. Why was her nightgown out? Had they really left it like that? It was possible. He couldn't remember the last time they had been to her room or even upstairs. But the window, they wouldn't have left it open. The truth is that what felt real at 3am this morning felt just as real now. This garden, her room, the house, it had all started to run down; it had all started to run wild. And if someone didn't tame it soon, who knew what would happen. The chimes of the clock tower struck, the vibrations rippling across the town, up the hill and through the trunks of the trees. Eight long chimes. Bobby looked at his watch; it was ten minutes to nine.

They descended Elm Hill together as the wind whipped up. Leaves flew at them as they walked, sticking to the arms of their jackets. Bobby struggled to keep up, and had to raise his voice to be heard above the wind.

- You must have felt it. It's like she's still there. It's like she's in the walls of the place.
- She isn't Bobby. It's an old house. And neither of us has the time or money to look after it. The ceilings creak, the roof leaks, the wood cracks at night. It's an old house and if you let it get to you it'll spook you. But there's nothing more.
- It's more than that and you know it. What are we gonna do? Keep living downstairs and pretending it isn't happening? How long can we do that for?
- And just what are you proposing?
- I don't know...
- Exactly.
- How about we get someone to visit? ... like a medium?
- A medium? Dammit Bobby, The only thing that will make that house creepier is inviting a medium round. Why don't we light candles and get a Ouija board out? Set up a fucking altar in the kitchen?
- I don't know, okay? I just feel like she's unhappy there.
- She isn't unhappy there. The only thing there is our house and our imagination. She left it to us and whilst you're in school we're staying. But you finish next summer, and then we'll sell it and move away, okay? We can live there till then.
- I....
- Look, I've got to head to the library now. And you've got to get to school. We'll talk about it tonight, okay?
- Okay.
- Now, go learn something, I'll see you tonight. I'll pick up some

real food. You'll see, it'll be fine.

And with that Charlie ran off down the path to the red brick library and disappeared through its doors.

Bobby trudged the halls of Ashenbrooke Community College, his echoing footfalls bouncing off the tiled floors. The school was comprised of four large corridors forming a square, with occasional windows affording a view of the hidden quad within; an enclosure filled with a landscaped garden and benches for the students to read between classes. There were a couple of students sat beneath a dull cherry blossom, with their textbooks open by their sides and their coats done up to their necks. Everyone else was either in class, or huddled in the canteen. He watched the garden. It was funny, it followed him around on days like this and wouldn't let him go. Was it that he was sensitive to the cues, and merely saw his mother in these things where objectively she was just as present as any other day? Or did he draw it to him, the way flames drew a moth? It was a common misconception that moths liked the fire. In fact they were trying to navigate as usual, by moonlight, when this bright ball of light blinded them and they thought it was the sun. Attempting to recalculate their course, they became confused and flew round and round the flame in orbit, until the inevitable collision. Perhaps his mother's ghost was like this; he'd drawn her from her course and now she flew round him, alighting in his field of vision wherever he went. It didn't help that she used to teach here. A few of the teachers still smiled at him sympathetically in the corridors, and he knew that he and his brother had been a source of talk in the staff room for many years. He stood and looked at the cherry blossom with its little plaque beneath: 'In loving memory of Eleanor, beloved teacher and friend'. The bell sounded out for class, disrupting his thoughts. 11am, English, Room 402. He walked down the hall, into the classroom and chose a seat near the window, affording him a view of tree-lined hills, extending in arches towards the horizon. The shadows of clouds rolled steadily across the land.

Miss de Winter stood at the white board waiting for the class to fill up. Her straw coloured hair fell to one side, and she absentmindedly spun a pencil between the fingers of her left hand. The desks shuffled, book bags opened, paper spread out, and the lesson began.

- Okay everyone, today we will continue our discussion of William Faulkner's 'A Rose for Emily'. Please turn to page 78 in the reader. I want to look at some specific passages from the text. Now, as we spoke about last week, Faulkner's short story is an example of southern gothic fiction. There is a sense of horror hidden just behind the surface of the buildings, something being covered by a thin veil of civility. But as we progress this hidden horror seeps out slowly from the cracks in the town. Now, who can tell me broadly what this story is about? How about you Jack?

- Uh, it's about an old lady who died and everyone wants to take a look at her house because she's stayed indoors for a long time.

- Uh huh, that's right – Miss Emily has been a recluse for twenty years, she has always been a mystery to the town and this is a chance for them to sneak a glimpse behind the curtain. And what do they find?

- That she collects lots of roses?

- Did you just read the first page?

- …Yes…

- I set you all short stories. The operative word is short. Okay, show of hands, who actually finished the story? Hmm. Okay, Lauren, can you tell me what they found?

- They found the mummified body of her old lover, lying in the bed that she sleeps in.

Shocked laughter bubbled around the room.

- See, you're interested now aren't you Jack? That's right Lauren. They find the preserved body of her fiancé, which she clearly sleeps next to at night, and it becomes clear that he has been dead for 20 years. Now, let's return to the beginning. Lauren, how are we introduced to this story?

- Well, we are told the story by an unnamed member of the town. She is part of an aristocratic family so they are all curious about her, she is a sort of mystery that the town wonders about.
- Exactly. Emily stands apart from the town, she exists in an antiquated world of social manners and arrangements which the common members of the town are not subject to. We are talking about arranged marriages, family lineage, maintaining a certain respectability. I'd like to look at a specific section of the text from the opening of the story. Bobby, would you be so kind as to read out the description of Emily's house, from the bottom of page 88 in our book.

It was a big, squarish frame house that had once been white, decorated with cupolas and spires and scrolled balconies in the heavily lightsome style of the seventies, set on what had once been our most select street. But garages and cotton gins had encroached and obliterated even the august names of that neighbourhood; only Miss Emily's house was left, lifting its stubborn and coquettish decay above the cotton wagons and the gasoline pumps – an eyesore among eyesores.

- Now, Bobby, what does this description tell you about Miss Emily?
- That she is like her house; she was once beautiful and stately but now everything has aged and decayed.
- Okay, yes. In some ways, she stands for the Old South in this story, a style of sophistication and society that has left the land, being replaced by capital, and the automobile, a dangerous symbol of the future. A grand way of life has gone, gone with the wind, if you will. But there is something else going on here that Faulkner is hinting at. Look at how he describes this decay, as 'stubborn and coquettish'. What does this mean?
- That there is something desirable about this decay, that it has a power to draw things towards it.
- Yes, I agree. It is a potent word for Faulkner to choose, it ties together the worlds of death and sexuality, a theme which

will continue in the story, and it also inverts the idea of decay and depression as something we want to run away from. Think about this in terms of horror stories themselves. They are full of gruesome images, they frighten us, and they are concerned with things we want to avoid: death and ghosts. But at the same time we are drawn to them, titillated by them. Just like the rest of the village, we want to know what lies behind the walls of Miss Emily's house. This is why we read on. And perhaps this is intricately connected to revelation. So let's think about that. Jack, can you read us the concluding two paragraphs of the story, the discovery of Homer?

The man himself lay in the bed. For a long while we just stood there, looking down at the profound and fleshless grin. The body had apparently once lain in the attitude of an embrace, but now the long sleep that outlasts love, that conquers even the grimace of love, had cuckolded him. What was left of him, rotted beneath what was left of the night-shirt, had become inextricable from the bed in which he lay; and upon him and upon the pillow beside him lay that even coating of the patient and biding dust.

Then we noticed that in the second pillow was the indentation of a head. One of us lifted something from it, and leaning forward, that faint and invisible dust dry and acrid in the nostrils, we saw a long strand of iron-gray hair.

- And so I have to ask: Is Homer a rose for Emily?
- Perhaps the way you would save a petal from a rose? In a book?
- Yes, exactly. I think so. And perhaps the most shocking or the most disturbing elements of these stories are not what we run from but what we cling on to.
Yes, it followed him around on days like this. The bell rang out.
- Okay, that is it for today. Now, you all have the mid-term questions, and as you'll see there are a couple about this story. Remember, you need to answer two of the questions, five sides each, and I'll be expecting them in two weeks from today, at the beginning of class. Think about the themes we've discussed

here; revelations, uncovering the secrets people keep until they die. I'll finish with a quote from Faulkner you should find useful: "The past is never dead. It's not even past." I'll see you all next week.

A moment of silence descended on the classroom and then broke as the bell rung out into the room once more. Books slammed shut, bags were hoisted and then the steady soft smack of trainers as the pupils fled the room.

As the sunlight fell, rich orange light from the house on Elm Hill burned brighter against the twilight. Bobby sat at the kitchen table, his work from class spread liberally across the surface. He sat staring at a collection of Faulkner's short stories but the text had become impermeable, where before he could have fallen through the sentences into the story, tonight the page merely sat there glass like, reflecting his own thoughts back at him. *Keeping alive what had died.* Were they doing that here? Living together in this room, pretending the rest of the house hadn't changed, that the darkness had somehow preserved it. Maybe. But it was clear that something was happening here, that the more they tried to forget what had happened and make a life here, that something wouldn't let them. In the night when he felt her presence at the door, watching over them, when he'd wake to the blue light beneath the curtains and feel the house moving, creaking, sighing. Perhaps they had succeeded, kept her alive. Part of her anyhow. Taking slow steps around the house whilst they slept. Sitting in their old bedrooms. Looking for them. Sitting, crying softly to herself, wondering where they had gone. And so they slept here, in this bright room, missing her, wanting her back, and she paced the darkness, crying to herself, wanting them back, neither knowing for sure where the other was.

The front door opened and Charlie walked in.

- Hey bro, how's it going? Good to see you're working hard. I'm impressed. There's not even an Empire magazine hidden under there or anything, is there?

- I can't stay here any longer Charlie, I think we need to move out.

Charlie set the brown paper bags down on the counter and turned to look at him.

- You're just upset because of last night. We worked ourselves up. It's bound to happen. The nights are drawing in, Halloween is almost here, you're reading all those horror stories for class, which is…okay, it's pretty cool actually, but should they really be setting this? And this house is old, it creaks, it's creepy. I get it. But we can't leave because of that.

- You know something isn't right. Can't you feel it?

- I'm telling you, we will be fine. We're fine here. We just need to look after the place a little, that's all. When was the last time we didn't just pass out here after watching TV? We've been stuck in here for weeks. And it's probably making us both a little stir-crazy. So I tell you what; on Saturday, when we're both off, we'll give it a good once over, tidy a little, and start using the rest of the place again. You'll see there is nothing to be scared of. Okay?

- Okay. Okay, Fine. But I just need a break – a few of us are going round to Ed's tomorrow after school for a movie night- is it alright if I stay over at his house?

- Uh, yeah, sure. Of course. Now, let's get some dinner.

The following day Charlie arrived at Ashenbrooke library and was greeted by Susie's smiling face.

- Hey hey Charlie bear, good to see you. The big man is waiting for you in the office.

- What? Why? I am entirely on time today.

- It's not that. Just go see him, okay?

- So mysterious aren't you?

- Yeah, now get lost.

- Fine then.

- Fine.

- You want me to grab you a coffee on the way back?

- Yeah, thanks.

Mr Brayman's office sat at the back of the library. The room had originally been Teddy Ashenbrooke's private study and many of the original features remained. The room was hung with a series of framed black and white photographs of the town in the 19th Century, the walls were lined with several glass display cases and locked bookcases containing rare manuscripts and first editions, and in the centre of the room stood an antique writing desk which legend had it contains a colt 45 revolver secured in a hidden compartment somewhere within, which Teddy had kept on hand in case there were any differences of opinion concerning the ownership of said rare editions and manuscripts.

One apocryphal tale had it that during a tradesman's visit/week-long bender in Baltimore in the 1840s Teddy engaged a particularly drunken Edgar Allan Poe in a game of poker, ultimately winning Poe's shoes, pocket watch and the original manuscript on which Poe wrote *The Raven.* Another variation of the tale is that Teddy actually lost the game, but gave Poe some particularly pure and potent opiates as payment, then proceeded to secure the contents of Poe's pockets and knapsack once the writer had slipped into an unconscious stupor. Hence the locked cabinets and handgun provided insurance on Teddy's 'investments'.

Mr Brayman sat behind this large oak desk, looking like a man who had just lost a wager with Teddy himself.

- Charlie, come in, sit down.
- Sure.
- Mr Shurdach is dead.
- Max?
- Yes. I spoke to Sheriff Sullivan this morning. They found his body yesterday and they found one of our library books in his pocket.
- Oh, yes. About that, he was just so fast and I tried to stop him but...
- Don't worry about the book Charlie. I just wanted to let you know and to tell you that the sheriff will be coming in this afternoon to talk to you and Susan.
- Oh. Sure.

- Are you okay?
- I...yeah. Did they say what happened?
- No, not much, just that they found him way out by the Atalonga.
- What was he doing out there?
- I'm sure that is one of many questions they will be looking to answer.

Later that afternoon Sheriff Sullivan sat at the large oak desk, writing notes on a yellow legal pad. Susie and Charlie were seated across from him and Mr Brayman was bringing in a tray filled with tea and biscuits. He placed these at the desk and then perched near the window whilst the sheriff interviewed his employees. Mike took one of the mugs filled with coffee and pressed on.
- Okay, so we've established that Max came here on Monday afternoon. Did you both know him? Was he a frequent visitor?
Susie answered first.
- He wasn't a regular, I'm sure I'd seen him here before but not many times. I don't think so anyway. I mean, Max was a nice guy but he did tend to fade into the background a little, he kept himself to himself.
- And on Tuesday, did anything strike you as out of the ordinary?
- Yes, he was rushed, rude even. He didn't really even stop to talk to me, he just went off with Charlie to the catacombs.
- The catacombs?
- Oh, the book storage in the basement.
- Okay. Charlie, how did he seem to you?
- Susie's right, he seemed...skittish. Like his mind was elsewhere. When I found the book he wanted he just bolted, straight out of here, was gone before I could stop him. And I'm fast.
- Just not in the mornings.
- Suse, I'm still fast in the mornings. Just because I'm late, doesn't mean I'm not fast. If anything, the opposite is true; it makes me faster.

- Okay, so just so I've got this straight; he comes in, then goes with you to find a book downstairs, and then runs out of the library?
- Yes.
- Did you talk about anything?
- Not much. We talked a little about dreams. The book he took out…well, stole really, was about dream interpretation.
- Okay, and anything else stick in your mind?
The image of a mud-caked leather shoe laying in the long grass flashed suddenly into Charlie's mind.
- …No. Nothing special.
- Well, I think that about does it. One last thing, what time did he leave?
- Around 2?
- You agree with that Susan?
- I'd say more like 3. Charlie is not the one to ask about timekeeping. Seriously, don't get him started.
- I'm going to take your advice on that. Okay, thank you all for your time, and thank you for your hospitality James. I will certainly be taking you up on that offer. Have a good day now.
And with that the sheriff collected his notes and left the library.

When Charlie got home that evening the house was unusually quiet; all he could hear was the tapping of the tree branches against the windowpanes and the wind in the eaves. With his brother gone, the place was too quiet, and so he quickly turned on the radio and grabbed a beer from the fridge. Some classic rock would keep this place in line for the night. He knew what his brother meant, of course he did; there was something off about the place. Had been for months. He stared out into the black backyard and heard the rain coming down on the trees. The only thing he could liken it to was her sickbed, that timeless room that they would sit in with her and watch movies. A room at once dangerous and safe, sad, and heartbreakingly happy. That death could seem so harmless for so long. That was the thing you didn't expect, the dailyness of it all, the routine. Teas, and movies, medicine and sleep. That time ran down too as she got sicker, as if the pace of the world followed the pace of her heart, slower, slower, slower. That room became the still point of the turning world, a place they would return to each day and find unchanged. Teas, movies, medicine, sleep. It was endless. Until one day, just like any other, when it ended. Charlie watched the shadows fly across the lawn as the wind whipped the trees back and forth.

Scratch. Scratch. Scratch. Claws stroked the wooden walls. He was getting bolder, that furry little bastard. Outside the windows were chickens heaped up in piles, their guts thrown liberally across the lawn. Each time I look out the window I see the blue swish of his tale as he rounds the bend, and the trail of destruction in his wake; trails of muddy blueblack blood plastered across the grass where he dragged their carcasses across the ground. There is a shoe, sticking out of the wet muddy mass.

Let him come. If he gets in he won't be getting out. That's for damn sure. Come to me blue fox. If you dare. But he doesn't. He prowls on the threshold, keeping his ground, scraping rhythmically at the walls. Mocking me with those scuttling claws.

Charlie woke in the unknowable hours before dawn, aware of a rhythmic noise at the back of his mind. He lay listening to the staccato tapping of tree branches against the kitchen windows. At first that sound seemed to occupy the whole world but before too long, he heard something low between the notes; a soft sighing. Of wind perhaps, rustling through the last leaves on the trees, whisking them away. But steadier actually, the sound was familiar, and then he placed it; the intake of breath. The slow steady sobbing had returned, he heard it gently on the wind, coming from somewhere nearby. He lay there for an indeterminate amount of time, just listening to the sighs, focussing on the taps, and wishing the wind would die down, would cease for the night and leave him in peace. As he lay there in the darkness, memories of his mother returned to him and he saw her laying there in her bed. It swamped her emaciated form, the crisp white linen contrasting harshly against the sallow yellow of her skin, crumpled tissues falling from the pillows as she moved and the hollow sockets of her eyes where the tears wouldn't fall.

The shutters banged suddenly against the side of the house; the storm was rising and had clearly torn one shutter loose. It was now flapping madly against the wall, knocking against the window pane. He heard raindrops (footsteps) falling on the upper floors of the house. The floorboards were creaking softly above him as someone paced from one side of the room to the other. He sat still, unsure whether to get up and investigate or to lay back down and attempt to fall back into fitful sleep. So he lay half-awake on the sofa, in a halfway position between action and rest, as the rhythmic sounds swelled and the grotesque phantoms above began to form wilder and more menacing shapes in his mind. The image of his mother crossed into his conscious mind; her jaw contorted, her eyes unfocused, pacing the halls on outstretched feet. Quietly, creeping, her slender brittle body stalked the house, clothed in a rotting nightgown, as she wandered, lost, through their home at night. She no longer knew where she was, was looking for something, something she could no longer remember, and couldn't find. He heard the loose step on the staircase creak and knew that she was descending, was flowing towards him. And he was up; the swift shot of adrenaline rushed past his heart, making his chest leap and fall. He heard her descend the stairs. He acted fast, pushing the sofa across the floor, up against the door as a barricade. The shutters seemed to grow louder, smashing against the side of the house, and the rain howled against the window panes. The noise was now cacophonous, the storm outside shook the house and Charlie felt each rattling window and door further fray his stuttering nerves, the adrenaline and fear coursed through his body and all he could do was sit on the sofa pressed against the door, hoping his weight would keep the door shut and this room safe. He sat there in the semi-darkness, looking around the room, at the storm outside and listened; listened to the branches patter against the roof, the rain lash sideways against the window panes. He listened to the decaying ghost of his mother, as she shuffled down the stairs. He saw her vacant eyes, her white skeletal form as she stumbled from room to room. Something scratched against the door behind him. Scratched softly against the woodwork. He hunched down, planted his feet on the floor, and pressed his weight into the sofa. He would hold this room, keep this door shut. He sat tight as the door handle began to shake and he felt a steady pressure push against the door behind him. He would hold this, he would hold this door closed. The rain lashed louder, the shutters slammed, something wanted in. But he stayed there for as long as he could, frozen in the darkness as the storm whipped around him, as the door shook and windows rattled, as the house itself creaked and swayed in the wind.

Was she here? A body that faded from the world, its echo reverberating in the walls of this house. He braced himself against the door, wishing it to quiet, and praying for the sun to break through the darkness. He closed his eyes and visualised her dying, leaving them. She wasn't here any longer. They'd said goodbye and watched her leave. They'd held her hand and said goodbye to her.

The rattling ceased suddenly, and a hushed stillness fell over the house. Charlie felt the pressure ease on the door and he allowed himself to listen, to focus. Nothing, an absence of sound, the wind whispering at the door. Nothing more. The sky was brightening ever so slightly and he could see rich blue at the windows, the faint beginnings of another day.

FICTIONS

Emily awoke to the familiar feel of a paperback pressing into her shoulder. She rolled over and extracted it from between the pillows. Ah, Rebecca. She longed to roll back under the warm covers and plunge back into Manderley; its happy valley and wild coastline, the splendour of the house, the locked doors and hidden corridors. But as she retrieved her phone from underneath the other pillow she already knew she was late. 7.32. Yep, definitely late. This meant today's breakfast would be a coffee and pastry from the school café sometime between classes. She was up and in the shower, the warm flush of water running down her back, warming and waking her body, her mind fresh and airy, rising like steam in the air. She liked mornings like these; she'd scarcely left her dreams and here she was already, awake, stepping into the day. Where had she been? In Manderley perhaps, standing at dawn on the fair English coast, the mist of morning hanging low in the air, crafting a silhouetted nowhere world of grey and shadow. Someone was with her, she was sure, but she looked in every direction, strolled into the mists and nothing, just the shore extending in either direction and the surf slowly slapping the rocks. She felt it still, as the water caressed her body, warm tendrils of heat flowing down her shoulders and back, and the steam hanging in the air, fogging the mirrors. She leant backwards, letting the water flow over her hair, the combination of cold air outside and warm water on her head sending waves of sensation shivering down her back and making the hairs bristle on her arms. Yes, she liked mornings like these; the fresh chill October air coming through the slightly open window, the special warmth that comes from the cold outside. Cold and heat mingled in the air making mist. She liked Ashenbrooke, was glad she'd moved here. From her classroom window she could see the leaves falling from the chestnut trees. The town was quiet and sleepy, slightly strange. It felt like the towns in Washington Irving stories; isolated misty towns secluded from the world. Yes, she liked it, was happy here and enjoyed the solitude of her own apartment. She read late into the night, letting her imagination roam in ways only possible when alone, falling into vivid fictions and then floating back up each morning, ready for the world to begin anew. In some ways moving to Ashenbrooke felt like stepping out of her own life into a story she'd read as a child, stepping from the grey London streets into the bright American page. She'd experienced it a million times; nestling into the nook of the sofa with a new book, letting the rainy afternoons become nothing more than background noise, a percussive beat in the background. Only this time it was real, she had stepped fully into a world of her own imagining.

Was moving here a choice? In some way it felt like the logical conclusion of her life, stepping in to a story she'd half-written. But then there had also felt like no choices left at that time - well, perhaps one – that choice that had whispered to her on empty nights. And then what did you do? You let it end, or you hurled yourself headlong in to a new one – hoping the speed would create momentum; a reassembly of self. Yes. She had chosen Ashenbrooke, had found the passport she'd kept tucked away at the very bottom of her chest of drawers, and then had boarded the plane and disappeared somewhere in the vast web of time zones that crisscrossed the globe. And here she was, four months later; alive in the tremendous freedom of her solitude.

To be alone in another country is not the same as being alone in your own – there is an added comfort in the life around you and it is right that you are in some sense separate from it, an unobserved observer. Since arriving Emily had reread many of her childhood favourites – Sherwood Anderson, Fennimore Cooper, Melville and Hawthorne – she couldn't help but picture Ashenbrooke in this light. An American town half shrouded in the mists of myth, the insubstantial world a presence in the forests and rivers on the edge of town. She imagined half-formed monsters in the trees, waiting for wary passers-by. Decades could slip here, ten, twenty years drifting away and the town stood still, in its own pocket of time. She felt this world, wanted to be like it, to drift from the present to somewhere, at once old and without time, a clearing in the forest where everything happened.

Emily sat in the corner of the canteen sipping coffee and staring out the window towards the forests. A paperback sat with her, she still couldn't quite get used to the idea of e-readers. To read pretend stories on pretend pages felt one step too far. Instead she liked the feel of stories in her hand, their smell and their weight. The books in her own apartment seemed to have taken on a life of their own, they roamed around from room to room and would plonk themselves down wherever they chose, on counters, reclining on couches, their pages spread out lazily. They would hide under pillows or nestle down the side of the bed. She shepherded them as best she could but without the wall sized bookcase from her old apartment in London it was a losing battle, and she watched as they took over. She remained as vigilant as she could be, but they had now taken to following her to work and were already accumulating in the staff room. She took this one and restrained it in her bag, it couldn't disappear until she was done with it. Then she got up and strolled down the corridors of Ashenbrooke Community College, enjoying the last few minutes of quiet before the students arrived.

Bobby knocked on the half open door of the English department staff room and Emily beckoned him in. To call it a staff room was to exaggerate its grandeur. It was really an old storage room that had been converted. There was just enough room for a kitchenette, a sofa pressed against the wall, a small table with 4 chairs, and bookshelves. Lots of bookshelves. But it did have a small window that looked out over the inner courtyard. It was pokey, but pleasant.

- Come in Bobby, take a seat. As you can see we don't go into teaching for the glamour, hey? You fancy a coffee? It's, well...it's drinkable. That's really all I can say to recommend it.
- Sure, that sounds good.
- Milk? Sugar? It needs it by the way.
- Yeah, just milk please.

Bobby put his rucksack down on the table and pulled out one of the chairs. There were lots of posters on the walls, for raffles, lectures, school events. Others looked like national geographic shots; a savannah here, some earthenware pots there. He took out a notebook.

- So, Bobby, what essay were you thinking about choosing?

Emily brought the coffees over to the table and pulled out a chair to sit down.

- Thanks. Well, I was thinking I wanted to try the one about hauntings and locations, I mean, place. I was thinking about the houses.
- Aha, yes – 'the haunted house'. It's potent, isn't it? Practically a genre of its own. Would you like a cookie?

She opened a tin that was on the table, revealing a handful of biscuits that could easily have been there for months.

- No, I'm okay thanks.
- Yes, probably wise, I'm not sure when these are from. Okay, so – what's your take on it?
- I guess that the houses are always connected to people. The ghost of Rebecca is part of the house, it, her things, they live on after her. And with Emily too, all the ghosts of her past still live in the house with her. Like the dead are living on, in a way.
- Hmm, yes, I like that. In a way you could say that the dead are 'preserved' in the house. The way we talked about in 'A Rose for Emily'; she preserves Homer the way a young girl may preserve a petal from a flower. She keeps the memory but kills the thing she loves in the process.
- That's the feeling I get from those stories; something not quite alive, not quite dead. The houses are like that, like something is trapped. There's this unsettling feeling to them.

- Now that is a good place to go with your essay. I see you've got your notepad, so write this down: Sigmund Freud, 'The Uncanny'. It's a brilliant essay, it'll really bring this alive for you. I'm afraid I didn't get a copy for here but you can get it from the big library, the Ashenbooke Library.
- I know it, my brother works there.
- Hold on…Older brother? Lighter hair?
- Yeah.
- I've seen him there, I'm sure I have. You look alike.
- Yeah, he looks more like our dad though. He'll help me find the book.
- That's good. It's quite brilliant; and focuses on that feeling of being unsettled, that sensation of knowing something is wrong but not knowing what. What you're going to write about is a perfect example; 'the haunted house'. I mean, I don't want to spoil it but what I will say is this; it's exactly what we talked about, the past haunting the present. These houses were once homes, they were once places that were alive, vibrant. That's why the haunted house pops up in these tales so much, why it is such a recurring trope in this genre; because it is an inversion. This unsettling, uncanny feeling can only exist in somewhere that was once associated with happiness. The haunted house is the dark mirror of the happy house of memory. Ha, I get carried away with this; there's more, about the words, reversals, but I'll let you come to that on your own.
- Miss…
- Emily, please.
- Emily, do you believe in it?
- What? The idea? Yes?
- No. Not just the idea. I mean the hauntings.
- I believe a person can be haunted. By their past, by their memories.
- And a place?
- Hmm. Yes. I suppose so.
- It's just, that's what it's felt like since…my…our mother died last year.

- Oh, Bobby, I'm so sorry...
- That's her plaque over there, by the cherry tree.
She saw his shoulders stiffen and a wateriness at the edge of his eyes.
- It's just, since she's been gone I've felt it, and then your class and the stories we're reading, it feels the same at home, and I didn't know who to talk to but I thought you might get it...
She reached out and placed her hand on his arm, his jaw clenched and tears spilled from the side of his eyes down his cheeks,. He looked away, down towards his bag.
- It's okay. Bobby, It's okay. You can talk to me.
- She...
He paused, gathering his breath.
- It's like...like she's still here. I can't...I feel like she's not gone...
Tears started to well up again.
She plucked some tissues from the box on the nearest bookcase and handed a few to him. Tears fell from his eyes and his jaw trembled for a while, then his breaths got under control again, he looked at her and half-smiled.
- Bobby, that is the least convincing smile I've ever seen. But you get points for effort. Listen, I heard a little about it. The teachers here, you know they like to talk but really they're just concerned about you and your brother. It's just the two of you in that house right?
- Yeah, since last February.
- Look, to be honest I'm not surprised you feel like this. The two of you have been through a hell of a lot and you're alone in that house together. Have you talked to anyone about this?
- Not really...I...
- I don't know about ghosts per se, but it has to be oppressive; living alone where you all lived together, carrying on your lives. Can you talk to your brother about it?
- Sort of. We can't always talk about it so well.
- Look, If you need to talk I'm here, you can always come find me. And what you need is to get out of that house for a bit too. Spend some time with your friends, get some distance. Are you going

to the Halloween parade? I hear it's a pretty big deal around here.
- Hah, yeah, that's to say the least. Yeah, I think a few of us are planning to go.
- Good. Okay, I've got to get going to the next class now. But I mean it, if you need to talk come find me.
- I will.
- Good. And I'll see you in class tomorrow.

That night Emily climbed into bed and retrieved her paperback from beneath the pillows. She fell back into the world of Manderley, letting her mind take light steps down dark corridors, listening to the sea lapping against the rocks in the distance. She followed the story until the sentences began to blur, falling into each other. The story flowed into her dreams and then out as she followed the new lines between the old ones. This lasted for mere moments until her arm fell, the paperback dropping onto the pillow beside her. Suddenly she was standing outside Manderley, hidden by the dense foliage of the trees, staring up at the house. The lights in the lower rooms blazed brightly against the darkness and she could see figures silhouetted against the window panes. She allowed herself one glimpse over her shoulder to see who was behind her in the bracken, but all she saw was darkness. The waves rolled on ceaselessly, lulling her back to sleep. As she relaxed again she felt her body begin to float as she flew weightlessly towards the house. She could see Rebecca sat at her writing desk, her luxurious dark hair hiding her face as she concentrated on the letter she was writing, the dark calligraphic symbols unidentifiable on the page, inked out in her slender hand. She flew around the side of the house, peering through the windows of the library where she could make out the figure of Bobby, walking from shelf to shelf, searching for something, scattering books on to the floor. Neither of the inhabitants of the lower floor seemed to sense her presence, and she flew onward, rising, until she found herself at the windows of the west wing. One window stood open and she was drawn towards it, peering into the darkness within. She could only just make out the faint outlines of objects; a bed, a dresser, and a figure, creeping silently around the bed. She squinted, trying to discern more about the figure, when it stopped creeping and turned toward her, its dark hollow eyes alighting on her own. She felt an instant of sheer panic as she was frozen immobile in the air, looking into the dark sad eyes of the figure in the bedroom, and then she fell swiftly to the ground, landing abruptly on her own pillows and sitting up with a jerk, sweat prickling on her brow, her heartbeat racing. She stayed there for minutes trying to expunge the image and feeling her heartbeat return to normal. Then she retrieved the paperback from the pillow beside her and placed it on the floor next to her bed. She turned out the light and lay back in bed, feeling her heartbeat slow and her panic subside. She tried to forget the feeling of the figure's stare, and felt herself awake once more by the house. But this time she stood and strode away from the dark house, tramping through the woods and walking away from night and into day, coming out in the clearing of the happy valley. Here she lay in the sunlit garden as the endless waves beat quietly against the shore, dozing in the warm light, oblivious to the dark house and the footsteps in the bracken.

THE STATION HOUSE

Sheriff Sullivan opened up the station house and turned on the lights. He liked arriving at the empty building and watching it slowly come to life as the ceiling lights sputtered on in rows, illuminating the ordered boards and disordered desks of the squad room. He could hear the heating kick in, and smell the old radiators as they came on. The building was waking up. He felt the rhythm coming together, establishing itself; there was a steady heartbeat, a steady progress, and they would solve this murder, he could feel it just as he felt the beat of the building itself.

Carter arrived a little after 8 and found Mike sat with the coroner's report open on his desk.

- Good morning boss.
- Hey, morning Carter. The machine is on, go get yourself a coffee, I have some news.
- Okay, will do. What time you get here this morning?
- Hmm, 6. Maybe. Seriously, you want to prepare yourself for this. Go get a coffee right now.

Carter hunted for capsules in the kitchenette. Mike had insisted on installing a Nespresso machine last year, and had managed to get budget approval from the finance committee by selling them on the idea of improved staff efficiency and alertness. She couldn't really argue with that; a lungo in the afternoon certainly kept her going on the slower days. Somehow, she had a feeling today was not going to be a slower day.

She leant against the wall whilst the machine whistled. The original station house had burned down in the late 70s and the temporary set up in the old town hall had somehow become less temporary over time. The current police department now took up the large central meeting room; a couple of the old benches remained at the far end of the room for visitors but most had been removed and replaced by four large L shaped desks in the centre of the room. The main entrance and reception desk were at the south end and the northern wall was where the current case boards were situated, next to Carter and Mike's desks. Today Max Shurdach's picture was up there. The two smaller meeting rooms on the eastern side had been completely overhauled and were now a self-contained interview room, and a holding cell respectively. The two larger rooms on the western side had been maintained in their original fashion and were used for press conferences, meetings, and quilting and baking clubs. The benefits of hosting community events in the station house were twofold; firstly people got to know them and provided a steady source of rumour about the town. Secondly, they tended to leave the detectives cakes on a morning. Carter spied the tin, found what she hoped was a piece of fresh carrot cake, grabbed her coffee, and headed over to sit down next to Mike.

- Okay, listen to this. The doc finished his autopsy of Max and inside one of the facial lacerations he found a broken shard of nail.
- Does that mean we can trace the type of bear?
- No, you see, that's the thing; the doc says it was a tough shrivelled old nail, but he's pretty sure it's a fingernail, a human nail.
- What? You're messing with me.
- I am not messing with you. He's had to send it off for further tests but this might not be a bear attack at all. It could be a murder staged to look like a bear attack.
- I don't know. I've seen bear attacks before, and it was messy as hell. It looked pretty realistic to me.
- Yeah. I know, but maybe he fought someone else first. Maybe he was already dead and then his body was dumped there, in the hopes that a bear would destroy the evidence. We need to keep an open mind on this one.
- Damn, Potemko is going to have a field day with this.
- Ha, yeah. The kid has a creative mind.

- That's one word for it.

Once Lewis and Potemko had arrived Mike began the day's briefing.
- Okay, you've all heard about the unusual developments of the day so far. I want us to remain focussed, there is a time and place for speculation, and that is at the end of the day when the work is done. For now, we run this like any other investigation. Okay, in summary: The autopsy report is back, and the cause of death is a heart attack. Likely this happened due to the shock of a violent attack. Time of death is between midnight and 4am. We are working under the assumption that Max died by the river, and the scene indicates he was running and was brought down. Now, we don't know if he was savaged by a bear pre or post-mortem, which means the possibility remains that he was already dead and his corpse was savaged by the bear. We will continue to pursue both avenues until some hard evidence surfaces. Lewis and I have been reconstructing the timeline of Max's day. So far we are drawing a blank between the time he left the library at 4pm and his body was discovered at 5am the following morning. Lewis, I want you to keep manning the phones today, we are looking for any indication of his whereabouts yesterday evening. Carter and Potemko, we have a meeting set up with the Fairmount Sheriff's department at 2pm this afternoon so I need you both to travel there and gather all the information related to bear attacks in the greater Atalonga region. One more thing. Who is free to work at the Halloween parade in a couple of weeks? The organisers have asked for a police presence this year at the event. I'll be there so I just need one more person.
Potemko was quick to volunteer.
- I'll do it Sir. I was planning on going so I'm happy to help. You think I'll be able to take half an hour out to show my little sister some of the rides?
- I don't see why not, I don't think it's going to be too taxing a gig.
- I don't know boss. If I was the manbear, I think it might be the

perfect opportunity to strike.

- Potemko, don't make me sorry for keeping you in the loop. Okay everyone, you've got your assignments. Any important developments you call me. Otherwise, we regroup here at 6 this evening. Happy hunting.

The tall pine trees sped past the car windows as Carter and Potemko drove north to Fairmount. Carter kept her eyes on the rolling scene ahead whilst Potemko rummaged through the glove compartment. Carter could tell the questions were coming and was trying to maintain an air of indifference and to give off the impression that she was concentrating hard on her own thoughts. But despite her efforts, Potemko began.

- Carter, do you think there's some sort of half man half bear wandering around in the woods?
- No. No I do not think that.
- But you have to admit the evidence is weird. I just have this image of like a Yogi Bear wandering around the woods. What was his deal? He was a half man half bear wasn't he? I mean he could talk.
- He was not a man bear. He was a bear bear, a regular bear.
- But he could talk, and he walked around on his hind legs, like a man. And he stole picnic hampers. I mean, it's not the level of criminal activity we're looking at here, but it's something.
- He was a cartoon Potemko. That's why he spoke. Like bugs bunny speaks. Like Garfield speaks. That doesn't mean they are part man.
- Now, with all due respect, we don't know if Garfield speaks.
- What? Of course Garfield speaks. I've watched that show a hundred times.
- With Garfield it's a voice over. Like, we are privileged to hear his thoughts. But he doesn't converse with Jon. It's just Garfield's thoughts. He's a regular cat.
- Who thinks aloud?
- Yeah, all cats must think aloud in their own heads. We just can't hear them is all. With Garfield, the voice over is our glimpse into

his thoughts. Yogi Bear, on the other hand, speaks. He's not your average bear.

- I don't know why I even bother having these conversations with you. Okay, for argument's sake let's say you are right and yogi bear represents some sort of hyper intelligent bear. He still doesn't seem prone to fits of rage in which he tears ranger smith to pieces.
- I'm not saying our killer IS Yogi Bear.
- Good, I'm glad we agree on that.
- I'm just asking – do you think something strange is out there?
- No. I do not. It's clearly either a wild bear, which I'm inclined towards, seeing as we are currently driving up to Fairmount to review the details of three *wild bear* attacks in the area, or possibly, just possibly, it's some fucked up guy who wanted to kill Shurdach and make it seem like a bear attack.
- It couldn't be an intelligent bear trying to make it look like a man's attack?
- I...stop fucking with me Potemko and pick a damn radio station alright?

By the time that Carter and Potemko returned to the station house the sun had set and darkness crept through the windows to settle snugly in the corners of rooms. The room was quiet and the others sat at their desks, going through the paperwork for the day. When Mike saw them arrive his eyes lit up.

- Hey guys, what have you got for me?
- It was actually a very informative trip. And I also managed not to throttle Potemko during the course of the day, which I consider a win on both counts. Have we got a map of the greater Atalonga area around here anywhere?
- Yeah, I'm sure there are a few over in the information centre. Give me a second and I'll go take a look.

   The information centre and gift shop were part of the old town hall – it was a small building attached to the south of the main house and had been used as a visitor centre since it was built. Ashenbrooke still got a fair few tourists each year that based themselves in the town, before heading out on the trails of the Atalonga national park, and the information centre provided maps, trail guides, postcards, novelty pens, and bear-shaped chocolates. Mike took a left down the corridor to the connecting door. The lights were off and it was closed up for the day but he had keys for all of the buildings on the property, which had come in handy on a few occasions. This time he let himself in to the quiet store, took one of the maps from the back of the pile, and let himself out. He brought the map back to Carter and helped her pin it up on the board.

- Okay, so we spoke to Sheriff Elson over in Fairmount and she filled us in on a few things. There have been 12 suspected bear-related deaths over the past year in the greater Atalonga area, 13 if we include Mr Shurdach. This is not an uncommon amount for the year. 9 of these incidents were open and shut cases, the bears were tracked down and euthanized. However, the other 3 incidents were never resolved. They all remain classified as suspected bear attacks but all 3 were notable for their crime scenes. Typically, with bear attacks there is a large amount of evidence left at the scene; scat, stripped trees, the victim's innards spread liberally across the area. They are usually cases where a lone traveller has gotten lost and accidentally wandered into known bear territories. In most instances the cases are open and shut, with the rangers called in to track the bear and euthanize it, this typically achieved after merely a week or two. However, all 3 of these other scenes, 4 if we include Shurdach, are comparatively tame. They are bloody, sure, but the shredded bodies were still in one piece and the scenes were fairly undisturbed. There was no subsequent evidence of bears in the vicinity and on one of the victims autopsies the coroner noted that the teeth marks on the body were inconsistent with a bear attack. In all cases the investigation has gone cold, no further evidence has appeared, meaning they've been listed as bear attacks and filed away. It was only because Sheriff Elson had earmarked them that we even know about them. Now, Potemko, throw me that marker will you? I'll get these up on the board.

Carter marked small black crosses on the map.

- Okay, so we have the first site north of the Atalonga, at the White Fells, towards Fairmount. The second is further east along the Atalonga River, near the Bayliss Woods. And the third is further west, by Oakwood Ridge. And Shurdach is here, fairly central between the 3 points. So, the intersection of these sites is on the northern bank of the river, a couple of miles further east from where we found Shurdach, with a radius of around 25 miles covering all the sites. As you can see there's not a whole lot around there, just the forests and the river.

Suddenly, Lewis sprung up from his seat.

- Give me a minute. I think there is something there.

And with that he disappeared round the corner into the darkened gift shop, returning minutes later, with another fold out map.

- Check this out; this is the booklet they give out to hikers, it's the historic Atalonga trails. I remember this from when I was a kid and my parents would drag me along with them on a Sunday hike.

He pinned this one up on the board too.

- See? The Fairwater mill is right in the middle there. They probably don't keep it on the main maps anymore as it burned down when I was like ten. It's huge though, I remember trekking out there, it has to be five years ago now, but when I was there a few of the old cabins were still standing. It used to be a bit of a local landmark, people would go there as a dare. It's just been left now, falling to pieces. But it has to be the only vaguely habitable place in that area.

Mike stepped up to the board and peered at the map.

- Well, it isn't much, but we sure as hell don't have any other leads right now. Carter, do you mind holding this place together tomorrow? Get some good rest tonight guys, looks like we are taking a trip in the morning.

ASHENBROOKE

Charlie descended Elm Hill, the town laid out before him. He watched the slowed clockwork motions of the town's residents as the chimes called out a time that meant nothing at all. To the birds who nested in the high trees surrounding Ashenbrooke the town was a rough circle in shape, similar to the stone pools in which they stopped to wash on stifling summer afternoons. To those birds passing by on longer journeys it was a mere break in the endless seas of green below, a small town nestled on the southern ridge of the Atalonga forests – a patch of greys and lights already long forgotten by the time they reached their destinations further north. The smaller birds stayed well within the limits of the town, for to head north in to the forests was to pass over in to the domain of eagles and ospreys, to face a swift death in the quiet forests. They were quite content to limit their explorations to the many parks and squares within the town. From their aerial perspective they had a sense of large squares and a series of grids crisscrossing the land, a faintly disordered pattern of lines and squares surrounded by forest.

The centre, both in terms of geography and the social calendar, was Monument Park. The 100 acre plot of land had previously formed the private Ashenbrooke residence but was bequeathed to the town along with the library in Teddy's estate. The park occupied a central place in the lives of Ashenbrooke's residents; they would all flock here to watch the Fourth of July fireworks and the Halloween parade. On an ordinary day, almost everyone would pass through the park (or around it) to reach the different neighbourhoods of the town.

Ashenbrooke Library sits on the eastern edge of the park and looks out over the splendour of Teddy's old private land. To the west the land rises sharply, and at the crests of Elm and Willow hill sit the older neighbourhoods of Ashenbrooke. Large wooden gothic structures can be seen high on the hills, their imposing structures and the street's gas lamps casting shadows over the hill that rises from the park. These are the finer neighbourhoods of the town with small boutique shops and cafes nestled in the streets. To the north of the park lies Ashenbrooke College and the high school; the site pressed right up against the forests.

South of Monument Park lies downtown Ashenbrooke; the lights of bars, cafes, apartment buildings. What passes for a metropolitan life takes place here. The Southwest is the old civic neighbourhood and this is where the courthouse and the police station are both based. The Southern neighbourhood sprawls but this is not the case in the north, where the forests form a distinct barrier. The local hospital is located in the Southeast district, and this is where the roads swell and eventually lead away from the town towards the highway, and endless white lines on black tarmac.

*

Charlie woke in a room that was not his own. He felt an arm on his chest that was also not his own. He felt hot and butterflies began to float in his stomach. Echoes of the previous evening returned to him; whisky chasers on the bar, dancing on a table with Casey, falling in the street outside Odell's. The ache in his left hip returned in sympathy with his memory. Black hair cascaded down his shoulder and he remembered. The girls outside Lucky 13. They'd shared a smoke. His mouth tasted like ash. In one slow breath he inhaled the room and wanted to open the window but any movement could wake her and he wasn't quite ready for that. He took in the posters on the walls; the Stones, Gustav Klimt, one of the Yeah Yeah Yeahs. There was a bureau under the eaves and an assortment of CDs scattered across the floor.

He heard footsteps along the corridor and the sound of the

shower being turned on. Indistinct whistling. She stirred next to him.

- Hey.

- Hey yourself.

- Charlie right?

- Yeah. Uh…

- Karen. I'll try not to be too offended by that, I hope last night wasn't entirely forgettable.

- It wasn't. Just not entirely rememberable at present.

- How's the hand?

He retrieved his left hand from underneath the covers. The first two fingers were bruised and swollen, turning a rather nasty bluish purple. His fingers pulsed.

- Shut in the door at Odells. You kept trying to get back in. Suffice to say they stopped finding it amusing after a while.

- I guess you can like a place too much.

He sank back into the pillows, breathing in the peace of an unfamiliar bedroom. The shower stopped and footsteps ran along the ceiling.

- That's my cue. Don't get too comfortable. I've got lectures at ten so you need to be ready to go by the time I'm back. Take your chances now if you like but if you want to escape without the tenth degree I'll have to distract the guys and sneak you out.

And with that she jumped over him, grabbed a towel from the closet, and disappeared upstairs in a blur of long black hair and underwear.

Once she was gone Charlie rooted around at the bottom of the bed and found his boxer shorts crumpled up in the sheets. It didn't take long to find his shirt under a pile of cushions, and his jeans behind the door. The right leg was frayed at the bottom, and there was a dark stain on the left that smelled like stale beer. He pulled them on, careful not to jar the fingers on his left hand, and tried to find a mirror in the room. He opened up the closet and took a look at himself in the long mirrored door – his hair was standing up in the back, his eyes looked like they were coated in film, and he had a few days' stubble on his cheeks. He rubbed his face and tried to smooth his hair as best he could. His left hand hurt like hell and his hip still twinged – what the heck had they done last night? He lay back on the bed and listened to the constant patter of the shower through the ceiling. He felt warmth around his eyes and his head fell in to the pillow as he imagined the water cascading over Karen's body above him, the suds from shampoo rolling down her back.

He felt a hand shake his shoulder, his heart jumped and his eyes snapped open. Where he expected to see his brother was Karen, fully dressed and ready to go.

- Hey, get up, we have to go. You sleep like the dead, you know? Now follow me. I'll distract whoever's in the kitchen and you head straight out the front door.

Charlie waited for his cue and once Karen was in the kitchen he ran quietly across the living room, flipped the latch, and snuck out of the house. He immediately recognised the tree lined streets and could see the lake ahead on the right – he was in the dorm houses just east of the college. It wasn't unusual to wake up in someone's living room after a party when he was back visiting friends at college. He'd wake up, sneak out of the house and find himself somewhere in the Poplars – the name given to the few blocks of student housing on this side of the park. And here he was again, but this time knowing no-one in this part of town. He waited for Karen beside a tree next to the path that led to the lake. She came up and joined him.

- I thought you'd be long gone by now.

- I can't move so fast this morning.

- Yeah I guess so.

- And besides, I live on the other side of the park. You're heading that way, I thought we could walk together.

- Lead on kemosabe.

They strolled through the brisk October morning. The sky was a bright light blue with swift white streaks stencilled in the air.

Leaving the college, Charlie took the long route through the trees. He checked his phone – seven missed calls from Bobby. It was almost eleven. He was due at the Library by noon. Maybe he'd go. Maybe he'd stroll. Now that the adrenaline had left his body he felt cold and wrapped himself up in his jacket. Why didn't the world continue without you for just a little while? You can turn off for a few hours but then you had to catch up on all the bullshit you missed. It would all be about the fucking house. He turned off his phone and paced his way towards the Library, kicking the leaves as he went.

Charlie rolled in to the house a little after nine.

- Hey Bobcat.

- Where have you been?

- Around and about – met a few guys from college and the night sort of got away from me.

- Okay.

- You been alright?

- Not really. I tried calling you.

- Yeah, sorry, I lost track of time.

- It happened again last night.

- Bobby, I don't want to hear about it.

- It…how can you not want to hear about it? This place is fucking haunted.

- It's not haunted. It's…look I really need to hit the hay.

- We need to do something.

- What?

- I don't know.

- You're making it worse.

-I'm…

- Yes, just leave it okay.

- What if she's trying to tell us something?

- Fuck Bobby. She's dead. She can't tell us anything.

They sat there in silence for a while.

- You know what's happening.

- Oh fuck this, I'm out.

- You can't!

- Watch me.

And with that he strode out the house and made his way down Elm Hill, through the park towards Lucky 13. He saw the town, he saw the light, and he saw the shadows in the trees. He watched the slow clockwork of the town's motions and felt the beginning of another night. The chimes of the clock tower reverberated through the park. He listened to the wind howl, the cars pass, and didn't even bother trying to count.

THE ABANDONED MILL

A pale mist hung over the river and the surrounding areas of the Fairwater mill. The remains of the mill were sprawled across the old site; the millwheel had rotted years ago and floated downstream and all that remained of the main structure were a few rotten boards caked in years of mud. The mist hung over the mill like a thin veil of time, and to look at the site it was impossible to tell if the place burned down one year ago or twenty. The walls that still stood showed signs of indeterminate aging; they had swelled each summer and contracted in the winter, crafting intricate patterns in the wood. The misshapen buildings hunkered over in the mists. Viewed from above the site looked like scattered dominoes; some walls still stood, others had collapsed, taking the buildings nearby with them.

When the Sheriff rolled up that morning, he parked his car by a copse of trees on the southern side of the mill's outskirts, and waited for Lewis and Potemko to arrive. They'd set off together in the morning but somewhere along the hour long journey, Mike had let the radio wash over him, gone into cruise control, and lost track of the other car. In truth, he couldn't remember the whole journey now, just the seemingly endless woodlands passing by on either side of the road and the empty roads slipping by, punctuated by the very occasional truck passing on the other side of the road. There was nothing really out here, a few deserted gas stations nearby and the odd signpost pointing to property out in the sticks but any semblance of the old Fairwater was gone. There had never been much here, but when the mill used to run there were enough food and convenience joints to make a community. Since it burned down, it seemed most of the businesses had gone bust.

Sitting here, on the edge of the forest, with the mist lying still on the river, it really felt like he was perched on the edge of the world. Perhaps there was nothing there on the other edge of the river. The world would just fall away into the dark chasm below. Mike sat there watching the weak wooden structures wallow in the slight breeze, letting the quiet emptiness of the place wash over him. The structure of the scaffold hung in the air. Oddly it reminded him of the skeleton of a dinosaur he'd seen in the natural history museum, held together with pins; the echo of an animating force that once took it trekking across continents. In another twenty years it would surely be nothing but rotten planks of wood, misshapen makeshift plaques commemorating the graves of forgotten men and women. So here they were, at just the right moment to pay monument to its decay.

After a little while, the white beams of headlights announced the arrival of the others, and Mike watched them pull up and park on the other side of the dirt track which led from the woods to the mill. He got out of the car and cracked the trunk as Potemko and Lewis strolled over towards him.

- Geez, this place really is the ass end of nowhere isn't it?
- You know, it actually used to be quite something. I remember the big mill wheel going round. They used to give tours of the place. It was busy, popular. Damn, it really has fallen to bits.
- Mill tours, hah, sounds like the crazy kinds of excitement kids get up to around here. Seriously, Lewis, why weren't your folks taking you to laser tag or something?
- They were…outdoorsy, I guess. Look, it was fun, alright?
- Yeah well I think the only tours they'll be doing out here now are ghost tours. Or some sort of ripper serial killer trail, if that's what this turns out to be.

Mike unloaded the trunk, handing flashlights and evidence bags to the others.
- Okay kids, now we're here to survey the area. We're looking for signs of habitation; food, blankets, clothing. Anything that looks out of place here, which I suppose is anything at all. You find

something, you bag it and radio me. I'm going to check out what used to be the offices over on the west side of the mill. Potemko, I want you to go explore what's left of the main building. Lewis, you take the storage huts on the eastern side. If you need help, an extra pair of eyes, you radio me. And we'll reconvene on the northern side. It shouldn't take us more than an hour to cover the area. And I know it looks abandoned, but keep your wits about you okay?

Lewis set off towards the smaller buildings on the eastern side of the mill. There were still charred planks of wood after all this time. They were mostly hard to distinguish blackened clumps of wood, but you could tell there had been a fire. The first hut that he stepped into was almost preserved, black scorch marks had climbed halfway up the walls, but it must have been one of the few structures that remained relatively unharmed. Well, undestroyed. The place was a mess. And he didn't expect to find much amongst the ruins. Most of the buildings had been reduced to a few walls but there were some that remained standing on the far north eastern side, and so he made his way towards them. The mist hung around the buildings, clinging to what was left of the place. The air was strangely still and as he walked further to the north side of the mill, the sounds of the others faded away until he could hear nothing. Well, almost nothing. There seemed to be faint scratching sounds, floating rhythmically towards him from the huts by the river. He walked closer, following the sound. It sounded like a small creature might be hunting around inside the remaining store houses, perhaps drawn there by the ancient scent of grains or oats. He found the door of the nearest hut, and with a light touch it swung all the way in on its hinges, crashing into the wall and shaking the entire building. The whole structure seemed to lean precariously to the side as the door made contact with the walls. Something scurried away but when Lewis flashed his light around the corner all he saw were piles of old boxes stacked against the walls and animal droppings all over the floor. This was useless, there was nothing out here but a burned out building and rats picking off the carcass. He scanned the room but there was nothing there, so he headed back outside. The beam of his flashlight cut through the mist but it seemed to have gotten thicker. He could see the mill, but not the buildings on the other side of the site where Mike was. He arced the light over towards the river and thought he saw a small rodent disappearing into the waters. The river rolled by slowly, the mists hanging over the water and flowing along after it in undulating currents. Both became a sort of mirror of each other, the watery world below and the misty world above, gurgling away, running down, running down, pulled along by some vast dark current. Lewis felt the world sliding past him, the concrete world running away, and looked around him. The solidity of it all had gone, walls that were once strong had faded, their molecules slipping away from each other, crumbling into light barriers. The blue sky had rolled away, leaving greyness all around, nothing to separate distances. This world here was empty, still, it was always the same but it was dead, inanimate. There was a quiet beauty to it, the still beauty of a tomb, or a graveyard. What was it about the soil in a graveyard? It belonged in two places at once. Like an embassy. The way American soil could exist in far off lands. Well, the soil in a graveyard existed in our land, but in another too. The same space was both, and none, all at once. That's what this place was, its own graveyard, a space between worlds. An urgency crept over Lewis. The stillness was beautiful, but suddenly he wanted to be done with this, and to be back with his partners on the other side of the mill. He flashed his light, found the next intact looking building and headed over towards it. It was quiet and he pushed the door, expecting it to give easily, but it didn't. It must have been wedged shut, the water swelling the wood and warping it, creating a solid barrier. He set his shoulder, and threw his weight against it. It barely yielded on the first attempt, but on the second it flew open, leaving Lewis off balance from the momentum. It took him a second to steady himself and raise his light. He barely had time to register the figure in front of him, the gnarled features, and the wet yellow teeth, before the force of it hit him square in the chest and he felt himself flung backwards. He felt the wind leave his chest and heard a very loud cracking sound that seemed to come from within his own chest. He tried to cry out but his breath was gone and his lungs weren't filling. He was on the floor and he rolled to face the man (was it a man?) and found himself looking into its cold black eyes. His body was thick, muscular, dirty, and he felt the man's sharp nails digging into the skin of his left arm. He tried to act fast, and as he pulled the pepper spray from its holster with his right hand, he heard the man's wheezing breath and felt sharp claws tearing open the flesh of his arm. He felt unfathomable pain and the sharp, warm falling of his own blood pouring from his body. His stomach felt like it was floating and it took all his effort to raise his right hand, push down the trigger and release the contents of the pepper spray into the thing's face. He held it down, gripping with all his might and spraying, aiming for its eyes, feeling its grip release, the dull pressure of its claws pull away from his muscles.

Potemko was leaving the mill and heading down towards the river when he heard the heavy slam and thud from over by the storehouses. He starting jogging over that way and called out.

- Hey Lewis, you okay? One of those cruddy old buildings fall over on you?

That's when he heard the sound that made the cold stream of adrenaline flow through his veins; a murmuring growling sound, dark and deep and guttural. He drew his pistol and ran towards it. The mists parted and he could see Lewis sprawled on the floor, something hunched over him.

- Hey! Get the fuck away from him!

It turned towards him and Potemko could see it was a man (was it a man?). He was as dark and charred as the buildings around him, his hair fell over his face in grey straggled clumps. His eyes were dark, and there was blood dripping from his red right hand.

- Get the fuck away from him and get down on the ground or I will blow your fucking brains out! You hear me?

That sound, a dark deep guttural sound, rumbling out from its chest. It was fast, it glared at Potemko for what seemed an age, and then it sprang, sprinting towards him. Potemko fired, low and straight. The revolver shot out fire and the bullet pierced it straight through the chest. He saw the impact but the man kept coming, barrelling towards him. He fired again, this time blood sprayed out from its shoulder but it was too late. Potemko felt the force of it slam into his side and lift him off his feet. For a second he was airborne flying backward through the air, and then he came down hard as the ground swiftly came up to meet him. The force of the blow threw his pistol away into the grass. He scrambled toward it, knowing he'd have to be fast. He crawled across the floor, the pain of the fall obliterated by the adrenaline in his system. He rolled, picked up the gun, and sat up, aiming at where he thought it would be. But it was gone. It had barrelled straight past him and kept going; it was already disappearing into the mist to the south. Potemko leapt up, feeling the pain dance up his left side as he ran over towards Lewis, whilst radioing Mike.

- Sir, we need you right now, the storehouse next to the river. Lewis is injured. Call an Ambulance. Get the first aid kit from the cars. Fast.

He knelt next to Lewis; he was babbling senselessly, and his left arm was torn to shreds. There was blood everywhere.

- Lewis, Lewis! Listen to me, this is gonna hurt like hell but stay with me, okay?

Potemko unbuckled and removed his belt, ran it around the top of Lewis's arm, and pulled it as tight as he could, forming a makeshift tourniquet. Lewis screamed out and rolled in pain, the whites of his eyes rolled up and his eyelids flickered frantically.

- Stay with me kid, the boss is on his way.

His breath came in fits and starts and Potemko could see blood seeping through his uniform.

- Shit! Shit! Lewis, Lewis! I know it hurts like hell but stay with me. What the fuck was that? What was that?'

They sat there for what was probably mere minutes but felt like hours until Mike came running out of the mist, the static chatter of overlapping conversations babbling from the radio pinned to his hip.

- The ambulance is coming. What happened? What do you need?

- We need to staunch the blood. We need the bandages, anything absorbent.

Potemko took the first aid kit and covered Lewis's arm and chest with the dressings, they clung to his skin in sodden bloody clumps.

- Boss, we need that ambulance now. That thing really fucked him up.

- What happened? Was it a bear? Is it coming back?

- No, it's gone. I shot it. Twice. Just call them, find out how close they are.

- They're minutes out, I'll call them again.

Mike stood there, pacing the site, looking for any sign of something coming back, and directing the ambulance to their location. Potemko sat with Lewis, keeping him conscious and keeping pressure on the wounds. They stayed like that until they heard the wail of sirens approaching, and saw flashes of blue and red light heading towards them through the grey.

LINES

Emily woke to the sunlight streaming through her curtains and a slow steady throb pulsing through her head. At first she put the aching down to one too many glasses of red wine the night before, and rolled her head into the other pillow, but then she realised that it was getting louder and more insistent and wasn't coming from within her head at all (well, mostly not from within her head) but actually from the other side of her bedroom wall. She got up and opened the bedroom door and there it was; that steady drone of the alarm from across the hall. Bloody hell. She stormed across the living room, pulling her dressing gown closed and tied the cotton belt as she walked, opened her front door, found the key behind the painting in the hall and opened the door to Mike's apartment. In here the noise was deafening, the pulsating beep synchronising with the pain in her temples. Her head seemed to swell and contract with the undulating sound. Was this some sort of industrial alarm he had taken home from the station? It was as loud as an ambulance siren, the Doppler scream that assaulted your ears when an emergency vehicle careered past on the street. She ran over to the wall and pulled the plug from the socket, stifling the last blare mid scream. He must really be a deep sleeper if he needed this thing as a backup. She surveyed the apartment; it was empty, no doubt about that. Everything was in its right place, tidy, clinical. The bed was tucked in, hospital corners. No signs of anyone at all. She picked up his phone and dialled his number. He picked up on the second ring.

- Hello?

- Mike, this is Emily. Why am I calling you at 8am on a Sunday morning you may ask? Well, I don't want to be calling you at

8am on a Sunday morning and that is for sure. This is either contrived to get me to call you, in which case I'm flattered. Or this is sheer thoughtlessness, in which case I'm annoyed.

- Fuck. Fuck. I set the alarm didn't I?

- And I'm annoyed. Seriously, I'm going to throw it out. Why can't you get a normal alarm? Like one that doesn't sound like an air raid is imminent?

- Shit, I'm sorry Em.

- And where the hell are you this time anyway?

- I'm in Fairwater, at the hospital.

- You're in...are you okay?

- I'm fine. It's Lewis, one of my partners. We got attacked yesterday and he's pretty badly hurt. They say he's going to be alright, but I've been here all night. I wanted to be here when he wakes up. I...shit, I totally forgot Em. I'm sorry.

- Hey, um, don't worry about it. You, uh, you need anything?

- No, we're fine. Thank you. I've gotta go now. Listen, I'll call you later.

Mike hung up the phone and stopped pacing the waiting room to take a look out of the window. He'd been up most of the night, except for falling into a strange dreamless sleep sometime around 3am and waking up with his limbs aching and crushed into the shape of the waiting room chairs. Lewis had been in surgery for most of the day, and they had finally stabilised him by the evening, but he wasn't meant to wake up for a while. So Mike had waited with Potemko in his room and then spent the night down here. He wanted to be there when Lewis woke up, to see him before he went home. And fuck it, he needed to know what he saw. Potemko was going on about some 'crazy Charlie Manson fucking feral old bastard' and he needed to know what Lewis had seen too. He'd spoken to Carter last night, put out a bulletin about the attack but without some sort of description of the guys' features what good was it? Fuck, he hadn't seen it coming at all, hadn't seen or heard anything. Just that fucking grey mist, and then the gunshots. Lewis returned to his mind, laying there, his blood seeping from his chest into the long grass. He shook his head to clear his thoughts. Emily was up, and his alarm had gone off, that meant the day had begun. He'd sat here so long in this timeless waiting room, drifting in and out of sleep that he'd lost all track of time but it must be 7.30am now. That meant visiting hours had almost begun. He trekked to the café to get himself and Potemko a cup of coffee. And he'd forgotten that damn alarm again. What else was he meant to be doing today? He picked up his phone and dialled the library.

- Hello, Ashenbrooke Library, James Brayman speaking.

- Hello Mr Brayman, this is Sheriff Sullivan.

- Oh, hello. Yes, I found those books we spoke about. I have them all ready to go so you can come visit anytime.

- Thank you. Thank you very much, but you see, I'm afraid there's been an incident and I won't be able to visit today.

- Nothing too serious I hope?

- It's… I'm going to be busy for a while. Is it okay if I come to see you next week?

- Yes, of course. Don't worry, these books won't be going anywhere. You can visit anytime.

- Thank you. I'll call you later on in the week.

- Of course, speak to you then.

Mr Brayman set the receiver back in its cradle. The dappled light fell through the mullioned windows onto the large maple desk. The phone was illuminated for a moment in a spotlight, made significant for an instant and then forgotten; the light moving on to cascade in leaf like patterns over the books and papers scattered across the desk. Charlie walked into the room carrying the next box of papers.

- Okay, where shall I put this one down Mr B?

- Just over in the corner if you wouldn't mind. How many more are there?

- Another 3 I think.

- Okay, well, if you get those and put them in the same place, I'll put on a pot of tea and then we can have a quick break before we get to work.

- Sounds good to me.

Mr B prepared the tea and set down the biscuit tin on the small table by the window. Once Charlie had deposited the last box, he took a seat in one of the large red reclining chairs by the window. They afforded a view over the grounds behind the library; the large pine trees out on the horizon and Teddy Ashenbrooke's private garden in the foreground. Mr B maintained the small patch of land very well, it had a small herb garden and many small plants that thrived in the winter snows. The garden had the feeling of epic in miniature; like the Japanese rock gardens that were so popular; a grand garden reduced to a manageable size.

- How long has it been you've been working here Charlie?

- Coming up to a year at Halloween.

- Hmm. Time just presses on doesn't it? Though perhaps it doesn't in quite the same way here. This place doesn't change much does it?

- No, you're right. But I like that.

- Me too. You get to a point where you don't really crave change anymore. You're just happy to feel the slow accumulation of days that fall on a place, and make it more significant if anything. But...surely you must still want something else from your life?

- I'm quite happy here Mr B.

- But you're so young. Don't you want to travel? Explore?

- It's not really on the cards. If I can enjoy my work and see Bobby through school, then I'm happy. I don't need any more excitement for a while.

- Yes, I know what you mean. I knew your father you know?

- Yeah?

- Man was a fool to ever leave. I guess that's what running after excitement gets you in the end.

- Yeah. I guess so.

- Well, I suppose we better get back to it.

As the sun began to set outside the windows Charlie's phone rang.

- Excuse me a second Mr B. Hello?

- Hey.

- Hey. How's it going?

- Fine. You planning on coming back tonight?

- Yes, I'll be there.

- Look, can you do me a favour? I need a book.

- That I can help with – what's it called?

- It's an essay called 'The Uncanny', by Sigmund Freud. I'm not sure which book it's in but my teacher thought you had a copy of it there.

- Sure, I'll speak to the big man; I'm sure he'll know where to find it.

- Thanks.

- No problem. I'll see you later. I'll pick up some take out on the way home – you up for pizza?

- Yeah, sure. See you later.

Bobby put the phone down and looked at the books he had spread out on the kitchen table. He'd been revising for his mid-term physics test all afternoon, if you considered wandering around the living room bouncing a tennis ball off the walls, sitting on the back stoop reading short stories, playing PlayStation, drinking cups of coffee, watching YouTube clips, and perhaps 30 minutes of actual textbook revision revising. Which he did. He was glad that Charlie would bring that essay home. Since they'd started reading Faulkner's short stories for his English class he'd become addicted; he'd just sit in the garden and fall into the page. There was something just right about the setting too; it felt right to read those stories whilst sat in that garden with the calligraphic branches and the sun low on the horizon, shadows arcing up the lawn. Well, at least he could hope for a good grade in that class at least. But for now, Newton must be faced; different type of trees altogether. He sat there as the sun fell below the horizon, reading until the light was finally gone and then got up to turn the kitchen lights on and grab a drink from the fridge. This place had gotten darker, more frightening over the past few months, he never felt entirely safe when he was here by himself but he couldn't imagine leaving like Charlie suggested; the truth was that he loved the place, had always loved the place. Even now, in its fractured form, when they only really used the kitchen, living room, and the garden it was still home. There was a certain magic, sometimes it felt like it existed in some nowhere place, that it was their island cut off from the world. It could be terrifying, he knew that now, but really it was something special too; mystical, he'd sit on the stoop outside, feel the electric charge in the air where the warmth of home met the stimulating cold of fall, and he'd look straight through the veil of this world to the next, feel time fall away and just stay there, at the still point of the turning world. Just then the house phone chirruped. He picked it up but all he could hear was static on the other end of the line, the ever changing crackling pitches of disconnection.

- Hello? …Hello?

- …

He almost put the phone down when he recognised a faint voice on the line, distorted but there. He recognised it and shivers rippled from his neck to his shoulders, the hairs standing alert on his arms.

- Mum?

The voice faint but unmistakeable in the static.

- …obby…tchzz……he….tchttt….kzz….ng…

The next instant the phone was dead in his hand; as mute as the stark darkness that now enveloped the house. Bobby stood in the dark, unable to move, listening to the silence all around him. The only sound was his own heartbeat thumping in his ears. Everything was stillness, no light, no noise. A fuse must have blown as he couldn't even hear the fridge humming to itself. He reached for his mobile, turning it on so that the faded blue display would at least show him the outlines of shapes in the room. Once he'd gotten his breathing under control, he found the cupboards and the flashlight stored there. The beam broke the darkness, and threw grey light into the furniture. He pulled a chair over to the front door in order to reach the fuse box, forcing himself not to look over his shoulder into the darkness, stood on the chair, removed the cover and flipped up the red breakers. The house came back to life; the lights blinked on, the fridge chuntered and started back up, the spotlight in the garden flickered on and then off. The noise of the house returned and the steady sad flat line of the dial tone broke out from the phone. Bobby quieted it by placing it back in its base, and then sat at the table watching it, willing his brother to come home.

TURN, TURN, TURN

The following morning Bobby awoke with the sound of his mother's voice still echoing faintly at the corners of his mind. The sense of foreboding he'd felt for weeks was getting stronger and his feeling that big changes were coming found expression in the turn of the seasons outside his windows; the last leaves were falling from the trees and the charred end of the year approached. Smoke began to rise over Ashenbrooke as the residents burned bonfires in their backyards and lit fires in their living rooms at night. The wispy trails of smoke wove together over the town, making a blanket of haze that lay softly over the houses, lulling the residents to sleep in their homes. But for those who stayed outdoors and wandered paths at dusk, there was still a crackle in the air as the night caught alight and the last few weeks of October burned away.

True to tradition, the residents of Ashenbrooke were making preparations for one last grand civic gesture before winter truly arrived and they would take solace in their homes; lighting fires inside as the cold sunk into the land. But for now the air maintained its electric crackle in the dying fall and preparations were made for the Halloween parade and bonfire; the last great spark of the year. This was a tradition that brought the whole town together and preparations had now been underway for weeks. In the fortnight preceding the parade the town was made ready for the celebrations; bales of hay and pumpkins would arrive on street corners, assorted root vegetables pushed forth from wooden stoops and a fine layer of cobwebs fell from the streetlights in town. School groups at the elementary were putting finishing touches to their floats and costumes for the parade, and the great bonfire grew tall in

Monument Park as volunteers stacked the broken birch branches high. The old town made its preparation for the coming crowds and stores on Main Street stocked their shelves with candied bats, chocolate ghouls, and toffee apples in abundance.

In the time since the sheriff had walked down to the Atalonga and the first hesitant leaves had fallen from the trees, time had sped past swiftly and days were now deposited in great burnished piles on the lawn. Charlie and Bobby took rakes and cleared the yard as best they could, creating large colourful piles at the base of the great elm trees. They had come to the uneasy conclusion that they needed to tackle the house; that the only way to take it back was to live in it, and so they had resolved to confront the ground floor. For too long they had sanctioned off the kitchen and lounge at the back of the house and today they moved the long sofa from in front of the hallway door and watched dust motes swirl in the new shafts of sunlight. The hallway led down to the front of the house and the front door. Neither could remember the last time that the front door had been opened. The coat stand stood at the foot of the staircase, and the hallway was empty, echoing. To the left of the entranceway was the door to the reception room, they pushed it open and stepped inside. The forgotten room greeted them; dusty paintings of ships on the walls, and the stacked record player in the corner. In happier times this room had been used when guests came round. There were board games stacked up under a large wooden table in the centre of the room and a functioning fireplace on one wall. Bobby remembered games of monopoly that lasted multiple days and the crackle of the radio in the corner, churning out seventies classics. The room was incredibly cold and they began by kindling a fire in the hearth. The light from the fire flickered off the frames of the paintings, lighting up the steep crests of waves and the sails of ships. It was a small victory, the first they had had taken in a long time. The smoke rolled up the chimney and ascended into the grey haze hanging over Ashenbrooke.

The smoke formed a canopy of cloud that sat low over the town, hanging over the hills. On the other side of town, at Ashenbrooke General, Lewis's convalescence was progressing slowly. The white walls and syncopated beeps of his hospital room had become his home away from home. At night Lewis would watch the framed woodland scene at the foot of his bed as he drifted through codeine-infused states of consciousness, and would wander endlessly through wild woodland as the birds chirruped in time with his heart rate. The doctors had set his broken ribs and had fought hard to save his arm. There had been significant damage to the nerves and ligaments and now it lay motionless on the bed next to him, wrapped in bandages and gauze. Occasionally it gave out sad pulsating waves of pain that rocked his body, but mostly it lay there dead and motionless, the cold clammy skin of his fingers shocking him briefly when he rolled onto them at night.

He'd come to feel at home here, and each day that he spent surrounded by the white walls and machinery he felt like he'd drifted further and further away from reality, as if he'd come untethered and was being carried downstream by the current, allowing himself to let go. The hours had lost all semblance of shape or conformity; at 5am when the pain set in and he waited for the dawn one hour could last forever, when the medication took effect and he sank down under the waves he'd lose handfuls at a time. He watched the paintings; irretrievable time washed away like wheat down streams.

In his dreams Lewis returned to the misty mill, but now it was alive with movement and light. He stood in the long grass at the perimeter of the site. The lights lit the mists in an array of yellows, blues, and orange. He heard music filtering through on the wind. It was a party. As he got closer figures began to come into focus. Revellers dancing on the lawns, couples speaking conspiratorially over wine glasses, a lone smoker puffing away under the eaves. The mill was whole again, like he remembered it from his youth. There were people on every balcony, and they spilled out on to the lawns. Men in suits threw beer bottles in graceful arcing loops through the air and into the river, the splash of sound bouncing off the walls eerily. Time seemed to flow unevenly in this world too. He would approach the party in slow motion, watching the dancers sway, and listening to the elongated vowels of the singers as the music slowed down. Then time would speed up, and he would be propelled through the throngs and up the staircase towards the warden's office. The walls shook and he could hear a fight breaking out inside as things were thrown against the walls.

He stood listening at the door, the wall of sounds pulsing through his body. For a second he saw the faint outline of the hospital walls though the woodwork, and then it was gone, the world seemed solid once more. Chatter and music swam all around him as he floated through the party. He caught glimpses of something at the corners of his vision. A flash of red, a grimace in the darkness. The laughter began to sound more hysterical, higher pitched, more like screaming. He woke up drenched in sweat, his yell catching in his throat.

Potemko visited every day in the fortnight after the attack and on his days off he brought an old set of board games he'd found in the station house – a reversible board suitable for chess or chequers. The key was to focus on games that could be played one-handed – cards were out of the question. He would keep Lewis busy during his lucid periods and when the meds kicked in and Lewis rolled off into the medicated haze, Potemko would sit in the chair by his bed, thumbing through a worn paperback.

The view from windows across town was grey and still but for those who still forayed outdoors it was a different story. The nip in the air quickened the senses and there was a feeling of urgency and excitement. Even the old men sat huddled around their chess sets in the town square were not immune to the feeling of festivity in the air. Their campaigns were conducted with renewed vigour as the decorations were erected around them in the square and they would nurse take-away coffees they'd bought from the new refreshment van set up for the imminent crowds. A few solitary figures would be seen throughout the winter but for the most part the Halloween parade marked the ending of the year's battles, and the inhabitants of the square would relocate themselves indoors. Hence there was a renewed sense of urgency in the air, a need to settle scores before the winter kicked in and the battles would cease for the year.

Emily and Mike made their way through the square and past the players on their way to Main Street and the Hitchcock marathon showing at the Harrison. The street was lit up and more popular than ever as couples sat sipping cocktails at Dukes, and groups of kids shopped for outfits in the pop up Halloween store. As they still had half an hour before the movie began Mike and Emily popped into Tart to Tart, the café next door, which stayed open til Midnight, to satiate the coffee and pie cravings of Ashenbrooke at all hours of the day. They bought a couple of coffees and a slice of cherry pie and found a table in the window looking out at the street.

- You know, I just love this time of year. The charge in the air – It feels like we're getting ready for a real pagan festival, worshipping the old gods. Halloween is nothing like this back in England. You'd be lucky to get 2 trick or treaters and a firework through your letterbox. But this…it feels potent doesn't it?

- You don't think it's just a little over the top?

- Well, yes. But then, I think that's what I like about it. America isn't afraid to commit to something.

- Yeah, one hundred and ten percent.

- Exactly.

- So, how long have you been here? In the states I mean.

- Not long actually, just since the start of the year.

- You mean you arrived when you moved in across the hall? In February?

- I'm touched you remember Mike.

- I have a very good memory.

- Yes, I guess it comes with the job...

- And, I mean, it was a memorable event. So, how come you moved to our sleepy little town?

- I don't know. I'd lived my whole life in London. And it felt like it was time for a change. I'd always had the passport, tucked away in a drawer. My dad was American. And it felt like time for something new, an adventure. I haven't been disappointed so far.

- So does your dad live here too?

- No, he passed away a while ago.

- Oh, I'm sorry.

- Thanks, It...It was a pretty crappy time to be honest. And that was part of it, I needed a fresh start.

- So, why Ashenbrooke?

- You're just full of questions tonight aren't you?

- Sorry – that is also something that comes with the job. I find it hard to break the habit.

- Yeah, I imagine so. Let's turn this interrogation around hey? You grew up around here?

- Not that far away actually. My parents still live out in Fairview.

- Let me guess – on a little farm?

- You know it has been called that. But it's actually a school they run. You've heard of Montessori?

- The one where you get report cards with the smiling suns on?

- Only if you find maths fulfilling…

- And if not it's a sad division sign?

- Or a forlorn square root. Yeah, the place is full of kids. They just never retired, kept it going.

- That's sweet. That where you grew up?

- Yeah, there were books everywhere, half built railways running across the carpet.

- That explains a lot.

- About my finely honed habits of attention?

- Yeah, something like that. Speaking of which – any news?

- No. Absolutely nothing. Lewis is getting better. Slowly. But it's been over a week since the attack and we have no new leads, no reports of anyone matching the description of the attacker. Not from the rangers, not from the hospitals. It's like he just vanished. And I've got Potemko, he's the one who put two bullets in the guy and probably saved Lewis's life too, telling me this crazy shit about how the guy was some otherworldly killer. I don't really know what to do with that. I mean, the guy's a fucking hero but he's…how do I put this…an imaginative kid. It all happened so fast, who knows what he saw.

- Well, it would certainly seem the time of year for something otherworldly wouldn't it?

- Now, I know you've gone native. Just because there are skeletons hanging from the streetlights doesn't mean this place has slipped off the map just yet. Anyway, tonight is about a different kind of horror. Have you seen this movie before?

- Psycho? Yes. It's great. I'm a bit of a Hitchcock fan – I was made up when I saw that the Harrison was doing a season for Halloween. It's such a great cinema. You haven't seen it then?

- No, never have.

- I would have thought it would have been required viewing for the job.

- No, not this one. Silence of the lambs, now that was mandatory.

- Another classic. Well, I won't spoil anything but I think it's safe to say the title gives you a fair clue about the subject matter.

- I'm looking forward to it. And speaking of which we'd better get going if we want to get some popcorn first.

And so Mike and Emily headed to the Harrison and took their seats. On the streets outside the theatre leaves blew steadily across Main Street, getting tangled in the cobwebbed street lights. The steady procession of people still passed by on the streets, making their last preparations for the parade and letting the dynamic force of the festival ferry them along towards the darkest day of the year.

ALL HALLOWS' EVE

The fete arrived and ghosts and ghouls drifted past on the streets. The crowds packed in close to watch the floats as they passed down Main Street, snaked through Monument Park, and marched up to the square. First came a tribute to Dracula, complete with a vampire bride that rose slowly from her coffin and a series of great black bats stuck hastily to the float, some of which detached themselves as the float moved past, falling into the sawdust that lined the path of the procession. One of the bats fell at Emily's boot. She plucked it from the floor.

- This actually goes pretty well with my costume, doesn't it?

The staff from the English department had elected to go with an Adams family theme. As Morticia, Emily's outfit was now well accessorised with the black bat on her shoulder.

- You know if you could just bite the head off that bat we could all modify this a little and go with an Ozzy Osbourne theme. When you think about it the Osbournes are the Adams family of our generation.

The floats rolled past: there were mummies, vampires, ghosts, werewolves, zombies, ghostbusters, skeletons, and a particularly inspiring float of animated pumpkin-headed scarecrows with rotating swords. The crowds buzzed and cheered as the floats rolled past, they applauded the costumed freaks, and prepared to burn things. As the last floats rolled past the crowds joined the procession and headed up towards the square where a funfair had sprung up overnight; there were candy floss vendors, hook-a-zombie-duck, a haunted house ride, and assorted stalls to draw in the punters. As they walked up Emily saw Bobby at the shooting gallery standing next to a taller fair haired boy.

- Whoa – nice shot bro! Okay, now focus, you can do this, just two more hits and we can win one of those…stuffed bears. Okay, it looks like it's just stuffed bears, but you know that is just what our living room needs.

- Don't worry, I've got this.

He loaded the air rifle and aligned the sight with the target. He realised this gun fired a little low and to the right so he raised the sight, targeting the upper left corner of the next ring, breathed out slowly, pulled the trigger and…ping-bulls eye!

- Yes, yes! That furry little guy is gonna be kicking back on the sofa, enjoying a beer and a movie before you know it. Okay, one more, you've got this.

Bobby loaded the final pellet into the gun and snapped the barrel back. The whirlitzer's music jangled manically at the edge of his mind. He heard the other contestants sighing in frustration as their shots winged the target. He breathed in, aligned the gun, and then breathed out, letting the world wash away from his mind. His finger squeezed the trigger gently and…ping-bulls eye!

- Yes! Yes! That was fucking awesome. How did you get so damn good at this? We'll take that big fat bear at the top please sir. Haha, nice work bro.

- You're very welcome. You're holding on to that bear for the rest of the night though.

- This guy? I wouldn't let him out of my sight, he's my trusty companion now.

A figure in black floated towards Bobby and tapped him on the shoulder.

- Hey Bobby. That was some nice shooting, I'm impressed.

- Oh, Hi Miss de Winter. Thank you. This is my brother Charlie.

Charlie took her hand and kissed it.

- Charmed, cara mia.

- Ah Mon cher, It is a pleasure to meet you. And your bear.

- Ah yes, Terence, he is very pleased to meet you too.

- Please call me Emily. I like your costumes. They're...marines?

- Zombie soldiers. Hence the steady aim.

- That'll explain it. You planning to take a cache of bears home?

- Yep, some bears, a duck or two, maybe even one of the scarecrows.

- Great. Well, good luck with that. I should get my spot at the bonfire. See you both later.

Emily re-joined her group at the bonfire. It wasn't especially hard to find them, as Uncle Fester had rigged up a secret battery pack to power the light bulb he occasionally put in his mouth. The crowds had gathered and were jostling for a better view. Emily caught sight of Mike standing by the side of the stage and smiled at him. He smiled back, and then the AV equipment crackled into life and a voice echoed across the park.

- Ladies and Gentlemen, Ghosts and Ghouls. People of Ashenbrooke, welcome to our parade. On this night each year we gather together when the veil between worlds is at its finest, when the dead return. We honour the spirits and remember them. The nights draw in and the curtain is pulled back, revealing what we always knew was really there. So hold those dearest to you close whilst we light, and keep the fires burning bright into the chary night!

The torch was touched to the doused wood and the flames licked the bonfire, dancing high into the black sky, climbing wildly in the wind. The spectacle of the fire drew each person's gaze and united the town in defiance of the night. As Emily watched the flames they shaped themselves into patterns, moving incessantly, forming and dissipating swiftly so that they were never one thing but always many, always new but gone the moment they arrived. The longer she watched the flames and felt the heat flicker against her face the dizzier she became, and eventually she stepped back, pushing past people to get out of the crowds. They closed in on her and she began to panic. A sea of arms and feet blocking her path as she pushed past, feeling immaterial, her limbs becoming fuzzy, as she pushed past person after person, the crowds seemingly endless. After what felt a long time she broke free, out into the cooler air. She filled her lungs and felt her strength return. The tension eased from her body and she walked through the smoke filled park to find a quieter spot. She stood in the quiet night watching the trees drift in the breeze, the shadows of the trees darkening. After a while the trees shifted in the haze and a face appeared within. She saw it and her heart leapt. He appeared in the haze drifting towards her, his arms were branches, his face leaves. When he reached the tree line she ran. She could hear the branches parting and his steady footfalls as he followed her. She ran, and over her shoulder she saw him. In the fire on the hill, in the leaves on the wind. She ran and the haze got denser and soon he was nowhere and everywhere at once. She passed the crowds looking out for Mike – where would he be? The crowds were still standing around the bonfire and now drinks were being served – he was probably keeping watch. As she passed she couldn't see him, so she kept going, trying to get away from the haze. Soon she was back in the square. It had gotten later and the crowds were thinner. Some had gone home, others has moved to the bars on Main Street to keep the night going. She remembered that her colleagues were going to Lucky 13 after the bonfire and so she headed in that direction, looking all around her as she ran.

Candles flickered in red glass holders, throwing shadows over tables and up the walls. The music kicked up another notch as

Bobby returned with two pumpkin beers from the bar, elbowing his way past a troupe of zombie cheerleaders. Lucky 13 was the place of choice for two distinct reasons. Firstly, the dark corners, red walls and giant stencilled black cat provided a very suitable atmosphere for this night of nights. And secondly, they had a "don't ask don't tell" approach to asking for ID from their more fresh faced customers, which was very handy as it would be another 4 years until Bobby could legally drink. The bar was comprised of dark candlelit corners and so he made his way towards one of them, where Charlie was sitting talking to a couple of his old friends from school. Bobby let the conversation drift over him as the bar hummed and customers shrieked over their cocktails. He heard the crack of pool balls as they collided, the bars of a Kansas song thumping in the background, and watched the jack o lanterns grin maniacally on the bar, the flashes of light from their teeth jumping scattershot around them. Beer pong contests took place on the far side of the bar, and Frankenstein's monster roared as he hit the last cup and made the mummy down 5 cups of beer. The party raged indoors and out on the street leaves flew past. Bobby kept one ear on the conversation to his left, his brother was talking with some guy about what they'd been up to since university. But then he saw a dark figure he recognised come up to the glass of the window and peer in to the bar. Emily looked worried, as she hurried up to the glass and scanned the bar through the window. He doubted she'd be able to make out much in the gloom. He waved, trying to get her attention but she was distracted. She looked to her left and then ran off in the other direction.

Emily walked swiftly down Main Street, keeping an eye on the shadows cast by streetlights as she moved. She'd lost him, somewhere after the square. She'd managed to cut out of the western gate, take a circuit around lower monument park, and cut up to Main Street. She kept checking but she thought she'd lost him. Now she just had to find her colleagues and she could forget it ever happened. She skipped up to the window of Lucky 13 and looked inside. She could make out almost nothing; the front section of the bar was full of ghosts and zombies. Trying to find people in this dark crummy bar on a normal night was hard enough but trying to find an undead family amongst the masses? Forget it. At least she'd be amongst the revelling crowds inside. She turned to the entranceway and there he stood, watching her. She jumped and felt her blood turn cold. Fuck. She bolted; turned on her heel and ran down the street. He'd followed her this whole way. Of course he had, this is what he did. She ran down Main Street, looking for someone, anyone, but they were all inside now. The breeze blew up, the cold had sunk in, and everyone had moved inside. Fuck. She ran. Whenever she stole a glance over her shoulder he was there, striding silently towards her. How would she lose him? She saw the alley that cut down to Sycamore Street and she took it. It was only about 10 blocks to her apartment from here, if she could cut across a few streets she'd be there in 10 minutes. She picked up speed and ran as fast as she could, past industrial sized bins full of empty bottles and leftover food, the remains of nights out. She could hear the bass of music behind doors that led into bars and kitchens. She ran. And then she felt a strong grip sink into her shoulder and throw her sideways into a fire escape. Her face hit the side of the rusted metal and she felt hot blood course down her cheek. She lost her footing and landed on a sack of hot garbage, its warm putrid smell billowing out into the cold air, disturbed by the impact of her fall. She looked up and there he stood above her, his cold dead eyes looking straight into hers.

Bobby put his beer down on the table and stood up. He headed straight out of the bar onto the street and looked around. The street was empty, but he could just make out a figure striding into an alleyway halfway down the street. That must have been where she went. He wasn't sure why he followed but there was something in her face that told him she was scared and he found himself out on the street before he'd even made a conscious decision to follow. He jogged down the street towards the alley and just as he got there he heard a scream yell out in the dark night. It pierced him and he ran; all he could see were shadows moving in the darkness and he had to pick out his footsteps carefully so as not to trip over on the garbage strewn floor. The night was now unnaturally quiet and he kept running down the alleyway, and the shadows ran too. Up ahead he heard movement. Then he saw her, laying in a pile of garbage to his right, blood and tears coursing down her face. She was breathing uncontrollably.

- Emily! Emily, are you okay?!

Her eyes came into focus and she realised that he had gone and that someone else was standing before her.

- Bobby?

- Yes. Here, let me help you up.

He put his arm around her and helped her get to her feet. He felt her body shaking as she stood up. Once she was up, he ripped some of the bandages from his costume and used them to clean the blood from her cheek.

- What happened?

- I was…someone was following me and…they…I thought…you must have scared them off.

- My god. Are you hurt?

- No. I'm, I'm okay. The rubbish broke my fall. I'm okay.

- Good, but we should get out of here. Come with me, there's a café just down the street where you can sit down and have some water. Then we'd better call the police.

- Mike, the sheriff, he's just over at the bonfire.

- Okay, I'll get my brother to find him. Come on.

Bobby took her arm and they strode out of the alleyway and back onto Main Street. They found a quiet seat in Tart to Tart, there was still a steady stream of customers at this time of night and so they easily sank into the crowds. Emily dabbed at her cheek with some more of the bandages that Bobby had given her. The cut had closed up and just left a line of tacky dried blood on her face.

- I can probably pass this off as part of my costume, right?

- Yeah, it doesn't look too bad now. Can I get you something? Some water? Chocolate? My mum always said chocolate was good for your nerves.

- You know, I could really go for a cup of tea. And I never turn down the offer of chocolate.

- Okay, I'll be back.

Bobby joined the queue at the counter. Whilst he waited he took his phone from his pocket and dialled his brother's number.

Carter and Mike watched the flames of the bonfire die down. Most of the crowds had dispersed now. Just a few brave souls stood out in the black night, wrapped up against the cold, their beers in paper cups providing a little extra warmth within. The fire had burned down and now gave a steady red glow, a cloud of grey smoke rising into the air. One of the park wardens would stay to make sure the fire burned down safely overnight but for now the detectives' duties were done.

- Well, I think we managed to keep the peace for another night, hey Carter?

- I was worried there for a second boss, when they threw the scarecrow on the fire, but the lords of darkness seem to have kept their wrath to themselves for another year.

- Yeah, no human sacrifices. No visits from the dead. I consider this another successful night. Hey, I wanted to thank you for stepping in for Potemko at short notice. I know you had plans you had to cancel. I appreciate it.

- It's no problem boss. I feel sorry for him. Can you imagine Potemko taking it easy on Halloween? I've never seen anyone go so mad for a holiday. I bet he's at home carving a hundred pumpkins, just to take his frustration out.

- Ha, yeah. Well, he certainly carved enough at work this week. He's probably keeping the pumpkin patches in business.

- I'll just be happy when they're both back on their feet.

- Me too. Me too. Right, I think we can officially call this a night. You fancy getting a drink in town? I said I'd catch my neighbour in Lucky 13 after the festivities tonight.

Just then a figure came running across the dark square towards them. It took Mike a second to place the face but then he remembered sitting in the library with him. Charlie came running up to him. He caught his breath and began to explain.

- Hi, Sheriff Sullivan.

- Hi Charlie, I like the costume...its?

- Zombie Soldier. Look, you need to come with me. It's Emily, your neighbour. She was attacked. She's okay, but my brother is with her in Tart to Tart. She said you'd be here so I came to get you.

- She's okay?

- Yes, Bobby said she was fine, just shaken up. He was going to call the police but I think she'd appreciate a friendly face. She asked for you.

- Of course, let's go.

The three of them made their way swiftly to Main Street. Carter went to grab the first aid kit and the incident report book from the car and Charlie and Mike headed to the café. Mike threw the door open and saw Emily sitting at the back of the café. She smiled at him when he walked in. There was a thin cut covered in dried blood across her left cheek and her hair was matted against her temple on one side, but she looked okay. The three of them strode over to Emily and Bobby.

- Emily, are you okay? What happened?

- I'm fine. Really. I've got a cup of tea and I'm being well looked after. Let me introduce you to my knight in shining armour. Mike this is Bobby, one of my pupils.

Mike shook his hand.

- Nice to meet you Bobby. And thank you for looking out for her. We're going to need to take a statement from both of you about what happened tonight and my partner will be here in a minute, she'll take a look at your injuries Em and make sure you're okay.

- I'm okay honestly, come, sit down.

Mike pulled some more chairs over to the table and Charlie made himself useful by going over to the counter to buy hot ciders and coffees for everyone. When Carter arrived she took Emily to the bathroom to disinfect her cut and dress the wound. Then they all sat down together and went through the sequence of the evening's events whilst the detectives wrote in their note books. Whilst the five of them sat in the café talking the other customers gradually disappeared until there was nobody else left. The owner was closing up the store and the crowds had either all gone home or were moving on to the local bars. As midnight passed and the new day began, Mike thanked the owner for staying open and drove Emily back to their apartments. Carter took the boys home. In the trees by fire a figure watched them all.

PART II: WINTER WAS A WORD OBSCURED BY FOLIAGE

Or when the lawn
Is pressed by unseen feet, and ghosts return
Gently at twilight, gently go at dawn,
The sad intangible who grieve and yearn.

- T.S. Eliot, 'To Walter de la Mare'
The Complete Poems and Plays of T. S. Eliot, ASH 828 ELI

One does not become enlightened by imagining figures of light,
but by making the darkness conscious.

- Carl Jung , 'The Collected Works', ASH 150.1954 JUN

ALL SAINTS DAY

Sheriff Sullivan woke up to the sound of his alarm beeping rhythmically on his bedside table. He reached over to hit the snooze button and knocked a half full mug of coffee over. It spilled over the alarm and onto the floor, the alarm squealing and falling out of synch as it cycled through pitches, gave one last strangled cry, and fizzled out. *Fuck, the rhythm was already ruined.*

Mike rolled out of bed, found some kitchen towels to mop up the mess, and threw the alarm unceremoniously into the trash. He remembered getting home the night before, making sure Emily was safe, and then coming back to his to write up his notes from the night. He must have drifted off at some point, and he found his notebook wedged down the side of the bed. He threw some clean clothes on and wandered across the hall to knock on her door.

She was already up and preparing coffee in the kitchen. He noticed there were books scattered in the living room, and an open paperback, fanned out on top of a set of boxes on the living room table. She set the percolator on the stove top and turned towards him.

- Am I mistaken or was that the death throes of your alarm clock I heard earlier?

- Yes. Death by caffeine.

- It'll get us all eventually. Speaking of which, can I tempt you? To be honest, I can't say that I'm terribly sad to see it go.

- Hey, I've had that guy since college.

- You had an alarm clock in college? Why does that not surprise me?

- Oh come on, you didn't have an alarm clock in college?

- The schedule for literature degrees is a little more...flexible. And we actually had a particularly conscientious rooster near our dorms. So these recent rude awakenings are almost kind of nostalgic.

- Well, I think he's actually toast, and besides, with all these early morning phone calls I probably won't need an alarm any more...

Carter listened to the phone ring and then set the receiver back in its cradle. She watched Potemko gathering up the pumpkins from around the office and putting them into a container for composting. They had multiplied in the office day by day. Last week she had come in to find one sitting next to the coffee machine in the kitchen staring at her menacingly as she hunted for coffee pods. Then they'd started to appear on the tables in the office, now they took up most of the squad room – smiling to themselves stupidly. A few of them had begun to rot and a stale vegetable odour hung in the air of the office.

- I can't get hold of him. You feel up to coming out to a crime scene with me Potemko?

- Do I ever, I am so ready to get away from this desk.

- Grab that Camera will you? I think we might need it.

Potemko and Carter grabbed their equipment and set off in one of the squad cars. It had been a week since he'd been back at work and the doctors had assigned him to desk work for the following month. He felt fine in himself, mostly a little bruised and battered. He'd get lost in stacks of paperwork for the day and forget the pain, then turn around too quickly or reach down to one of the lower desk draws and suddenly it would dance swiftly up his right side. He'd gotten off lightly, especially compared to Lewis. A couple of bruised ribs. That was all. He'd taken a week off, finished two paperbacks whilst sitting in the hospital with Lewis, lost nineteen games of chess, won four, watched a late night John Carpenter marathon on the small television suspended from the ceiling in the hospital room, and spent four days in the station house, going through old incident reports and turning up nothing. Since that day two weeks ago they had no new leads, no further attacks had been reported, the guy had vanished into thin air. And here he was, laid up in the station house. This was exactly what he needed. Some excitement to get him back on track. He loaded the camera with fresh film, feeling the seatbelt digging into his ribs.

- So, where are we going on this glorious morning?

- I just got a call from one of the attendants in Monument Park; they've found a body.

- Shit. In the park? Is it?

- Yes, I think it is. We better get there and move it before people are up and about. I think the communal hangover of the town should give us an hour or two but I don't want pictures of somebody all cut up in the centre of town getting into the papers.

- Whoa, that must have been one hell of a Halloween party. I miss all the fun.

- Count yourself lucky. Remember what happened last time you were there for the fun.

- Good point. Well made.

Carter and Potemko parked on the far side of Monument Park and found the attendant tending the ashes of the bonfire. He led them over to the body in the grass. Empty plastic cups, discarded boxes of popcorn and half eaten toffee apples lay strewn around the site. The smell of the bonfire still clung to the sodden earth. It was a mess. In the copse of trees twenty feet away lay the discarded body of one of the erstwhile revellers. Her legs were twisted in the mud, and her throat had been torn open, strands of ligaments lay matted in clumps of leaves, mud and blood. Her face was partly ripped open, revealing the red muscle beneath which now sat muted and gray against the bright white skin of what remained of her face. Carter stared down at the body lying in the grass.

- My god. When did you find her?

- About 20 minutes ago. I was just walking around the site when I noticed something lying under the tree. I called you as soon as I found her.

- Thank you. Do you think you could fence off the area while we photograph the body and then get it moved? I'd really like to stop the press getting hold of this for a little while.

- Of course, yes. I'll call the office. We can say it's clean up after the festival.

- Thank you. I appreciate it.

Whilst the park attendant set up a makeshift fence around the bonfire site, Potemko took photos of the body. Orange light was breaking through the cloud cover, and forcing its way through the leaves of the trees. It crept up the savaged body, running up her leg and over her arms. Potemko had to reposition continually to get good photos of the wounds.

- Boss, this is even worse than Shurdach. Look at her throat, it's been torn to pieces.

- I know, this fucker gets worse and worse. We should have stayed out longer last night. Of course he was going to strike again.

- There's no way you could have known he was out there.

- We should have. Mike's girlfriend, Emily, got attacked in town. We thought it was...well I don't know what we thought it was. We focussed on getting her home. But we should have been more careful, more alert.

- Wait, Mike has a girlfriend?

- I don't know Potemko. His neighbour, Emily. I think they're seeing each other.

- You didn't ask?

- No I didn't ask. I had a few other things on my mind. Look, just finish taking the photos okay? I'm going to chase up that ambulance.

- Okay, okay. I just mean, you know the Sheriff. He's terse. But he'd probably open up to you.

- Potemko.

- Yes, sorry – taking the photos.

Carter walked away from the scene and strolled around the bonfire, kicking the still smouldering branches with her foot. The ash shifted, and a quick flame lifted itself up out of the embers before dying down once more, just grey ash in a grey park on a grey morning. She took out her phone and dialled the Sheriff once more. This time he answered.

- Carter, sorry, I was next door. What can I do for you?

- I'm with Potemko at Monument Park. There's been another body called in. It's...It's a mess Sir. I think you'd better get down here.

- I'll be there in 15.

The minute the door closed Emily felt the silence settle over the tables and book shelves. Empty plates and cups sat at the table, and a sadness coated them now that their owners were gone. She sat on one of the sofas and wrapped her dressing gown around her. How quickly a room changed. The presence of someone could change the light of the place, make the room brighter, the fittings jovial. Now the room was silent. She wandered from room to room, just silent grey light hanging in the air. She wanted the easy feeling back that she had when Mike was there, the animation of his presence. But as she sat there she couldn't dispel the images that pressed to the front of her mind; the leaves forming shapes in the darkness, his shadow strewn face staring down at her. A cold grey light crept from the windows across the living room floor. She resolved to break the silence and so she picked up the phone, and dialled the first number that came to mind. First she heard the shifting static of international phone lines flowing in the wind, and then the far away ring that came back to her, echoing across continents. Dietrich picked up on the fourth ring and Emily heard the connection establish itself with Berlin.

- Hello?

- Hi, Dietrich. It's Emily. It isn't too late there is it?

- Emily, what a pleasant surprise. No, not at all, it's only just gone nine, and anyway you know that I'm a child of the night.

- That I do, you are a veritable night walker.

- I prefer the term night stalker, it holds more menace. How are you?

- I'm fine. You know, next year you'll have to make it out for Halloween. It really is wild here.

- Were they sacrificing goats to the overlord?

- No, just scarecrows. And please tell me this is not how you celebrated.

- Not me my dear. But I did find a small group on the outskirts of Grabendorf who were planning it. I decided to give it a miss in favour of a Bela Lugosi marathon at the Friedrichshain. But tell me, really. It's always lovely to hear from you but what is happening?

- D, I think I saw him again...

114

Mike found Carter at monument Park.

- What do we know so far?

- It looks the same as Shurdach boss. She's a mess. But check this out.

Carter led Mike round to the copse of trees where the body lay. In a mound of dirt near the body a backpack was discarded.

- You've opened it?

- Yes, we've got her ID and check this out.

Carter emptied out the contents of the backpack and passed Mike two books.

- Both from Ashenbrooke Library. Same as Shurdach.

- You think it means something? It is the only library in town…

- I don't know. But it can't hurt to go back can it?

- No, I've been meaning to go actually. Things just keep getting in the way. But you're right, I'll make a priority of it.

- Right. Let's get this body moved. The meat wagon is on its way.

Emily set the phone down on the table. She reached over and picked up the open book from the table but then put it down again. Instead, she went to the closet and retrieved a wooden box that she kept at the back beneath a pile of shoes. She found the catch at the back and flipped the lid, and removed an old Polaroid from the box. A girl of eight with eyes like hers looked back at her. And a man in his forties, with eyes like hers, held her hand. He smiled at the camera, a blue fedora hat tipped back on his head. The lines around his mouth crinkled upwards, the left side of his mouth slightly higher than the right.

She looked in to those grey blue eyes. She'd seen them.

Last night. In the trees. She was almost certain of it. Watching her. Sometimes they watched her. From reflections in shop windows. From the edges of mirrors. From the dark shade of an Elm tree as the Halloween bonfire blazed high in to the night. Why did they still follow her? And why had he returned?

CHARRED

The story of the murder in Monument Park could not be kept out of the papers for long. The detectives did their best to keep the gorier details out of the public eye, but the news that a killer had struck in Ashenbrooke passed through the town faster than the November winds. An unofficial curfew took hold; parents collected their children from school rather than letting them walk home, people huddled together in public places, and a healthy respect for darkness returned. There was still a sense of confidence in the days when the shopfronts were open and the daily rituals continued but very few people walked alone through the town in the evenings. A feeling of menace floated on the winds, a charge of excitement in the air, and the heart would race as travellers made their way home.

The station house received more calls than ever reporting strange figures lurking in their neighbourhoods, and the detectives found themselves being called out more and more frequently on wild ghost chases. More often than not it was just the caller's overactive imagination, or a couple of teenagers playing a prank on their friends. But Mike was keen to respond and to make the residents of Ashenbrooke feel safe in their town. He felt that a police presence would make the people feel safer and so he established a twice daily patrol where one of the detectives would walk the streets of Ashenbrooke, providing support to the residents, and keeping one eye out for any signs of a return. He enjoyed his turn patrolling the streets, finding that the fresh air and motion allowed him to organise his thoughts in new patterns. The highlighted circles on the district maps revolved in his mind as he sought to distinguish areas of overlap, transections, cues, spaces of connection. The bear angle seemed less and less plausible as the circles moved ever inwards towards populated areas. And then there were the reports of a figure on the edges of town, coupled with what Potemko claimed to have seen – these things pointed to a man. But he'd seen the bodies – was a man capable of that?

As November rolled along, the temperature dropped daily and soon Mike could see his breath misted in the air as he walked. He watched it swirl and he watched the people as the town got quieter. Winters tended to hit the area hard and by early December the townsfolk usually began retreating into their homes. But Mike felt it would happen earlier this year, feeling the temperature continue to drop each day. With each patrol the town got quieter and quieter, and on many evenings he was the last solitary soul on the streets.

One person who enjoyed this new sense of solitude in the town was Charlie. He would leave the Library at night and not pass a single soul on his journey home across town. The table top chessboards in the square sat deserted, abandoned by their generals, as muddy brown leaves blew across the ground. Wind whistled through the elms on wintry eaves as he wandered through the silenced town. His thoughts blossomed out on these walks, grew to greater and greater proportions, spreading out over the square and town, the rolling hills. A tide had turned in the town; its lethargic state replaced by something heavier, more sinister. Now a weight was laid on top of it, keeping it quiet under bed sheets, no longer having the strength to fight. It was a time for moving inwards, looking inwards, each resident wrapped up alone in his or her solitary world. The charred end of the year approached.

The brothers had decided to face the rest of the house. What they found did not surprise them greatly. Rooms unused, under a thick coating of dust. Objects left alone too long, that in the long night of their solitude had grown odd, grown mad in the darkness. The landing sat still and the closed doors stared back at them, daring their next move. This was the first time that they had come upstairs since that strange dreamlike night at the end of September when they'd found their mother's dressing gown, floating softly in the breeze at the top of the house. Charlie crossed the carpet and pushed open the door on the right; Bobby's room. The Superman lamp greeted them, still grinning crazily from its safe perch on the bedside table.

Bobby's room was much the same as it was when he was 15; the bunk beds took up the left hand side of the room, its wooden frame carved with symbols and games of tic-tac-toe they had played as kids. His bookcase stood to the right, with its complete collection of Harry Potter novels, and 2000AD comics. On the far wall, next to his bed, sat his desk, with the beaming superman lamp, and piles of maths books from his old school. Posters for Linkin Park and Blink 182 lined the walls. Another time capsule kept safe in this house. Charlie left Bobby in his room tidying and going through his old books, and crossed the landing to find his own room. He opened the door and there it stood, almost unchanged since he'd left for college 4 years ago. The red walls and Japanese prints that decorated the walls welcomed him home. He walked over to his bed and tried the switch on the paper lantern on the chest of drawers. To his surprise it turned on, shedding a dull dusty light over the room. The room felt abandoned, even more so than Bobby's. He had loved this room. It was an ode to his love affair with Japan when he was a teenager. The walls were painted red, with a light grey futon in the centre of the room. The window had a rice paper blind, with a view of Mount Fuji and the rising sun etched onto it. Wind chimes hung from the ceiling. The blind was now grey and faded and there was a small patch of damp in one of the corners of the ceiling where water had leaked in from the roof. Time had stilled, and stopped. Left alone like this rooms lost their warmth, as if the presence of their inhabitants gave them life. But they didn't cease to exist when their owners went away, they just sat still, waiting, as the light falling from the windows crept slowly across the carpeted floor, and up the wall. Day after day, these rooms were here. A mausoleum of youth.

He'd loved this room but then he'd left for college and would only come back once a month for the weekend. Later on, in his final year when their mother got sick he came back every week, but keeping the place well maintained was not a priority. As her body decayed, so did the house. Dishes sat in sinks, dust filling up the hallways. The wood of the windows warped, slowly, allowing cold breezes and airs to float around the house. And then, last summer, after she'd died and he'd finished his exams, he moved home but hadn't wanted to sleep in this room any longer. By not acting he'd somehow hoped that time would stop, that they would delay the inevitable day when she passed away. Time grows long and weary around the dying. But that room still reminded him of hope, and therefore he didn't want to see it anymore, didn't want to be reminded of the happier days, when he would fall asleep, safe in the creaks of floorboards and sounds of his family moving around the house. And so he'd set up the sofa bed downstairs, initially as something temporary until he had a chance to change the room upstairs, and then it had gradually become permanent. At the start of this year Bobby had also started to sleep in the lounge more and more. At first falling asleep in front of movies, and then just making up the bed in the evenings, and then just leaving it made. Neither had said anything, they were happy to keep each other company on the ground floor. And that is how they'd lost the rest of the house. Charlie looked around the room. It was time to take it back.

James Brayman strolled through the catacombs, bristling the spines of books. He was lost in thought when his phone began to vibrate in his pocket.

- Hello?

- Hello Mr Brayman. It's Sheriff Sullivan here.

- Oh. Hello.

- I'm sorry I didn't get in touch before. Especially as you'd found those papers for me. I was wondering if I could stop by tomorrow?

- Yes. Yes, of course.

- Any time good?

- Whenever you like. We open at 10.

- Okay, I'll see you then.

He returned the phone to his pocket and returned to the quiet of the library. On these evenings when his endless thoughts wouldn't quiet, when she walked through his waking thoughts, so close he could almost smell her, this was all he could do to keep the peace. All he could do to keep that sense that she had just left the room, that she would be back soon.

He reached the end of the row, knelt in the dust and found the catch. It clicked and the row released, sliding towards him. He slipped between the rows and found the hidden shelf, removed a cloth bound book and breathed out – felt his mind quiet and the dark pit that had rested in his heart expand and wash him away.

As the evening approached, Charlie came back upstairs with two cups of coffee. They sat on the floor of Bobby's room and watched the sun melt into warm orange liquid outside the window, throwing golden light across the carpet. The room was bright and Superman grinned quietly to himself.

- So, what are the chances I can convince you to take the top bunk tonight?

- I think I'm going to try out my room. But I'm reserving a space just in case the doors start shaking at two in the morning.

Bobby chuckled, and then felt a shiver crawl down his back.

- Consider a space reserved. Hey, look what I found. Wayne's World. You want to watch it tonight? We could order pizza.

- Yeah, that sounds good. But we've got one more room we should check out before we call it a day.

The books in their father's study sat silently on the shelves. This room was the first time capsule of all, it must have been ten years since their father had last sat down at the oak desk and rifled through the papers in the drawers. After he walked out, Charlie would come and sit in his room, take his books down from the shelves and rifle through them, go through the desk. One time he found one of his dad's cigars in the desk drawer and tried to smoke it. He inhaled and immediately felt nauseous, coughing out smoke until his lungs ached. He then unrolled the cigar, letting the tobacco fall out on the desk and breathing in its rich aroma that smelt like his father's face when he used to read him stories as a child. Their father had been a professor. He frequently went away on trips when they were children. When they were younger their mother used to tell them that he was at a conference with superman and the other super heroes, coming up with plans to save the world. Then when they were a bit older she'd tell them that he was travelling the world, climbing mountains, and swimming to the depths of the oceans. And then when they were older still she wouldn't make up stories. She'd just say 'your father is away' and no more.

The trips seemed to get longer and longer and then one year, when Charlie was 12, his father never came back. He asked his mother when he would return and that was when she sat him down and told him that he wasn't. Despite that, for the next year Charlie was sure that he would. When he heard the door open at an unusual time of day he would run downstairs to find his mother struggling with some shopping bags or the postman dropping letters through the door. He would hear cars driving past at night and listen for the one that would pull into their drive and turn the engine off. And then after a year he began to sit in his father's study and smell the cigar in his drawers and think back to his father's warm bearded face telling him stories.

After a while everything returned to normal and the world of his brother and mother reigned. They adjusted to life again, the three of them a solid group ready to take on the world. And then when Charlie was 15 he received the postcard in the mail from Belgium. He had it still, a note from the traveller. A postcard of pictures of beers and barges. More followed. He'd rise early to check the post before his mother, and when there was one he'd snaffle it and run away. He kept them all hidden in a box in his wardrobe. They were still there. And then in his first year he'd seen him for that weekend in New York. He'd gotten a letter when he moved into his halls. He'd never told his mother about that. He was going to be in the city for 3 days and he wanted to meet up. They'd spent the whole weekend together, drinking and talking and visiting galleries and music halls. The following year when his mother called to tell him that his father had died he hung up the receiver, sat at his desk and cried reading that letter again and again. She was just recovering from her latest bout of chemotherapy and they didn't have the money so he didn't go to the funeral. Instead he'd come home and sat in this room, rolling one of the cigars from the box in his hands, and smelling the tobacco. He walked over now and opened the desk drawer. The box was still there. The time capsule never failed, it could take you back in a heartbeat. He closed the drawer and looked at Bobby.

- On second thoughts, we've done enough for now. Let's call it a night.

They sat at the kitchen table eating pizza as the windows turned blue. Bobby was tracing the outline of grooves in the table.

- Just say it Bobcat.

- You've heard about the girl in the park?

- Everyone has heard about the girl in the park.

- Okay. Well...I think this is all connected somehow.

- What is?

- The murders, the ghosts, all of it.

-...I can't.

- Look, you don't have to say anything. I can show you.

Bobby turned off the lights in the kitchen and lounge. The darkness lay heavy on the room and the whirr of the refrigerator ticked softly to itself – an endless sound, eternally renewing its source. They sat still, waiting for something.

Bobby got up, took the phone off the wall, and placed it on the counter. The dial tone sang to itself. An endless sound, the frequency of the fridge and the phone cycling, shifting up and down the pitches. Another pitched tone, escalating and devolving. The noise occupied the room, imagined ranges beyond the single tone as the mind searches for sound...

* * * * * * * * dy * * * * * * * ou * * * * * * * * * * * * * * find * * * * * her * * * *

THE WALKING WOUNDED

Lewis returned to work almost one month to the day since their abortive trip to the abandoned mill in Fairwater. His morphine hued journeys through the woodlands at the foot of his hospital bed had restored his health, if not his mental fortitude. Each night after the nurses had completed their rounds and Potemko had left for the day he would feel the medication seeping through his veins, slowly cooling his body and mind, until it felt lightsome, air-like, and insubstantial. Then he would rise from the bed, his deadened arm no longer pulsating painfully but instead cold and tingling at his side. He floated up out of his bed and into the frame of the picture, crossing into the woodland scene.

He would explore for hours, looking behind the trees, finding secret brooks and woodland scenes. He chased deer that glided through the trees, and sat in shady glens, watching the warm white moon settle in the skies. Time never seemed to change; it was always the softly lit twilight as he floated endlessly through the woods. That was his life for almost a month and now he was back, seated at his desk, his bandaged arm pulsing with pain. They had insisted it was time for him to leave, that in order to return to the daylight world he would have to begin his old life again. Return to a semblance of order, a routine that would return him to health. And so the sheriff had agreed; he would return to desk duty, short days, followed by rehabilitation clinics in the late afternoon. But really he longed to feel the soft blue light of the codeine infused sleep sink into his bones and float freely around the outskirts of the station house. It would have to wait. In his bedside drawer at home he had enough to take him away for a while, to explore, and to find what secrets lurked in that woodland. But here he sat, on a bright Friday morning at a desk piled high with case files, looking around the sunlit squad room whilst the Sheriff made coffee out back.

Potemko came bounding into the station house a little after ten in the morning.

- Yes! Lewis my man, good to see you back at work! I see the boss is keeping you busy. You got everything you need?

- Everything besides some heavy duty pain killers.

- Well, I think we've still got something down in the evidence locker from that drug bust last year. I can go rustle up something special for you.

- Thanks Potemko, but once you've had the best there's no going back to the street stuff.

- Haha, you'd better make a good friend at the hospital then.

- I'm working on it.

- Glad to hear it. Anything going on here?

- About a hundred reports. Over the past couple of weeks people have seen everything from Charlie Manson to the Blair Witch.

- Yeah this is quickly becoming the supernatural centre of the universe.

- I just don't know what I'm looking for in these things.

- Clues my friend, clues.

- At this stage we might as well go out and get a Ouija board.

- Now you're speaking my language.

The morning rolled along slowly and Lewis let the files swim across the surface of his mind. He was just drifting into a paperwork haze when Mike called everyone together by the board.

- Okay, firstly I wanted to welcome back Lewis. We're all very glad to have you back here, and it's going to be very handy having someone who can man the station in the days. As you all know, the past couple of weeks have been full on. It's important that we have a presence in the town, both to reassure the people and also to deter any further attacks. To recap, we have identified the girl as Millie St James, 18 years old, attended the local college. The attack happened around 2am on the morning of November 1st. Since it took place in such an inhabited area we are ruling out the bear angle for now. Holloway also found traces of fingernails in the wounds. Not enough to get much info but the attacker was definitely human.

Since the body was discovered in Monument Park we have had numerous sightings reported. I know that some of these have turned out to be all kinds of hokum but we need to keep responding to each call as if it is the real deal. We've all seen too well how brutal these attacks have been and if we can prevent any further incidents and find a new lead on the killer this will be invaluable. Carter, if you can take the patrol this afternoon, Potemko and I will respond to any direct call outs.

When we're here, I want you to comb through the recent reports, see if there have been any more attacks in the local area, and revisit the old files from the previous murders to see if there is a pattern we can put together here. Lewis, I want you to focus on the locations of the attacks, find the connections between the places. I know we're on the back foot a little here, but we still need to think one step ahead. If we can predict something about where the next attack might happen, then we might be able to stop it. See if there is a connection between the locations. If our killer is a vagrant we need to see where he's already been and attempt to predict where he might be staying, or where he might strike next. The three attacks in town that we know of that are genuine, along with the body in Monument Park indicate that he is now based somewhere nearby. If he prefers abandoned locations I want a list of these put together. And I hope it goes without saying that I want you all armed and wearing protective gear. We weren't ready for him last time. That will not happen again. Okay, now get to work.

When Lewis got home that evening, the day's case files still echoed in his mind. It was hard to tell which of the reports were genuine and so he either had the killer spotted at almost every neighbourhood in town or nowhere at all. The only locations they could be one hundred percent sure of were Monument park, the Atalonga, and the Fairwater mill. He couldn't think about it anymore and so he turned the lights down, and swallowed two small white pills with water.

He lay his head down on the pillow and at first felt nothing, just the steady ache in his side, and his thoughts returning to the never-ending pile of papers on his desk in the squad room. But then he felt something wet and soft against his cheek. He turned his head slowly and saw; grass was growing up through the fabric of his pillowcase, the dew clinging to its blades. He rolled into it, felt the fresh water on his face, and smelt the heady aroma of fresh earth. It grew swiftly, and soon his bed was covered in grass. He rolled to the left and saw his bedside table was now a small tree trunk, and trees had taken back his room, growing where the walls had been before. He seemed to rise on the air and suddenly he felt well, the pain left his body and he floated once more through the mists of the forest. He flew through the air, watching deer run, and rabbits hide under rooted earth. And all at once the leaves parted and he saw it; the mill at the centre of the clearing. It was no longer abandoned, but was instead a wave of noise and light. Beams of light shot out into the misty surroundings, and waves of sound pulsated across the air. He could hear music, slightly out of sync, like a 45 record played on a 33. He walked around the clearing and saw people everywhere. They were spread out on the lawn, drinking champagne, swaying in the warm evening breeze. Talking, flirting, dancing.

There were people on the stairs, people in the workshop, everywhere. As he moved through the figures at the party he heard fragments of conversations, chatter all around him. He walked up to guests but they were oblivious to his passing, he was smoke in the room, background noise that sat somewhere below the threshold of consciousness. He was a half remembered song, playing just below the surface of memory. He walked amongst the guests and danced with them, felt their joy, the sense of ease, something had been finished, some pressure lifted. He felt drawn towards the centre of the mill, floated towards it. There was a large office raised above the workshop, with windows that looked out over the mill. It was clearly where the foreman worked. As he climbed the stairs towards the large wooden office on the second floor he heard raised voices. And then a slam against the wall. He rushed up and stared through the windows; there was a couple yelling, the man gesticulating wildly, his glass half filled with red wine splashing, leaving marks on the paperwork and the wooden floors. He yelled, pointing at a woman in a red dress, and then threw his glass against the wall, it shattering into a dozen pieces. Then time slowed, the fragments of glass hanging in the air, trapped in the viscosity of the slowing past. The figures were frozen, and he watched the woman mid scream, tears glistening on her cheeks, her soundless scream enveloping the room. He awoke, thrashing wildly in his bed, opening his mouth, but no sounds came out. Instead he was frozen there, his heart beating rapidly, his body locked down.

The medication had its knock on effects. It would stay in his body, slowing time. It was as if all the extra time he experienced in the woodland had created a debt, and back in the daylight world his body and mind seemed to function at half the speed they should do. The next day at the station house he felt like his body was out of sync with his mind. He'd think about standing up and then twenty seconds later his body would acquiesce. His legs were jerky, particularly unsteady, and his thoughts were even harder to control, wandering across the surface of the files and around the room. At one point the phone rang on Carter's desk but there was no one else there and so he left it, the rings echoing off the ceiling and against the walls. He couldn't do this today, he needed sleep, real sleep, and when Potemko came back to the station house after his morning patrol Lewis made his excuses and went home.

He got in and threw his bag down on the couch. He immediately went to the bathroom cabinet where inside they sat in their little orange vials, the keys that unlocked the door to another world, the one hidden behind this one. He just needed to swallow two with water, and then his limbs would relax, his mind would lighten, and he would begin to blend, to become consubstantial with the air, with the forest. They'd found it strange when he'd asked to take the picture at the foot of the bed home with him, but they had agreed, after all these hospital paintings were probably worth around twenty five dollars. They had seascapes, forests, mountain ranges stacked up in the janitor's closet. These scenes which were designed to lull the patients into a sense of peace, of oneness with nature, to remove their selves from their situation, to feel their troubles were not so bad in the scheme of things, they were bought in bulk from an art warehouse. They were designed to both be there and not, to exist on the fringes of the patient's minds, but nevertheless to soothe them somehow, to reassure them that things would be all right, the mountains were not going anywhere. So they were happy to let Lewis take it, if anything they felt slightly sorry for his taste in art. But he found it invaluable, a way to focus his mind. And so he sat down on the sofa and stared at it, as his body became lightsome.

He watched the trees, the way they began to take on depth, he watched the leaves falling, passing in front of one trunk, behind another. The red path in the middle where the daisies grew on either side. It led him through the woods, past purple trunks and into the yellow fields in the distance. Suddenly he was there. He was walking through the scene, through the thick green forests in the distance. Walking all night through the forests as the warm blue twilight settled. He could hear the music once more, through the trees, and he let his feet carry him towards the sounds. Walking through pines, stopping to feel the mossy bark and inhale the sweet fresh aroma from the needles. Feeling the crunch underfoot, the tangible touch of a world more real than the one he had left.

There were so many people at the party, it was the end of something. He could feel the relief and reverie in the dancers, in the carefree feeling of the crowd. His eyes were opening up to the reality of the world; time didn't exist anymore, nor distance. It was just a matter of focus. There were no floors beneath him, just a pocket of air that hangs there, had always hung there, before, and after. He saw back, through time, and through forests, to the bright lights emanating from the mill, before it fell. He stood at the doorway, crouched on the stairs, listening to urgent whispers within.

- *I saw you.*
- *We were talking Harry, we work together.*
- *Don't lie to me like that. Like I'm some stupid fool you just met in a bar. We've been together long enough. I'm used to your bullshit by now.*
- *Fuck you Harry. You're drunk.*

- *Doesn't mean I'm not right.*
- *You haven't been right for a long time.*
Glass shattered against the wall, the cracking pieces showering the room and the floor.

Lewis went to open the door, he reached for the handle

and his hand slipped right through it. The door seemed to sway and then fade. He walked through it, but all he could see were two shadows in the room. He looked around but everything was already faded, becoming darkness, swaying out of focus, and then he reached for the desk and his hand picked up a cup from his own coffee table. He was back in his living room, the world had faded into being.

By the end of the week the dream world and the real world had traded places. He only felt truly alert and awake wandering though the strong scented pines, but once he was awake the memories faded, seemed impossible, and as hazy as the office around him. He floated through the hours, the clock face on the wall juttering forward and then spinning around. At one point he was sure it started to move backwards and he would be stuck in the bright stillness of 11am. He couldn't keep this going. He needed to make it into the mill, the whole way. When he got home that night he took an extra pill. He might not wake up until later but if it got him there it would be worth it.

He felt the forest return almost immediately and sighed with relief as the warm pine infused his lungs. As the trees parted and the light was visible he knew that no time had passed. He was back and here was his chance. The moon still hung lightly in the egg blue sky and a plane sailed through the ether, leaving a trail of light orange as the sky darkened towards a rich indigo. The time is right now. He made haste towards the mill, and ran up the stairs.

- *You haven't been right for a long time.*
He waited for the crash and then felt it. He stepped through the door and saw shards of glass explode out from the wall and pass through the lady's face. It splintered into a thousand pieces, some turning to dust, others scattering across the walls and floor, a few flying through the lady's cheek and eyeball,

scattering blood and hair as they flew. The blood flew swiftly down her face and she gaped in shock. The man's face took a minute to register what was happening and then contorted. There was a second of stillness and then a scream that reverberated off the walls of the room, and out into the party. It could only have been seconds before the first guests arrived to the scene that confronted them; the lady stood with slivers of red glass protruding from her eye and cheek, thick blood flowing down her face.

THE TREES RUN WILD

The swift November winds shook the trees in the back yard. Bobby watched them dancing, their last leaves being stripped and carried away on the wind. The back stoop gave some shelter but in the yard it was a whirlwind of leaves and branches bending this way and that; the trees lost all of their rigidity and became a constant flowing stream of wood and leaf. In contrast to the storms outside Bobby was feeling calmer than he had in months. The chaos of the outside world seemed to have extracted some of the menace from the house, as if the wildness of the world soothed something that had been playing on his mind. That call from his mother felt far away, and the warning was forgotten: no one had come. The house had begun to feel slightly safer and brighter. They had even dusted the photographs in the drawing room, and could now sit in the evening with the images of their parents' safe on the shelves. They still didn't venture to the top of the house, and they left their father's study as it was, but now both Bobby and Charlie slept in their own rooms and there had been no midnight disturbances in the weeks since Halloween. As the storms raged harder outside, the house calmed down within. Another period of normality had begun; grief seemed to work that way. The truce with the house held for now and Bobby felt optimistic that one day, one entirely ordinary day, they'd wrestle it all back, the trees included, and they'd sit in this garden in the soft cool light of spring.

Emily stepped into the shower and let the mists roll over her. In the weeks since Halloween she had found the town less charming. Where before the thought of walking through sleepy hollow had filled her with an excitable nostalgia, now there seemed to be something truly menacing between the pages of her books. Seeing his face in the trees felt like something half-remembered, like a story read to her as a child. She tried her best to enjoy the warmth of the mist but a chill had set in and she found herself running from the shower, to feel the warmth of the hairdryer on her body, and then to hide in knitted sweaters, in cafes filled with people. It wasn't so bad when she was at work. The movement of the students, the rush and energy took over and she could find some distance from the stories she lived in, could enjoy them with others. It was just that when alone in her apartment, or walking back from the college, she felt his presence in the woodlands, she felt the weight of him on her thoughts.

Mike woke before dawn and made his way to the station house whilst the Morse code of colour was still a mixture of black and indigo. As the town's inhabitants spent more time within their homes the lights increased in both volume and variation but he had noticed their darkened persistence – low night lights left on – shades of quiet blues that set the base pattern of the town. The incident reports were outweighing his team's ability to respond but there hadn't been an actual attack in the weeks since Halloween. The patrols were working, and if anything, had engendered a level of overly cautious behaviour which seemed to be keeping the town safe. But even so he felt as if they were treading water, as if they were merely waiting for the next leap in the pattern, and more than anything he wanted to make progress before the technicolour clash of reds whites and blues returned to end the quiet sequence.

The storms raged over Ashenbrooke, tearing down trees, blocking off roads. The wind had blown in from the Arctic and in the first weeks of November the temperature plummeted. The

College Quad was mostly sheltered from the storms and Bobby sat out under the naked cherry tree, his duffel coat buttoned up to the top. Everyone in the school was talking about the murder in Monument Park after the Halloween Parade and they were already suggesting that the Thanksgiving parade would be called off this year. He'd needed a break from it; suddenly everyone knew Millie, had gone to prom with her, they'd had joint birthday parties, they'd sat next to her in French class. They couldn't believe this had happened. It was always this way when a tragedy struck the town. Those who hadn't known true loss gravitated towards it, took centre stage, wanted to be a part of the story. And those who really knew what it was like to lose someone sat by themselves in the college quad under bare branches because they just couldn't hear about it anymore.

Emily sat down next to him on the bench, stirring him from his thoughts.

- Taking a break from the chatter too?

- How many of them really knew her do you think? Ten? Twenty? I wonder how they are feeling.

- They're probably the only ones not talking about her.

- She was nice. I mean, I really didn't know her. She showed me around in induction week, that's all. She lost her mom too, people seem to have forgotten that.

- I didn't know that.

-

- How is...everything?

- Okay actually. We're...its better right now. Did they ever find that guy who was chasing you on Halloween?

- No. I actually wanted to say thank you for helping me that night. There are a few of us celebrating Thanksgiving at my place next week and I wondered if you'd like to come? You and your brother of course. We can't promise an authentic American take on it – it's a broadly international approach – but there would be games, and pie.

- Really?

- Yes, it would lovely if you could both come.

- I'll talk to Charlie but yes, that would be great.

- I have one stipulation – you need to bring an authentic American game. I need to continue my education.

- You've got it.

Charlie and Suze sat at the issue desk checking through the late returns.

- So, did you know her Charlie bear?

- No, she was younger, in the year above my brother.

- He knew her?

- No, I don't think so.

- I knew her, we used to play sleeping lions together.

- This was this year?

- Ha, yes. No, when we were five dumbass.

Charlie flicked the next index card across the desk.

- Speak of the devil.

- What? No way.

- Millie St John. 'Man and his Symbols' by Carl Jung

- You know what that means right?

- We're down another book?

- No, that means both Millie and Max Shurdach had overdue library books…

- And you're suggesting what exactly? That our killer has a serious problem with overdue books? This is a new form of zero tolerance policy?

- Exactly. Steal a book and he'll track you down, One week late? Throat torn out. You wouldn't do it again.

- ...because you're dead.

- Well yes, but I mean generally. The town would make sure they returned their books on time from now on.

- Okay, but actually this is an odd coincidence. I mean, 'Man and his Symbols' – I'm pretty sure that is related to dream symbolism too. So that means they were both looking into it.

- Krueger. Its Freddy Krueger isn't it?

- Yes, okay, it's Krueger. So it's time to cut out those afternoon desk naps.

Charlie knocked on the door of the office and stepped inside. Mr B was sat behind Teddy's desk, lists of this year's accruals spread out in front of him.

- Ah Charlie, come in. How are you?

- I'm okay. I've got the list of overdues here. You want me to send out the letters?

- Yes. Thank you.

- Mr B, this is probably nothing but Millie and Max both had overdue books from here.

- Huh, how many are on that list of yours?

- About two hundred.

- Two out of two hundred. I mean, I'm not a betting man, but I suppose it's something. What do you think it means?

- I don't know. They are both books on dreams and symbols so maybe they were both looking in to something. I don't know but Jung, he talks about these symbols that recur throughout history, ideas we share, so it is possible they both saw something.

- Saw?

- Yeah, crazy right? I don't know. Just thought I should tell you.

- Of course. Why don't you make me a copy of that list?

- Sure thing. See you later Mr B.

James Brayman sat in the study as the storm whipped leaves against the windows. Since his wife had died he spent more and more time at the library. He couldn't face the empty sofa, the sheets that still smelt like the lavender washing powder she'd used. She had never really visited him here and so it remained the same, a place that was his and his alone. Luckily Teddy Ashenbrooke must have enjoyed his solitude in a similar fashion and had designed a studio on the ground floor, adjacent to the study. Mr B boiled the kettle in the kitchenette and knelt down at the bureau in the study. He reached under, finding the worn indentation in the woodwork and pressed in the joist. He waited for the barely perceptible click and then pulled open the lower right hand drawer. He pulled the draw all the way out and reached in to the body of the desk, withdrawing a book wrapped in linen, and then replaced the mechanism as before. He brewed the tea, sat down on the leather futon, and removed the linen wrappings from the book. He traced his fingers across the raised lettering and breathed in, inhaling the rich dust of the book jacket. It smelt like something half remembered, an incomprehensible concoction of scents – the warm quiet of airing cupboards, the damp silence of tombs, and the heady aroma of lavender on the mossy peaks of hills.

THANKSGIVING

The thanksgiving fete in Monument Park was cancelled but this did nothing to stop the town from embracing the harvest. Squashes joined pumpkins on street corners, cardboard turkeys hung from shop windows, and a variety of pies from boysenberry to cherry were added to the menus at Salvador's Deli and the P & M Market. Emily's colleague Rosanna joined her at the market as they gathered the last items for the feast. Rosanna and Emily had bonded swiftly over a mutual fondness for William Faulkner and Toni Morrison and were currently lobbying the English department to add *Beloved* to the senior gothic module.

- This madness the same in England?

- Hardly. No Feasts. The most I remember from school is collecting conkers from the local park. We do have bonfire night though.

- Bonfire night?

- Yes…it's a celebration of…well, anarchy I suppose.

- Oh we have that. Black Friday. If you want to bludgeon someone to death with a flatscreen tv just get in line at the Walmart tomorrow at 5am.

- Ha. This time always makes me think of Shirley Jackson's 'The Lottery'.

- Yes, what is it about the coming of winter that makes you want to sacrifice a casual acquaintance?

- The season of ill will towards men.

- Yes, I like that.

- Bonfire night is essentially a huge celebration of burning Catholics.

- Well, I guess we repressed Protestants just have to let it out every once in a while…

- That we do. Well, let's try not to immolate anyone tonight.

The brothers arrived a little after six with a twelve pack of Sam Adams in hand. When they arrived Rosanna and Mike were drinking beer and lounging in the living room whilst Marco was attempting to pour mescal into an ice tray. Emily ushered them in to the room and made hasty introductions.

- Now I know you've met Mike. Rosanna and Marco, meet Charlie and Bobby Renyard. Although I have a feeling some of you have already met before…

Before Charlie had taken off his jacket Marco came over and hugged him so hard he almost lost balance.

- Charlie, It's been so long! How are you? I think the last time must have been the funeral.

- Yeah, it must have been.

- You know we all still miss your mom, she was a terrific lady.

- That she was.

- Well, it's good to see you. Let's get you guys a beer.

As Marco and Emily juggled dishes and serving forks in the kitchen the others steadily devoured crudités in the lounge. Rosanna brought in a fresh stash of beers and passed them round.

- So, Emily tells me you also share a fondness for the gothic, Bobby.

Bobby continued his steady decimation of the breadsticks and paused with one halfway to his mouth.

- Mm hmm. I've been really enjoying the books we've been studying. But it all feels a little close to home, what with everything going on lately...

- Uh huh. Yes, terrible business. Emily and I were just talking this afternoon – it is starting to feel a little like a Peter Straub novel around here isn't it? Speaking of which, have you had any breaks in the case Mike?

- No, we haven't. To be honest we're up to our ears chasing down leads but the victory of fiction over fact is precisely our problem. People are scared. And they're seeing what they think they should see. I've got people calling in with dreams that they've had. Premonitions. Predictions.

- Maybe you should start listening to them. No one ever believes in the monster until the final act.

- Unfortunately, I tend to think that the virtue of electric light is that now we see things rather more clearly where once we saw shapes in the shadows.

- Yes quite. You don't see shapes in the shadows then?

- You know, I have a colleague you would get on with very well. Excuse me a minute - I believe this is my cue for another drink.

The table was laid and the guests sat for dinner. At some point between the macaroni cheese and the sweet potatoes conversation returned to the murders. Bobby listened attentively, and as the wine warmed his mind he let the words flow over him. The sun was setting outside the windows and warm orange light filtered into the windows and across the room. It reminded him of the last rays of sunshine fading on the patchwork quilt of the garden. Would he ask? He would.

- Rosanna, do you really believe in hauntings?

Charlie kicked him underneath the table.

- Well, yes, in a manner of speaking.

- You believe they can really occur?

- I do, yes. But I would be quick to point out that in my experience hauntings are related much more to those who are haunted than any real ghost or poltergeist. I believe that Emily recommended Freud's essay about the uncanny to you for class and it reveals so much about what it means to be haunted. We call something uncanny that frightens us on an instinctive level, that tingling at the back of your neck when you think you saw a shadow following you through the trees, or hear the creaking of floorboards at night, and half-awake, believe that something is coming to find you. The word is revelatory; It is a translation of the German word 'Unheimlich', itself the inverse of 'Heimlich'. This word, Heimlich, has two meanings. It means 'belonging to the house, not strange, familiar, tame' but also 'concealed, kept from sight, so that others do not get to know of or about it'. So you see the word 'Unheimlich' and 'Uncanny' has in fact accumulated the opposite meaning of the first instance in the way that we use it, that something is unhomely or strange. But perhaps it is the subversion of the second meaning which truly illustrates what is disturbing about the uncanny, that it also means an uncovering of something which has been concealed. The haunted house is truly haunted because that which has been kept secret or locked away is coming to light. What appears to come from without really comes from within. That is where most of the truth lies in the few things I've seen.

- You've seen this before?

- Well, yes. I mean, nothing that was really corroborated but there have been a few cases in the area over the past twenty years.

- And how were they stopped?

- It is often enough to face the truth of what has happened but... I do believe that there are forces that are drawn to the haunted, that there are spirits which feed on these feelings of doubt and rage and grief, that when a house is full of that much anguish that over time something is drawn to it, will feed off it, and then...other measures are necessary...

Emily seized the moment to interject with the offer of dessert. She knew that Rosanna's enthusiasm for the subject was not always reassuring and the last thing she'd wanted when she invited Bobby was to upset him further and to lead him further down this avenue.

- Okay, I think we have successfully sacrificed the turkey. Who has room for pie?

The evening rolled on, the red wine flowed, and it was inevitably the time for board games. Emily sat up from the sofa and hunted in the pile beside the bookcase.

- It is a rare occasion that we have enough guests for a proper game of Cluedo, sorry...I mean Clue. I hope you will all humour me. Marco, can you set it up and I'll go fetch the festive spirits. Who is for port? Have you ever noticed how the clue house is so bright and cheerful after a murder?

She swayed slightly as she ducked around the sofa and to the kitchen, pouring the port into 6 short glasses, and bringing them back to the table. Mike and Bobby helped clear the plates whilst the other set up the board. The contenders took their places.

- Aha, 6 players, I'm not sure if this has actually happened before. And we have detectives amongst us tonight too. This promises to be the Clue to end all clues.

Mike sipped the port and watched Rosanna shuffle.

- I suppose you'll be channelling the spirit of the victim to discover the killer Rosanna?

- Ah, no, just some surreptitious use of mirrors and sleight of hand should do the trick.

She made one clue card dance over the back of her fingers.

- That does it, someone else is shuffling.

Charlie volunteered and then promptly spilt port over the cards.

- No, don't bow out yet Charlie, I'm counting on you.

Emily took the cards and shuffled, asking the boys and Rosanna to pick the secret cards and then dealing the remainders out to each player.

- I believe the youngest goes first. That will be you Bobby.

He picked up the dice and rolled.

After a couple of rounds Rosanna had eliminated all the suspects from her clue sheet and was fairly certain Mr Black had staged the whole thing himself, Bobby was keeping a fairly good count on things, Mike was insisting that he could work out who the killer was without needing to mark a single clue, and Charlie was trying to engage Marco in a conversation about the town's clocks.

- You've seen them right? If I was visiting I think it's the first thing I'd see. There isn't one that's right. Their jerky hands scuttling around their faces, always too slow or too fast.

- You are right Charlie, I've seen them; the end of time in this town is everywhere. It's a general running down. These clocks, these calendars, they are social inventions. We need clocks to know when to catch our train, when to get to work, to arrive at the party. We need calendars to plan our festivals, to ensure they are not far away, time is a civic benefit. Without it we lose the world, we retreat into our own private fears...okay, I think it is Mrs White, in the study, with the candlestick.

Mike laughed as he showed Marco the study.

- Marco, you talk and you talk, and this is not how you win clue.

Emily rolled the dice.

- He's not wrong though Mike, to quote Durkheim 'the foundation of the category of time is the rhythm of social life.'

Charlie was excited that someone was actually listening to him about this.

- Yes, you are exactly right. That is what is running down. Each person locked off in their own world, with their own clock, detached from the rest. I couldn't think of a better way to describe Ashenbrooke.

Rosanna went to show the kitchen card to Charlie but dropped it face up on the table and Bobby caught a glimpse before she retrieved it – that meant, if it wasn't – he had it. But then he saw that Emily's piece was already in the hallway and when she smiled at him he knew she'd seen it too. She rolled an 8, reached the pool, and made her accusation; Colonel Mustard, in the Library, with the Pistol. Such a classic murder. Right, right, and right.

As the night was winding down the brothers called a taxi and got their things together. Bobby knew it was now or never and took the opportunity to ask before he left.

- Rosanna, the thing is. What you describe, it's been happening to us for the last couple of months. Footsteps on the stairs at night. Things moving in the house. We've...Would you come take a look around?

- Bobby, I would be delighted to. Can I bring Emily too?

- Yes. Of course, You'd both be very welcome.

'That sounds splendid. We'd better make it sooner rather than later. How is this Saturday for you both?'

- Great. Yes. That's okay isn't it bro?

- Sure....I'm closing at the library on Saturday so won't be home til 7 but why don't you start without me? I'll join when I can.

Bobby knew Charlie would be pissed at him for this but it was his chance and so he took it.

- Okay, so why don't you both come around about 5?

CODEINE DREAMS

Lewis's investigations weren't merely nocturnal; in the days he searched through files for any information that he could find about the mill and its workers. Papers spread like small mountain ranges on his desk, with cups of coffee discarded on the hillsides as he made his way to the top. Sunlight streamed in over the hill of files scattered over the squad room and Lewis's arm was throbbing in waves of cascading pain. The days began to merge, to blend with the nights, and the continued debt of time accumulated in his body. His focus would come and go as the clouds shifted in the sky and sunlight scattered over incident reports and witness testimony. Seizing his moment to escape the world of his own creation Lewis jumped at the chance to join Mike on his visit to Ashenbrooke Library to meet with James Brayman.

Many of the guests had been interviewed that night but the cocktail of shock and alcohol meant that no two stories were the same. Rumour spread as fast as the fire had and by the time the police arrived on the scene in the small hours there were many stories making the rounds. A disgruntled employee taking revenge. A lover's tiff. A drunken accident. The textiles workshop had caught fire first, and then the structure went up. Thick black smoke circled into the night sky, and the truth became shrouded in a haze of smoke, booze, and rumour. There were a total of five deaths in the fire, and in the end it was the owner who took the heat, getting 25 years for criminal negligence. The authorities were lenient with him due to the severity of his injuries; he sustained major burns to most of his body, with most damage to his face and throat. He never spoke again after the fire. The case was closed, the mill was condemned, and Clarence Durkin sat in a jail cell in Fairwater for the next twelve years. The authorities kept track of him for a few years after his release. The last time they had him on record was for a drunken bar fight a few years back, and then they'd lost track of him. His record said that he had no fixed abode but he was assumed to be sleeping rough in the Fairwater area.

He researched the millworkers. The police had taken many statements that night. Each partygoer seemed privy to a new piece of information about the owner and the foreman, each had gleaned secrets from the gossip and theories that floated through the mill like an errant breeze. The foreman's wife had burned to death but somehow he had escaped, burned and disfigured but alive. There were many conflicting reports but none with the detail that Lewis had seen in his visions; the swift and frightening way in which the fire had spread, had burnt her alive with them watching. As she crawled to the staircase, away from the office, the skin already melting from her face, her hair singed and torn, the smell of cooking flesh that wafted towards the guests. They watched her, cry and drag herself to the stairs and then collapse, the bubbling white goo of her eyeballs running down her red and swollen cheeks. How could they forget that?

The investigations led to one inescapable truth; the mill owner was sentenced, but the details of what actually happened that night remained patchy and scattered. The first guests saw the fire spread quickly. There were some reports of an altercation between the foreman and his wife, some saw Durkin crawling from the flames, and others believed it was a drunken accident, one of the party guests accidentally igniting a bottle of spilled vodka. Each additional witness statement he read merely added one more conflicting narrative to the cacophony of voices in his head.

The woods parted and the mill was revealed once more. Light struck through the thin covering of mist and stepped enchanted into the forest fire. He approached, slipping easily through the crowds because this time they were frozen still, the music itself creeping on slowly, a shifting pitch of sound, a wall of noise.

He stepped into the office. Glass hung immobile in the air and a spark leapt slowly from the floor. The lady was pressed against the wall, and her cigarette had fallen from her hand, floated slowly down to the floor, and ignited the spilled brandy, which in turn had lit up the rug. Lewis watched amazed as the flames flickered across the floor. He watched in stop gap animation as the flames leapt and spread, crawling together deliberately towards the door. It was all stage lit from the hanging moon, that watched on blankly as the wall. And the actors appeared for him every night, ready to play their roles, he wondered if they were sick of it now? Having to show up every night and hold their positions as he wandered through their scene, disturbing them, and rifling through the props. They seemed absorbed in whatever it was they were fighting about.

He watched them, the blood trickling down her cheek where a sliver of glass had cut her, the man's face as it registered what was happening in slow motion, fear and surprise and then something else. His mask wavered, would he break character just this once? Lewis wondered what it was he was really thinking as he replayed this scene over and over. No matter how affecting it must have been the first time you had to think that it got tiring, he was probably thinking about the beer he was going to have once this was all over, or the next fire he was going to start. Lewis could not place him but he knew that something just wasn't quite right here. The flames licked around the office, and soon the rug was ablaze. The lady screamed and made her way towards the door but the fire was spreading fast and the doorframe was already alight. She reached for the handle but it burnt her hand as soon as she touched it. She looked around and the man was leaning against the desk, his trouser leg already ablaze. Time seemed to speed up then for Lewis and he witnessed it all, he saw the man snap into gear, and soon they were working together, trying to use his short sleeves to open the door. But the heat from the blaze had already wedged the door shut in its frame. They kicked, and threw things at it, but the door simply wouldn't budge.

Soon the mill roared with fire, and the flames announced themselves like uninvited guests; they leapt up in conversation, touched partygoers on their shoulders, swiftly ignited their shirts. The faces of partygoers fell, from reverie to despair as the warm feeling that they felt was recognised, not as a cocktail of alcohol and celebration, but as the imminent incineration of the mill. Due to the inebriation and impaired reactions, the crowd didn't act as swiftly as they should. It was really quite amazing how quickly a textile mill went up, but boy, when it did it really went. Guests fled from the party, their clothes alight, and rolled in the dewy grass until the flames were smothered. It was only once a crowd had gathered on the lawn that people realised where the screams were coming from. There were people trapped inside the building, but up on the second floor they could all see clearly into the foreman's office. The foreman and his wife beat at the door, but the room was already filling with smoke. They watched the flames encircle them and then they watched her hair catch alight. The image of smoke and burning flesh haunted many of them for years to come. Lewis stood in the room, the flames passing right through his body. He felt slightly warmed but it was far away, as if his body was in the room next door. He tried to look away but couldn't, and he watched them struggle. They hammered and threw themselves at the door until eventually, half burned, it snapped and exploded in to flame strewn pieces. They clambered over the shards of broken door and down the flaming hall, where she fell, her hair and face alight. He ran, jumping from step to step, and out in to the night.

Lewis began to watch the event through the eyes of each partygoer, feeling the panic rise in his chest, and watching the flames engulf the wooden mill, and chew ceaselessly through the woodwork. His vision blurred and his senses were overloaded until all he could feel was sheer panic and the sound of screams in his throat. He woke up in the night his eyes moving slowly, the room underwater. The images in his mind seemed to run in slow motion, overlapping each other, and that was when it became clear to him. The people running, the burning mill, bodies in the ashes of both the mill and the bonfire. He had it. Somehow, in some way, the connection was fire.

SHADOWS IN THE TREES

Potemko took the call a little after 7pm. It was Mrs Corrigan talking very swiftly about a figure tramping through the forests near to her home. He told her they'd be right there, put the phone down and went to find Mike.

- I think we've got a lead. Reports of a figure out in the woods by the Corrigan's place.

Mike dropped the report he was reading onto his desk, grabbed the keys to the squad car, and was already half out the door.

- Okay, Carter, you're with me. Potemko, the station is yours. Stay on the radio and keep us updated.

- Sure thing boss. Happy hunting.

Carter and Mike jumped into the car and sped off towards the Corrigan's place, out past Monument Park and up towards the woodlands.

- You got your vest on?

- Sir, I've got the whole kit; vest, pepper spray, the works.

- Good, because this has the ring of truth to it. Most of the reports we've had have been suburban areas. Local kids playing pranks. But the Corrigan's live out by the woods proper. This could be it.

- I'm ready Sir. Let's get this bastard.

The radio spluttered static and then Potemko's voice came out clearly.

- Boss, I've just had a further report from a gentleman who lives in the same area. He reports the figure of an old man on the treeline, scratting about.

- What's scratting?

- Searching, looking for something.

- Okay. Anything else?

- No that's all. I'll stay on the line and update you. And Sir, if it is him...the fucker is faster than he looks.

- Thanks Potemko. Over and out.

They pulled up to the property and knocked on the door. Mrs Corrigan answered, a shotgun in her hands.

- Whoa, ma'am. Would you mind lowering the gun please?

She lowered the gun so that the barrel pointed at Carter's left shin.

- Yes. Oh, I'm sorry officers. You just can't be too careful these days, what with this maniac wandering about.

Carter stepped forward.

- Ma'am, Can you pass me the gun please?

Mrs Corrigan handed it over and Carter held it in her hands, feeling the tension in her shoulders relax.

- Okay. Thank you. Now, can you tell us what you saw?

Mrs Corrigan led them both through to her kitchen, which afforded a good view of the woodlands on the other side.

- It's still there. On the treeline, you see.

Carter and Mike peered through the window but couldn't make out anything substantial. All they could see were shadows in the trees, as the wind blew them from side to side.

- Okay, you stay here ma'am and we'll go investigate. I'm going to hang on to this for a moment.

Carter and Mike left the property and began to cross the few hundred metres to the woodlands. The chill in the air bit more readily than before, and suddenly from the dark grey clouds above, specks of white snow began to fall through the air and settle on the ground. The snow began to obfuscate the air and both strained their eyes to look towards the treeline. Mike stopped to speak to Carter.

- Okay, I'm going to turn my radio off now. If he is there, we don't want to spook him, and with this cover we might just be able to get the drop on him. I'll take point. You stay on my left and keep me covered.

- You've got it.

They advanced and the snow began to thicken, swirling in eddies around them. As they got closer, Mike watched the pattern of the snow as it swirled through the trees and fell delicately on to the branches. The patterns of a landscape as they shifted. There were shadows, darkness in the trees that couldn't be breached. As he advanced the patterns formed themselves into shapes and he could see that snow was falling onto the figure of a man, leaving its trace in his wild hair and shoulders. Mike turned to Carter and gestured towards the man, who still hadn't seen them as they approached. Carter fingered the shotgun in her hands, held one hand low on the barrel and rested her right index finger on the trigger guard as she trained the sights on the figure in the distance. She remembered long summers spent with her mother in Bordan's Canyon, learning to shoot deer in the wild. Mike took his pistol from its holster and held it low and steady as he walked the last hundred metres to the treeline. Then the dark figure looked up, straight at him, its tangled matted hair cascading down its weathered face, obscuring the dark eyes beneath. He tensed and looked at them. Mike called out.

- Sir, stay right where you are. Do not move.

Mike carried on walking slowly towards the figure. Closer, closer. It looked around, apparently confused by its surroundings. Suddenly it bolted, running straight at the Sheriff.

- Sir!

Carter lifted the shotgun, and trained its sights on the figure but it was too fast and it barrelled straight into the Sheriff as he raised his gun to fire. The man hit him hard, the top of its skull smashing straight into his chin, as its shoulder dug into his chest and lifted him off the ground. Mike saw red stars in his vision and felt the warm blood blossom on his chin as he was lifted into the air. The man sprinted onwards, past Mike, darting off towards the west, and back to the treeline. Mike hit the floor hard on his back as Carter pivoted with the shotgun, breathing in as she tracked the figure's arc. It ran away from them incredibly fast as she trained the sights on the centre of its back, breathed out slowly, and depressed both triggers. The echo of the shotgun blasts shot out through the trees and the few remaining nesting birds took flight into the night. The figure was fast, but not fast enough. One shell shot straight through its left flank and dark red blood shot out in the snow filled night. It arced through the air and landed in a sickle shape on the snow dusted ground. The figure stumbled sideways and fell. Carter ran straight over to Mike.

- Sir, are you okay?

He rolled onto his front and pushed himself up to a kneeling position. Blood dripped down from the large open wound on his chin, coating his uniform. He kept his head still, waiting for the dark red spots to leave his vision.

- I'm fine. Just give me a second.

Carter looked up to see the figure had gotten back onto its feet and was stumbling towards the treeline. She put the shotgun down and unholstered her pistol.

- I'm going after him.

She started to stride off.

- Carter, wait. You hit him right? We'll be able to track him now. You saw how fast he was, you are not going after him alone. Help me get back to the Corrigans, then we'll call in back-up and chase this fucker down.

She kept walking away from him, scanning the trees for sign of the man.

- Carter, that's an order! Come back!

She slowed down and then returned to help Mike to his feet. They walked back to the Corrigan's house and Mike pressed his radio.

- Potemko, we've found him. I took a hit but Carter got him. I need you to call in the state police. We need back-up. I'm gonna get patched up and then we'll track this sonofabitch down. I need them ready to rendezvous with us when I radio in. You got that?

- Sure thing boss, I'm on it.

Carter knocked on the door and Mrs Corrigan answered.

- Ma'am, have you got a first aid kit and some bandages we can use?

- I sure do. Damn, that is a nasty cut. Come right this way.

- And, do you have some more shells for this gun? I'd like to borrow it for the night.

REVELATIONS

Emily and Rosanna made their way to the house at the peak of Elm Hill. Both were wrapped up against the chill wind; Emily wore her winter coat and Rosanna wore her trench coat buttoned up to the top. The temperature had plummeted even further since they were last out gathering ingredients for the Thanksgiving feast. Snow threatened itself in the wind, and when they passed the few solitary figures on their walk, Rosanna tipped her hat to them as they scurried past.

As they left the square and began to climb the hill, the house came into view, its impressive wooden structure backlit as the sun set. Yellow light spread out from the ground floor, billowing out into the approaching night. It was grander than she'd imagined, sat perched by itself on the hill; it was stately, even in its present condition. 'Coquettish Decay.' The words echoed in her mind.

Rosanna whistled.

- What a wonderful site for a haunting.

- Isn't it just?

They strode the last few hundred metres to the house, the warmth of the steady incline battling against the cold air, leaving them flushed and awakened when they knocked on the front door.

Charlie opened the red front door and ushered them inside. 'Welcome to our humble abode. Come in, come in, wonders await you inside.' He took their coats, hung them on the rack, and led them into the kitchen where Bobby was seated at the table. He stood up, and greeted them both.

- Thank you for coming. We really appreciate it.

Emily brushed his arm.

- It's our pleasure. Anything we can do to help.

She looked at his warm brown eyes, his quiet face. The resemblance was striking. She hadn't imagined it. What a strange and wonderful thing.

Charlie rooted around in the cupboards.

- Okay, what would you both like to drink? We have wine, we have pilsner. We have whisky…we have…schnapps?

Rosanna wandered around the living room, looking at pictures.

- A beer would be delightful.

- You've got it. Emily, beer?

- Yes. Please.

She took a seat at the table and watched him dart around the kitchen. His fast blue eyes. His careless hair. Not just one. Both of them. Like him, but also not. How strange. He darted around the kitchen, taking out glasses and bottles. He passed a beer to Bobby.

- Open this for me, will you bro? Okay, now we can't promise the same standards as the other night but Bobby and I have whipped a little something special up for you both. It should be ready in about half an hour so why don't you take a seat in the lounge and I'll bring over the drinks.

Bobby showed Emily and Rosanna to the lounge, which had actually become a bona fide lounge again since they had both started sleeping upstairs in their own rooms again. They took a seat on the sofa and Bobby brought the drinks in.

- This is a lovely house you both have.

- Thanks Rosanna. We've been trying to look after it better. After our mother died, lots of people thought we should move out but we couldn't do it.

- Well, you made the right choice. There was no need to lose any more than you already had. You feel the same way Charlie?

- Yes. I mean, with Bobby at school here for another year, and I've got the job at the library. It didn't make sense to leave. I think we probably will. But not yet.

Emily picked up a framed photo from the bookshelves.

- And is this your mother?

She passed the photo to Bobby. He took it and looked at his mother's smiling face and long brown hair. They were all there, sun baked and happy.

- Yes. This is from a couple of summers ago. When she was last healthy.

Rosanna asked the question.

- And when was it that she passed away?

- It was February. Last year.

- So you were 16?

- That's right. It was the week after my birthday.

Emily took another swig of beer.

- It really is a lovely house. I'm glad that you stayed.

The alarm in the kitchen bleep-bleep-bleeped and Charlie jumped up.

- Right, that is the garlic bread. Oh, I didn't say; tonight is Spaghetti Bolognese, I hope that is alright with everybody.

Rosanna downed the last of her beer.

- That sounds great. I could eat a small horse.

- Great, well, there is certainly enough of it. Grab a seat at the table everyone. Bobby, you know where the red wine is. Can you grab that?

- Um?

- Cupboard by the sink. On the right. Where the popcorn is.

Bobby's blank face lit up.

- Great. So, yes, take a seat everyone. And then after dinner we can give you the grand tour.

Emily watched the manic display in the kitchen as plates jumped from cupboards, spaghetti jumped onto plates, and bowls of bread and salad and Bolognese and dressings lined themselves up on the table, not in any particular order, but definitely giving the impression of bountiful amounts of food for all. She sat down and enjoyed the scene taking place before her.

The wine was opened, the bread was passed, and the subject was broached. Rosanna quizzed Bobby about the nature of the hauntings, what had happened over the past months. Bobby told the story, of creaking stairs, sobs at night, their scattershot journeys to explore the house at night.

- So, when do these events happen usually?

- I guess they usually happen at night. It's definitely once the light goes down. I don't think there is any pattern really.

- Now, forgive me for asking but neither of you have mentioned your father. Has he been involved since your mother died?

Emily took another sip of wine and looked down at the table. Charlie was the one to answer.

- He left. About ten years ago. Things weren't good between him and our mother so we never saw much of him. He died a couple of years back.

- I see. Okay.

Rosanna continued to explore the other parts of the house while Emily asked Bobby and Charlie to show her their father's study. When she walked inside she couldn't believe how similar it looked. His handwriting on the folders, books lined up along the walls. And an oak desk with a model ship sat on one side. She couldn't believe it. The room was a different size and layout but really it felt like stepping back into a photograph from her childhood, the faded image eroded by time. She'd sat in it many times after he'd left. She felt the panic rise in her heart as she looked around at this room, so much like him. All these relics that he left behind him in his wake as he barrelled around the world.

- You kept it like this too?

Charlie smiled.

- Yeah. I guess you could say we're making a habit of it. I like to think that we are keeping time capsules.

- Ha, yes. That's perfect. A crushed petal in a book. A photograph. All memories, preserved. Time capsules.

- We haven't touched it in years. We've never really touched it since he left.

She walked around the room, reading the books, taking them down, looking at the inscriptions.

- Did he keep a diary? Any letters?

- No, nothing I ever found. Just books and his old papers, his dissertation is up there somewhere.

She took a book down from the shelf that she recognized; *The Savage God*. A photograph fell out on to the desk. It was of her as a young girl. He'd visited in the summer and taken her to Paris for the weekend. And there they were, with ice creams, sitting outside Notre Dame. The photo sat on the desk looking up at them. Bobby looked down at it.

- Wow, I've never seen this. Check out dad's beard. Who's with him?

The silence hung in the air between them all.

Charlie looked down at the picture and their eyes looked back at him. Their eyes were his eyes. Light blue and piercing. And then it all clicked into place. He thought back to his conversations with his father in New York.

- How old were you then Emily?

- I was 12.

Bobby looked at them both and at the photograph.

- Why would…

SHOWDOWN

Bobby looked from Emily to the photograph. It was her, he couldn't deny it. But his brain had yet to make sense of it.

- I...what?

- You never knew anything about me? That he had another family before?

Bobby was stunned into silence and so Charlie spoke.

- I knew. He told me. When I was at college. We'd never heard about you before. Our mother never spoke about it and I was shocked when he told me. Well, I was half shocked. But I'm sorry to say I never really thought about it seriously. About you. We never knew you, and honestly, we had enough going on at the time. So I never said anything. But it's true Bobby, she is our sister.

Bobby sat looking at the photo, putting the pieces together in his mind.

- So, he...he was married before?

- Yes. He left when I was 4. That's when he moved back to America, and met your mother. And then a few years later Charlie was born, and then you. He would visit occasionally, if he had a conference in Europe he'd come visit or take me along. That picture is from when I was 12, so...I guess that's the year before you were even born Bobby.

- But how could he keep that a secret?

Charlie chipped in.

- You were 7 when he left Bobby. It's not that hard to keep secrets from a 7 year old. And our father could keep secrets for a living.

So, when he moved back to London did he live with you?

- No, no. His relationship with my mother was…turbulent. You know him, he never could stay in one place for long. But he didn't live that far away from me. We were close…I found him.

- When?

Suddenly they heard a tremendous crash come from downstairs as the kitchen door was ripped clean off its hinges. They looked at each other and then Emily called out.

- Rosanna?

There was no reply. They could hear plates and dishes being smashed in the kitchen. Charlie acted first, stepping out on to the landing. There was no sign of her, she must still be upstairs in their mother's room. But there was clearly something downstairs, and this wasn't the ethereal clattering of windowpanes. This was someone smashing their kitchen to pieces. He ran into his room and took the ceremonial sword from under his bed, a gift from his father on his eighteenth birthday. It was blunt, it couldn't be sharpened to travel through customs, but it still had a fair heft to it. Emily and Bobby were on the landing and Charlie told them to wait in Bobby's room whilst he investigated downstairs. They took a step inside as he walked to the staircase. At the bottom of the stairs he saw a figure, in rotted clothing, blood red seeping through the left side of its jacket. Emily looked into its eyes and the lights flickered, first dazzlingly bright, then a pop, and darkness. Bobby turned on the lamp in his room, which scattered dull light across the landing. Charlie yelled.

- Get inside, lock the door!

They started to edge in to the room as the figure bounded up the stairs. As Emily joined Bobby in his room Charlie swung with the sword and watched the blade smash into the man's left shoulder. Its reflexes were lightning swift as it grabbed Charlie's arm with its right hand, digging its ragged fingernails deep into the flesh of his forearm. Charlie cried out in pain as he lost his grip on the hilt of the sword and it clattered to the floor. The grip on his arm tightened and he heard the loud wild crack as the bone of his forearm snapped in two. The pain screamed out loudly as he swung his left fist into the man's face, knocking him off balance and feeling the grip loosen on his broken arm. He barely had time to register the misshapen forearm as he twisted loose and ducked toward Bobby's room. He was almost inside when he felt a force lift him off the ground as the man threw him sideways into the doorframe. His skull connected with the woodwork and then darkness. The figure lifted Charlie's limp body and threw it into Emily, who lost her footing and fell backwards on to the floor of Bobby's room. Bobby watched as the door moved of its own volition, slamming shut in the creature's face. There was a moment of stillness, the lamplight cascading over Emily and Charlie on the floor and then the awesome sound of the man trying to gain entrance to the room. He banged and barged, but the door would not shift. The door frame seemed to jump with the impacts, as Emily got to her knees. They both looked at Charlie lying on the floor, unconscious, blood trickling from his right earlobe.

Carter and Mike had traced the trail through the woods, and up to the peak of Elm Hill. They saw the door standing ajar and could hear screams coming from the house. Mike radioed in.

- Potemko, suspect is at 134 Elm Hill. Carter and I are proceeding into the property. Tell back-up to converge on this location. And I want an ambulance on standby too.

- Affirmative boss. Back up will be with you in ten minutes.

- Tell them to move their asses.

- Will do.

Carter stepped up to the property and peered inside. There were plates and glasses smashed all over the kitchen. The cupboard doors stood open, the place had been ransacked and torn to pieces.

- Sir, let me take point. You're injured...and I'm a better shot.

- We can settle that at the firing range. But okay, lead on.

Carter led the way into the building. They could hear a loud banging coming from the floor above but the yelling had stopped for the time being.

- Follow me Sir, I'm heading to the stairway.

The lights were out and Carter shone her flashlight ahead of her into the darkness. They followed the trail of fresh blood along the corridor to the foot of the staircase. The banging was now coming from directly above them. When they rounded the corner Carter shone the flashlight up the stairs illuminating the figure on the landing. It stopped and turned, its cold dead eyes looking through them both. Carter and Mike raised their guns in unison as the figure came towards them, pelting down the stairs. Mike fired, the shot clipping its right shoulder and ricocheting off the wall. Carter stood, lining up the barrels as it headed directly for her. It was too fast for her to dodge, her only chance was to take the shot as it came at her. Ten feet, five feet, she fired. The shots hit it square in the chest and chunks of flesh sprayed out backwards across the staircase covering Mike with muscle and blood. The figure carried on and hurtled straight into Carter, knocking her to the floor and landing right on top of her, crushing her into the floor. She struggled against it, trying to push it off as it held her down and sank its decaying teeth into her throat. She felt the warmth of blood flowing from her neck as she pushed against it and then she could no longer fill her lungs with air. She took sharp swift breaths but her lungs would not rise. She felt the strength leaving her arms as the weight pressed on top of her. Her breath came in short gargling bursts. Mike pulled at the man with all his strength, until it rolled off her, staggering to its feet, leaning against the wall. It stood looking at him, its eyes glazed over, blood pouring from the wounds in its chest, shredded organs dangling loose from its chest cavity. And then it pounced. With the grace and speed it had always shown. Knocking Mike backwards against the wall, it head-butted him, and he saw stars as its nails dug into his shoulder blade. He brought his knee up swiftly between its legs and pushed with all his strength. Its grip let up but it wouldn't budge. As he felt the nails dig into his flesh once more suddenly he heard a shot ring out. In slow motion he watched its head cave in, and saw matted blood and brain matter fly out the other side. The grip released, the figure staggered backwards, and then slumped lifelessly to the floor. Mike saw Carter drop the pistol as her arm fell to the floor and her eyes rolled backwards in her head. He dropped to the floor next to her, pressing his hands to her throat, trying to stem the bleeding. Her breath came in tiny wheezing noises. He thumbed the radio.

- Potemko! I need the ambulance now! Now!

- Got it boss. It's on its way. Hold on.

Then Mike saw a shadow jump in his left field of vision. He turned swiftly. It was Rosanna.

- What are you?

- There's no time. Towels, I need towels. Grab something from the kitchen!

Mike pressed the towels around Carter's throat. Her face was turning blue and her breaths were getting shallower and shallower.

- Rosanna, hold her head still.

- What are you…

- It's torn through her airway, she hasn't got long. I need to make a new one.

He pulled a pen from his pocket and a pocket knife from his jacket. He ran to the kitchen, returning with a half full bottle of vodka and some dishtowels.

- Do you know what you're doing?

- Hold her still.

Rosanna held Carter still as Mike sterilised the knife and made an incision at the base of her throat. He removed the ink and inserted the plastic body of the pen into the incision. Carter squirmed but Mike held her tight. No sound escaped her mouth. They waited for long seconds, and then her chest rose as her body took in oxygen again. The colour returned to her face and Mike staunched the bleeding with the dishtowels. They did all they could to keep her alive as the sound of sirens approached the house.

The door of Bobby's room suddenly relaxed of its own volition, swinging open gently. The noise of the rest of the house burst in and they could hear people running around downstairs. Emily put her hand on Bobby's shoulder.

- You stay here and look after him. I'll see what is happening.

She crept to the doorway. There were deep grooves in the other side of the door where that thing had attempted to claw its way through the woodwork. She was not prepared for the scene that greeted her; blood and flesh coated the stairs and wall and she could see Rosanna and Mike kneeling next to a body, their clothes and hands covered in blood. She called out and both turned. Her eyes asked them if it had gone. Mike answered.

- Carter shot him. He's down for good. Are you okay?

- Yes, I'm...the door shut and he couldn't...Charlie's been hurt badly.

- The ambulance is 2 minutes out. Shit, I need more towels. Emily, can you grab some from the bathroom?

Her steely expression faltered for a second and then she ran downstairs taking the towels to Mike. She couldn't help but glance over at the prostrate figure across the hallway. She couldn't make out much, blood pooled around his tangled long hair, seeping into the carpet, but it still threw shivers down her back. She turned to look back at Mike. Mike, when did they? Thank god they did. Mike worked feverishly, pressing the towels around Carter's neck and keeping track of her faint pulse. She was turning a waxy grey colour and he knew they didn't have long left at all. He held the towels tight but made sure she was still breathing, watching intently for the faint rise and fall of her chest. The sirens reached deafening proportions and then stopped. Mike's radio crackled.

- Sir, they've arrived.

He met Emily's gaze.

- Emily, I need you to take over. Place your hands on top of mine.

She did as he told her. He then slipped his hands out.

- Now, stay right there and keep pressure on her neck. I will only be a minute.

He unclipped his radio from his belt and ran out to signal the ambulance. The snow fell faster and faster over Ashenbrooke as the emergency vehicles threaded their way through the streets.

PART III: TO RETURN

The night sky is only a sort of carbon paper,
Blueblack, with the much-poked periods of stars
Letting in the light, peephole after peephole -
A bonewhite light, like death, behind all things.

Sylvia Plath, 'Insomniac'
Crossing the Water, ASH 813 PLA CRO

It was evening all afternoon.
It was snowing
And it was going to snow.
The blackbird sat
In the cedar-limbs.

Wallace Stevens, 'Thirteen ways of looking at a Blackbird'
Harmonium, ASH 813 STE3

THE LONG DARK NIGHT

Fluorescents flickered in fits, nerves jangled in discord. The walls stared blankly and orderlies shuffled softly, pushing trolleys down endless white hallways. Gurneys were rushed down corridors, and Charlie looked down at his body, spotlit on the steel table. There was a mess of action as surgeons operated on him, and a cacophony of instruments warming up for their performance as the beeps and blips echoed off the walls of the operating theatre. Charlie watched them for a while as they fought to stabilise his body, to keep him tethered to this world. And then he left, flying down long corridors as people ran past beneath. He found Bobby and Emily sitting together in the waiting room with the detectives, looking up anxiously each time a doctor came in to the room. The sheriff was there, pacing, and other detectives that he didn't recognise. The sounds were far away, muffled, as if travelling a great distance to reach him. He watched them all, and saw the snow falling in swirling patterns, nuzzling up against the windows, beginning to blanket the floor, pressing in small snow banks. The television set chattered to itself, as relatives sat waiting for any news. Charlie looked at the seat he'd sat in, all those times when his mother had been here for her chemotherapy. The magazines were even the same. Health magazines with smiling white-teethed grinning faces, that didn't match any of the sallow faces he'd seen here, pumped full of poison and struggling to focus. And here was Bobby again. He watched them together. A sister he hardly knew and his brother who he'd do anything for. The snow fell faster, fell faster, until the single snowdrops were indistinguishable, but merely a sheet, a slowly sinking white sheet of nothingness. It fell until it filled out the edges of the room. Everything was indistinguishable, and everything was white.

They sat in the waiting room and the clocks stopped moving. The darkness outside the windows was broken by swirling eddies of white snow, framed in the lamplight, and endless beyond. As endless as the night, sitting in plastic chairs, constantly moving, seeking comfort and failing. The stark lighting in the hospital revealed every worried crease in Mike's face. Emily watched his eyes scan the room, following the nurses, noting the announcements on the tannoy and compiling a picture in his head of what was really going on behind the carefully fixed faces of the doctors. His eyes didn't stop moving, instead they scanned, taking in all the information that was revealed in a furtive glance, a lazily held file. Bobby sat next to her, rolling and unrolling a magazine, and then tearing the edges of the pages. They sat like this for what seemed like forever, waiting and waiting, for something to happen.

Mike was outside the hospital, snow gathering on his jacket, his chin starting to ache from the cold.

- Potemko, I'm at the hospital with Carter.

- How's she doing?

- I don't know, they're…they're not telling me anything. Look, I need an update on what's going on. Can you get over to the house? I'd feel better if there was someone I knew at the scene.

- Of course boss, I can be there in 15.

- Great, thank you. When I left they were bagging up what's left of the body. Keep me in the loop yeah?

Sometime in the early hours of the morning two doctors walked into the waiting room with intent. Emily saw them coming.

- Excuse me, are you the relatives of Charles Renyard?

Emily looked at Bobby. He nodded.

- We've done all we can at this stage. He's stable but he's sustained substantial trauma. He's in intensive care now. You can visit him. At this point it is just a matter of waiting to see if he wakes up.

Bobby blinked and tears washed down his cheeks.

- I want to see him.

- Come with me and we'll take you to his room.

The room was a cacophony of tubes, lines going in and out of his body. Everything beeped in a staccato symphony; noises filled the white room completely, rhythmic, demanding, pervasive. They sat with Charlie for a long time, Bobby holding his hand, until the faint pink of the sunrise could be seen through the window, bouncing softly off the freshly fallen snow. It felt better to be in the room, to be this close and to watch his chest rise and fall, to hear the machines keeping him alive, to know everything in seconds, in constant updates. As the pink light warmed towards orange Emily broke the silence of the room.

- Bobby, I want you to come and stay with me. I have a spare room. We can drive by your place to pick up some things on the way.

- I can…they let you sleep here. They have a roll out bed.

- I know, but you heard what they said. He is stable, and you need some rest too. We're 10 minutes away, I swear it.

He nodded his head.

- Come back, get some sleep and a shower and we'll be back here before you know it, okay?

Potemko made his way to the scene. When he got there the street was painted with red and blue light from the 4 cruisers parked outside the house. Yellow tape roped off the house, and the kitchen door swung inwards on its hinges, snow already settling in small drifts on the kitchen floor. When he got inside the place was a hive of activity, troopers photographing the bullet holes, taking samples of the blood and sinew covering the walls. He found the officer in charge.

- Sir, my name is Potemko. Ashenbrooke county sheriff's department. That was my team that got taken out of here earlier.

- My god son, how are they doing?

- I don't know. Listen, can I take a look at the guy? I've seen him before and I need to check that it's who we think it is.

- Of course, follow me. I tell you though, I haven't seen a guy that messed up in quite some time. You can see through his fucking ribcage.

Potemko followed him to the ambulance parked outside and unzipped the black body bag. Seeing it there, torn to shreds, didn't take any of its power away. It still scared the shit out of him. He could see the bark and twigs embedded in its beard, and the stink was something else. It had taken one hell of a beating before being put down for good.

Emily and Bobby said goodbye to Mike and stepped out into the crisp white snow. It had stopped falling for a while and the tangerine sunlight reflected off the snowbanks. The world was new again. The cold crisp air woke them up. Emily couldn't quite believe they were returning to the scene of yesterday's nightmare but now that her tiredness had kicked in nothing felt quite real. They flew through the morning towards Elm Hill as she watched the road pass beneath the windscreen of her car. Neither said much as they drove, they were simply preparing themselves for the scene that would greet them.

There was yellow tape covering the doorways to the house, and a police car still parked outside. Emily pulled in nearby and cut the engine; the sounds slowed and ceased, and nobody moved. The house seemed oddly silent in the morning, but there was something ominous in its features; the faint menacing curl of the eaves, the darkness of the front door.

- I can pick up some things. You don't need to come inside.

- No. I want to see it.

Bobby took the key from his pocket and opened the front door. It opened inwards revealing the scene from last night; dark matted blood coated the walls and floors, and parts of the stairs and banisters had been blasted away, probably from the impact of the shotgun shells. Bobby climbed the stairs and headed up to his room, leaving Emily standing in the hallway by herself. Bobby stood looking around at the room, then picked up a bag, filled it with clothes and ducked under the yellow tape back on to the landing. He looked around the house; they'd truly lost it now.

Emily stood in the hallway looking at the patterns of dark blood spattered across the walls. Arcs of darkness with mottled pieces of white within. She reached up to touch the tacky matted brown substance and her eyes filled with a red haze. A memory half formed and then faded and she vomited on the floor. She recovered her footing and turned away from the dark symbols. She called up to Bobby. It was time to leave.

Once Bobby had fallen asleep Emily crept from the room and closed the door. She took a bottle of whisky from her kitchen cabinet and poured a glass. She took a sip, feeling the warm liquor tense her body and then relax it. She let her body fall into the cushions. She'd felt him. They were in his study when it started. That anger, that...it felt just the same as before. Emily let her body sink into the sofa. The whisky burned gently in her throat, and the adrenaline fell sharply from her veins. The door had closed and something had kept it locked, had kept them inside. Which one was still there inside that house? She felt it when she was there. Nothing was finished yet.

The hours swept by and the snow kept falling. Mike knew he should be back at the station house already but he just couldn't leave. He wanted to be here…if…he looked up as a nurse was walking towards him.

- Excuse me, Sheriff Sullivan? Will you come with me? We should really get that cut looked at.

- Is there any news?

- She's still in theatre. Come with me and I'll check up on her for you, as soon as we've got that stitched up.

She led him to a small room off the corridor and sat him down on the bed so that she could get a better look at his injuries.

- Can I ask what happened to you all?

- You know the killer that's been stalking the town?

- Uh huh?

- He happened to us.

- I'm hoping he came off worse that you all did.

- He did. She probably saved all our lives.

Mike stepped into the room. She was lying on the bed, her face pale, her body motionless, except for the steady rise and fall of the ventilator. A nurse sat at the foot of her bed taking notes, and adjusting the machines. He sat down next to her and held her hand, listening to the steady mechanical beat of the room. It was hard to look peaceful in a room full of so much noise but he thought she managed it. Fuck it, how could he have let this happen? Her hand felt cold in his, as if she'd already gone.

- What do we do now?

- We wait.

- How...

Her hand gripped his hard, and the tempo of the machines increased. The tones rose steadily signalling speed, signalling danger. She began to thrash on the bed and her hand spasmed in his. The nurse moved swiftly, hitting the red button above the bed and holding her down. Carter thrashed wildly and everything fell out of pace as the ECG spiked on the screen. It was mere seconds before the room was full and Mike was pushed back to the edge. They rushed to steady her as her heart thrashed in her chest, the rhythm spiking wildly. He watched transfixed as they applied the panels and electrical current seized her body, making it jump and still, shocking it back into a normal rhythm. The peaks decreased and began to slow, pacing steadily until she calmed on the bed. Mike felt the tension in the room ease a little as the doctors watched her calm, her body retire. Soon the stillness returned. Carter lay on the bed, the doctors withdrew, and the nurse sat vigilant at her bedside. She was stable for now.

- What do we do?

- We wait. You can stay if you like.

WANDERING

Mike arrived at the house just after midday. He'd had no sleep but instead had come straight from the hospital to meet Potemko. It was unbelievably cold; the state troopers and the coroners had all taken off, and the yellow ribbon still hung around the perimeter of the house, but now it had a feeling of abandonment. They'd taken what they needed and then left. Someone had attempted to jam the kitchen door back in to its frame but the wind and the snow had already taken it mostly off its hinges at this point. They kept their coats buttoned up to the neck and stepped through the corridor to the place where it had died.

- I can't believe you took him down boss. I took a look earlier, and he was just the same grizzly motherfucker as before, minus most of his guts.

- It was Carter, you should have seen her. She must have put five bullets in the damn thing before it went down.

- How's she doing?

- I don't know, it's not looking good. She's hooked up to all of those machines but they just don't know when she'll wake up. She lost an awful lot of blood.

- Shit. I'm glad she killed that fucker.

- I just can't believe it's over.

- Tell that to Lewis. Kid's back at the station house neck deep in reports.

- How's he doing?

- I don't know. Sometimes it's like he's not really there. Other times he's a man possessed. I can't get a read on him if I'm honest sir.

- Give him some time. He's recovering from this too.

I walk around the house, like a ghost haunting my old life. Feeling the empty corridors and quiet rooms settle around me. Staring past death and on to the other side, where everything is stillness, and mist around the edges of the frame. Now I think this house is what comes afterwards. These still quiet, empty rooms. Just a limbo world for spirits that can't quite move on. And so we shuffle silently around the rooms, looking at the remnants of our old lives, not ready to move on but unable to stay. Unable to be more than mere shadows of our old lives. They are there, their uniforms crisp and clear. My hospital gown is translucent in the sunlight that carries through the doorway. I feel as insubstantial as a shaft of sunlight. When did I get here? I can't remember, time doesn't really mean the same thing here. It moves slowly, like walking underwater, forceless against the weight of history. And so I creep, steady steps on the stairs, and they can not, will not, hear me.

Emily and Bobby came to visit Charlie every day that week. They sat with him and watched, listening to the steady beeps of the machines, the ventilator appearing to fill and empty itself ceaselessly. They talked to him, they drank coffee, they waited. For something, any sign that he was still in there, still somewhere inside his own body. But the truth is he wasn't. Charlie had begun to separate from himself, to flow out into the world around him. And now he could float freely in the corner of the room and watch them watching him. The haze made it difficult and his vision would blur occasionally, and then be drawn back into darkness. At these times, he would float off, down corridors, turning corners endlessly until he found himself in an old memory, a half forgotten dream. Many times he wandered around the house, creeping across the landing, watching his mother looking after Bobby, creeping downstairs to see his father. These dreams were half real, and he would get lost, sitting on the landing for hours, feeling the safe sounds of the house around him, content in his simple happiness. He felt warmth sitting on a stair whilst the past continued below. And time flowed slowly, slowly, around him, and he sat. And then sometimes he would wake with a start, open his eyes and sit up in the hospital bed. His heart raced and the machines panicked as he opened his mouth to cry out to the nurses. But no sound escaped him. None at all. And that was when he glanced around, and saw his own body still sleeping, silent and still. Well, not sleeping exactly. Repairing itself, his brain rewiring and triggering old memories, old smells and sights and sounds, and so Charlie spent his days, trapped within his own mind, content to replay the endless moments of his days. Until that one day, when he was awake, and alert, and sitting in his room, staring down at his body lying there. He looked at Bobby and Emily, sitting together and would listen to their stories, would hold onto their words, and then, when his skill became stronger, he would climb into their words, and be carried along on their sentences into new worlds, both like and unlike his own. One day, he left the room and wandered down the corridors, being careful to avoid the orderlies, and sidestep the trolleys as doctors ran past. The white shone brightly from the walls of the waiting room. Charlie stood in the corner watching them and waiting for the doors to open and close when the ambulance arrived and gurneys shot through the doors. Moments of action and inaction, shocking and repetitive. One time he walked straight out of the hospital, out into the fresh white falling snow. He watched it but didn't feel it. So strange, snow falling through his body. Didn't feel the temperature dropping, the settling on his shoulders. Vision was all he had, not feeling. But he saw the road, stretching away, and he began to walk away from the hospital. But as he walked away the snow began to fall harder, and faster, and a noise crept in to his mind, louder and louder the sound of crackling static, until it was all he could hear, and then a voice, booming in his ear.

- WHAT ARE YOU DOING? GET BACK!

It was ancient, a voice as old as the mountains.

- WHAT ARE YOU DOING HERE?

The voice of an ageless fear. Terrifying and awesome. The static chattered in his mind and he couldn't think anymore. He turned and ran backwards, towards the hospital and made it back inside, back inside his body, where peace and darkness took over once more. A river, a tide, thought ebbed and flowed in his mind, as the pain receded and his body felt calm once again. The next time he awoke he realised there were limits to his new life; that he couldn't escape the bounds of the hospital, but that there were ways to leave. He immersed himself in memories, sitting in his house, sitting in the library, whilst the clocks stood still. Until he learnt to enter other words, other memories, and was carried off by the stories of others.

Charlie stood in grand central station, under the turquoise sky, waiting, expectant, and cold. He wrapped his coat around himself, and stepped out of the path of hurried commuters. There was a band playing, set up on the promenade, outside one of the restaurants, and the tune filled the high ceilinged room. He'd been in the library when his father called, preparing for a mid-term paper due the following week. But he'd dropped it, and hopped on a train into the city. He hadn't seen his dad in two years and this wasn't an opportunity to be missed. So he'd ran back to his dorm room, grabbed his coat and some money, and hauled ass down to the train station. And here he was, ready for whatever the night would bring. They ran off together into the night, stopping first at a blues bar down on 52nd. His dad returned from the bar with two beers. The bluegreen potential night beamed down on them as they sat together by the bar. His father placed the beer in front of him and the candlelight flickered through the glasses.

- Where do we begin?

- The last time I was here your mother and I had just got married. We were staying in a hotel just up the street. We hadn't left the room in days.

- Okay, okay, there are some things I don't need to know.

- Yes, okay. Well, anyway, we thought we should see the city, and so we wandered down the street and that neon sign caught our eye. And here we were, listening to the band until the small hours.

- How long ago was that?

- How old are you?

- 21.

- I'd say almost 22 years then.

- You're shitting me.

- heh. Maybe I am. Who knows any more? You know, it's funny. I mean I love the music, I really do, but after so long my mind starts to wonder and I start to think – that girl on the trumpet. Those lips, so full, so talented. I bet she's got incredible technique, you know?

The New York night was a tapestry of blue and green painted light. The shadow puppet dance of the tall buildings splayed against the horizon. We walked, and then stumbled, around the town. I saw his eyes take in the rooms in a second, saw his hands moving slowly, rolling cigarettes, always moving, always moving.

- So, tell me something – what are you listening to at the moment?

- A bit of Dylan, the Kinks. I still listen to those Loudon Wainwright CDs you gave me.

- Now there's a guy who knows what's what. I still remember the first time I heard 'One man guy', it floored me.

The music sped up and carried the night away and Charlie was back in his hospital bed with the chords of a song stuck in his head.

When Mike and Potemko arrived back at the station house that afternoon they found Lewis and the coroner sitting in the squad room drinking coffee. When Lewis saw them he stood up and beckoned them over. It wasn't at the forefront of his mind but Mike had been aware of the changes in Lewis over the past few weeks; the bags that sat uneasily below his eyes, the stubble on his cheek, his crumpled uniform. He could easily put it all down to the injury, the toll that physio was taking on him, the stress after the attack, but for some reason Mike could tell it was more than just that. The way his mind worked now, the distracted look in his eyes, that intensity when he was working through the statements, something was different about him.

Doc Holloway stood up and shook Mike's hand.

- That's a hell of a cut you got there Mike. How's our girl doing?

- No news as yet. I'm on my way back to the hospital shortly.

- Okay, well I won't take much of your time, but I just came down to let you all know that the kid's hunch panned out. The DNA confirms it, the man in the bag was Clarence Durkin himself. From what was left of the body I'd say he'd been sleeping rough for years, probably out in the woodlands where you first found him.

- Huh, You don't say. And you're absolutely sure of that?

- Well, there wasn't much of him left but yes, the result are conclusive.

- So what's our story?

- I've rechecked everything with the guys over in Fairview boss. They confirm what we had, he was in the system for 15 years and then he's been MIA for the past few. A couple of disorderly conduct warnings, a temporary address in a shelter near Fairview, not much else.

- Hmm. But that makes him what? 65?

- 68.

- He was unstoppable though. Anything unusual show up on the tests doc?

- Best I can tell there wasn't anything strange in his system. He'd been eating berries, meat of some sort. We've taken samples and I should be able to match them to the victims once the labs are back.

- I appreciate it. Right I better be making tracks. No news from the hospital Lewis?

- No. I called a little earlier but they said there'd been no change.

- Good, I'll see you all later. Can I give you a lift Doc?

- I'd appreciate it.

And with that Mike picked up his keys and left with the Doc, whilst Lewis and Potemko sat in the squad room drinking coffee.

Lewis had the files spread out over his desk, showing Potemko the shots of the mill, the murder scenes, and the witness testimonies.

- I get it buddy. Nice work okay?

- If only I'd been a little quicker we might have been able to get the jump on him.

- Hey, there's no way you could have known what was gonna happen. And remember, they tracked him down – they found him, they followed him, and they took him down. This wasn't an accident. It was good police work.

- Yeah, you're right. I know. There's just…a part of me feels like it doesn't quite click, you know? Like it isn't finished yet.

- I saw the bodybag Lewis. Believe me – It's finished.

Despite the evidence Lewis couldn't shake his feeling that

something was a little bit off. Staring at the orange vials in the medicine cabinet he told himself it was important, he needed to do this to make sure it was right. Good police work, that's what he'd said. And so he swallowed the three little pills, his entrance fee for the ride. All night he wandered around the mill, reliving the raging fire. He watched Clarence Durkin's downfall again and again, searching for the answer to his feeling that something seemed wrong.

IT WAS SNOWING, AND IT WAS GOING TO SNOW

Emily lay awake in bed, watching snowflakes fall past her window. They fell lazily, dancing in the wind, but would then trip and throw themselves suddenly against the window panes. The town was being quietly submerged, cars hidden beneath hastily thrown blankets of snow, and Emily watched the whiteness fall. Had yesterday really happened? She watched the street; it felt as hard to imagine as the colours of the cars beneath the snow. But she felt it. In her shoulder, the bruises, in her gut. He never really went away, not really. He'd disappear for years at a time but he'd always be back sooner or later, just waiting to carry her away. She'd have to tell Bobby but there was so much to say and absolutely nowhere to begin.

The snow fell long and heavy, blanketing the town. Mike drove down the streets of Ashenbrooke listening to the new reports on the radio. The curfew had been lifted and residents were allowed, nay, encouraged to get outdoors and to stock up on everything before the long winter kicked in. It got to the point where Mike could no longer tell if the presenter was pushing the idea out a sense of civic duty, of wanting to make sure the residents of Ashenbrooke were well stocked for the winter, or whether, really, it was some sort of ingenious marketing plan. Either way, the fear of running low eventually won out (as it always did) and soon the shelves of the local Addison's market were almost bare, just the marshmallow pop tarts left sad and alone on the cereal aisle.

According to the forecast the snow would only get heavier,

and people could expect to lose the roads, and possibly power by the end of the week, so they were advised to stock up on flashlights and food, and logs for the fire, because the temperature was going to plummet. 'The coldest winter since '71', and they'd lost a few people then, so by all accounts it was time to start getting prepared.

Mike watched the streets change. By Wednesday, the crowds were thinning out. By Thursday the trucks were lined up in the supermarket carpark, and by Friday afternoon the streets were empty. He grabbed a coffee on Main Street and helped Mr Tarvis to shut up shop before heading home. By the weekend the town felt abandoned and the roads were becoming impassable. At least they had finished this before the snow settled in, it allowed the world to return to its usual rotation. A winter like this, Mike's priority was to keep the town running, keep the supply routes open as best as possible, keep the emergency generators stocked at the hospital, and allow folks a little rest and recuperation over the festive period, huddled around a warm fire. They just needed to put the work in this week, and then it should all calm down.

And then the phone rang late on Sunday night. Lewis was working alone at the station house. He'd expected it to be another request for extra gas from someone out by the forest, but he also half knew it wouldn't be, it was a lady gasping and shaking on the other end of the line. When they arrived at the house it looked abandoned, the front door writhing about wildly in the wind, smashing into the house as the wind thrashed. There was a light dusting of snow in the hallway and footprints that led into the darkness. When a dark shadow stepped out from the front room he jumped, but it was just Bea Croft, who'd called in to the station. She witnessed the slaughter, the carnage of it. Blood and ligaments strewn from the ceiling and cupboards. There wasn't much of the victim left, just a torn head by the sink, a body slumped against the kitchen cabinets, bone and sinewy flesh, exposed and gruesome. The blood had pooled on the kitchen floor, making the ground treacherous, slippery. Lewis was frozen by it, but then remembered Bea standing there. He took her outside and they sat in the car, huddled inside for the warmth.

- When did you find her?

- Just when I called you. I, heard this thumping all evenings, this rattling, and I just couldn't place it at all. It started to get louder and louder and that's when I saw the door rattling around. My kitchen is just over there, see, where that light is, and I saw the door smashing around on its hinges and that's when I went over, and oh my god, I've never seen anything like that. Never.

As gruesome as the sight was, something inside Lewis had known this was coming. The frozen blood drops on the kitchen floor reminded him of a trail of breadcrumbs leading through the forest. They'd been led here and soon, they would step into the clearing and the real nightmare would be revealed. It was time to face it. He picked up the phone and called Potemko.

- Buddy, you're gonna want to get over here. And Potemko, bring a camera.

Charlie walked the streets of Ashenbrooke at night and something returned to him. As he walked through the town square and the indigo night turned to a warm lilac mist he could hear the nightingales chirruping in the trees. The night became shadows; black birds nestled on branches. Tree limbs dissecting the world into a web of nerve endings. Fractal, self perpetuating, trees spiralling out of themselves. The warm lilac light hung over the town and Charlie felt a door open, and he stepped back through it into his own world, his own Ashenbrooke, a town quiet at night, a mixture of peace, the ending of all time, of hour hands standing still on clock faces. He wouldn't change it really; time had ceased and all the clocks hung still in the night; noiseless, immobile, and lightsome as air. He re trod the paths of his own footsteps and felt time move backwards. He felt like an archaeologist, walking the ruins of his own city, watching the past come alive in objects and stories unearthed from the ground. Time could always turn backwards. Could be lifted out of its earthen sleep. He walked in circles, from the library, up past the path of sycamores, through the town hall square, amongst buildings, down paths, up to the tennis courts and through building after building. He walked around and didn't see a single soul in the night. He could feel time stop, could feel it still. And suddenly he walked through it, to the still point of the turning world. Other Charlies were also walking around the town. He saw himself walking to school, his satchel full of Dark Tower novels, he saw himself sitting in his bedroom at night, listening to his parents listening to music downstairs, he saw himself walking to the hospital, wandering around town, taking off his glasses and sitting in the park, letting the unfiltered muddy light of the world wash over him. Time had ceased, time was ever present, he hadn't lost any of it, it was all still to come, and all irretrievably lost. A mess of styles, a heap of broken images. Words lodged in his mind like glass. This still quiet night soothed something in the very fabric of him, in his bones. The bushes rustled and the spell was broken. Walking through the woods the branches crept softly out of the gloom, brushing against his coat, slowing him as he rambled. He saw flashes. Flashes of a blue tail against a blue night.

Lewis trawled through the paperwork trying to find that single nugget of truth that lay buried in the soil of the witness statements. Everyone had seen something and nothing at once. Drunken, witness to a group spectacle and who knew where the truth ended and the fiction began. There were stories of her stumbling down the stairs on fire, of machinery exploding in the heat and bolts shooting across the mill. There were accounts of guests stripping naked and running into the river, of people pissing on the fire to put it out. There were people seen leaving the site in hooded masks, there was the tale of a lover's tiff that had gotten out of hand, some said that the foreman had just lost his shit and burned the place to the ground after one too many Mondays. It seemed impenetrable at first, stories and stories and stories, each more outlandish than the last. Without the owner, or the building left, the mill fell into a state of disrepair and was never properly cared for. The site was fenced off by the police but it became a source of wonder and horror for the local kids, who would dare each other to spend the night in the burned out factory, where it was said that if you lit a candle at midnight the ghost of the foreman's wife would return to set you alight too. The owner was sentenced 25 years, and over time the town began the process of mostly forgetting what it had vehemently cared about for over two years, but the name stayed on the wind. The site grew into legend, and became a sort of unofficial landmark of Fairwater – as much as tourists would flock for the cider festival in the summer, they would be sure to visit the abandoned mill on the edge of town whilst hiking in the local mountains. This was the context in which Lewis had first discovered it himself, trekking with his school friends when he was twelve, daring each other to go inside the mill and climb the charred remains of the stairs where she had died. He still remembered when he had first seen the black outline of the mill on the horizon and the chill he had felt on that balmy summer afternoon so long ago. Now here he was, sifting through the ashes of the story and trying to uncover what the hell had really happened on that night. The lights flickered around the station house and Lewis put the coffee on for a third time that evening.

The snow fell swiftly over the town of Ashenbrooke, depositing itself in drifts at the sides of roads, blanketing cars and shops, and piling high on the benches of the town. The whiteness fell, obscuring what lay beneath it. But under it something dark was growing, between the snowflakes in blizzard on the edge of town. Shadows encroached and the town was slowly cut off from the rest of the world. First the delivery vans for the supermarkets turned back, then the radio signals broke up, and then the power outages began. They would last for mere minutes or up to an hour, nothing that the town couldn't manage with for now. But it was a harbinger, a warning of the darkness that was coming in the night. The residents stocked up and prepared for winter, one of the coldest on record, and the snow fell and seemed like it would never stop falling. First thing in the morning when Emily would look out of her window the flakes were falling, and when she closed her curtains at night she could still see it coming down, illuminated in the beams of streetlights.

As Charlie's night walking continued he began to feel it, to understand it, and to have some measure of control. He walked through the hospital and the first time it happened by accident; he was standing watching the waiting room, watching the others waiting and the detective, the young one who was limping, opened the door behind him and stepped through, walking straight through him. For the briefest of seconds he tasted the dew drops on leaves, smelt pine in the air, after a fresh rain. The sensation was thrilling, completely new and unexpected. And then it was gone as quickly as it had come. Nothing but the sterile smell of the waiting room, the constant pervasive blips and beeps, and the sad faces sitting in the waiting room. But he was left deaf to the world, he could no longer hear their voices or talk. He walked (did he walk?) closer but he could hear nothing. He watched their lips move but nothing at all came out. What had happened to him? He took a step, tentative, towards the young detective. It felt intrusive to do this, to step inside the space occupied by someone else, even if they weren't quite in the same space anymore. Nevertheless it shared many qualities; he could still stand on the floor, still felt that objects had substance, even if they no longer did for him. In some ways the space was shared, part of him was clearly here, and part of them was too, but which parts shared this particular part of the world? He hazarded a guess and took a step forward, standing in the same space as the young detective. It was like stepping through a doorway; the white walls of the hospital became blinding and then disappeared completely. His left foot was still planted on the shining white floor, the right fell on soil, on a dense, green, and dark forest path. He stepped through and he was there, standing in the forest itself, green light falling through the trees. He inhaled deeply, feeling the still warmth of the forest fill his lungs up. He looked around in all directions, turning swiftly. He was – where was he? There was nothing but forest for as far as he could see. In every direction tree after tree, innumerable. It didn't feel threatening, like that night in the snowbank. It felt secluded, secret, a world he had been allowed into that belonged to somebody else. He started to walk through the trees, watching the blacks and greens part as he stepped through them, the openings smaller and then wider, perambulating. Until he found a yellow path of flowers in the forest, he followed it to an opening in the woods and was aware of the sound of water, flowing through the land. He became aware of a large building on the horizon down by the river when he took his next step and he stood facing the vending machine in the waiting room. He turned fast but all he could see was the familiar white walls, and the shape of the detective leaving through the automatic doors.

After this he began to experiment and found that he could step into anyone's mind, he could just touch them (brush through them), and he would be somewhere else. He lay in his bed listening to Emily and Bobby talk as they sat with him and began to enter their memories, and stories.

The house was firelit, the wood crackling in the hearth. That dumb cross-stitch on the mantelpiece – home is where the hearth is. He'd always pick up some piece of local art on his travels. It was hokey but not altogether untrue. The fire snapped and the house felt smoky and docile. The flames lit up the house in curlicue shapes and shadows and they sat around the living room, sleepy and full. The television flickered in black and white as 'It's a wonderful life' played to a full house. This shouldn't have to end. Ever. He'd returned from his latest trip just before Christmas, full of excitement for the season. He'd cooked turkey, cranberry sauce, parsnips, yams, and the whole traditional fare. They had just retired from a marathon 3 hour game of monopoly and the television played as they dozed in front of the fire. There was a game his father had taught them when they were both very young. It was called 'Ape shit in the dark'. You would turn the lights out, draw the curtains, and just go crazy. Running around, howling, hiding, dancing. Letting the wild rumpus begin. It was fantastic, easily their favourite game to play, and they would do it now, even full of turkey and Brussel sprouts. They drew the curtains, and ran around madly, lit up by the flickers of the fire.

The aftermath of snow is silence, streets left still and removed from time. Sound hung in the air and the snow ceased falling for a brief moment. The house on Elm Hill sat idle in the winter, snow piling up around the walls. Sunlight and shadows moved slowly around the rooms, illuminating open cupboard drawers, quiet table tops, and unused appliances. The house began to run down, to run wild. The stillness seeped into its walls, its foundations, making a still and wintry world. Emily rummaged through the ruins of the house, searching for something. She felt something in the house; a presence, pausing on the staircase. She knew he wasn't the only one there, but it wasn't necessarily a danger she felt, just simply something watching her as she wandered around the house. She tried the doors, they moved easily on their hinges this time. What had caused them to stick? Surely something else, some force of will. But whose? She took a seat at the desk, looking through the draws. Something was here, she could feel it. Every now and then the hairs would prick at the base of her neck, a sense of being watched from somewhere, but the house was as still and empty as the night.

INVESTIGATIONS

The snow fell endlessly over Ashenbrooke and by the end of the second week of December it was almost impassable. The town had stocked up for the winter, had stockpiled and ravaged the supermarkets. People loaded up their trolleys with gallons of water, enough gammon steaks and packets of pop tarts to see them through the next month. The forecast predicted a 'snowpocalypse' and there was no end in sight to the snowfall. Mike had put out an announcement on the local radio warning the people of Ashenbrooke to be vigilant, and to keep a weapon to hand. The spectre of the woodland killer still loomed large in people's imaginations and they were taking no chances. There was an equal run on ammunition too. Mike didn't want to unnecessarily worry the townsfolk but he knew they needed to be aware. To that end, he set up a helpline and arranged a system so that the station house was manned 24 hours a day. Running the assistance operation and trying to hunt down a second killer was going to take all the resources he had and this was no time to get picky about the help on offer. Carter was still recovering in the ICU, and Lewis was mostly constrained to the office. Which left himself and Potemko with the duty of responding to calls, and trying to get one step ahead of this fucker. By the second week of December it was decided that the schools would close early for the winter break, and would reopen once the weather abated. Unwilling to be left out of the investigation Emily and Bobby joined them at the station house and Rosanna had unofficially joined the team. Mike was convinced under the proviso that they didn't leave the station since it was, after all, one of the safest places to be in Ashenbrooke. They split their time between the hospital and the station house, visiting Charlie and then setting up a makeshift camp at the station house.

They would take it in turns to man the phone lines when the others got called out, or would sit with Lewis helping him to run through old case files.

Despite the damage to the body the DNA tests were conclusive; it was the owner of the Fairwater mill. Lewis returned to his investigations again, trying to reread the testimonies in this light, searching for a nugget of truth buried in the contradictory statements. With the snow looking like it wouldn't stop for the next month Ashenbrooke was all but cut off from the world now. Potemko had taken the opportunity to stock up at Addison's before all the supplies were gone.

- Okay, we've got pitta bread, we've got hummus, and we've got pirate biscuits.

- Great work Potemko. That ought to see us through the winter...

- You haven't seen how many packs of pirate biscuits I got.

Snow formed the barrier that shut the station house off from the rest of the world; as the whiteness fell outside the lights blazed brighter within. The power was unreliable at this point and occasional flickers and surges of voltage made the lights burn brighter in the corners. Shadows were thrown haphazardly across the sprawled paperwork and the scattered files on the desks. Mike was making notes on the whiteboard.

- Okay, let's recap here. Lewis, what have you got?

- Okay, I've been following on from the Fairwater mill angle, seeing as we have the owner involved in the attacks. I've focussed on the other victims. I've tracked down some of the original witness reports. Everyone was clear on the wife dying by the time the paramedics had arrived but it was not so clear about the foreman. Some people said it was too late for him, others that he was still trying to talk when they got him in the ambulance.

- Okay. And the other deaths?

- I can account for all of them. 4 died in the hospital that night, 1 succumbed to injuries a week later. The owner survived but was relocated to a prison hospital. It is only the foreman I am unsure of, he was checked out of the hospital at some point but that is where the records get sketchy; no details of a transfer to another hospital or a discharge.

- And his whereabouts now?

- No-one knows.

- No-one knows? That's very poetic and all Lewis but not really the police work that I'm looking for here.

- I'm sorry sir but I've been over it a hundred times. All the reports focused on the owner. The foreman was clearly a less interesting story.

- Well that wouldn't appear to be the case now.

Rosanna had been listening intently to the exchange and picked her moment to step in.

- If I may, I don't think we are necessarily asking the right questions.

- And that would be what exactly? Which planet was in alignment on his birthday?

- No. And I don't think his horoscope will be of much use to him now. But it is clear that there is a connection between the fire at the mill, the recent attacks, and the possessed mill owner.

- Possessed? The mill owner was possessed?

- You were there Mike, you really believe an ordinary man has that kind of power?

- Yes. Of course. Look at him, he's a vagrant. He could have been on anything. A little PCP, some steroids. He was fucking deranged.

- And perhaps a little bit more besides. I think that something has happened in this town. I don't quite know what but I feel it in the air as I walk around. The curtains drawn at noon, empty washing lines flying in the wind. It has run down, lost something, some fight, and now it's slow and dark and something has crept in in the night. Something that lives off this fear and sadness, something growing stronger each night as it devours the fears of the living, and prolongs the agonies of the dead.

- Where'd you take that from? An old hammer horror picture?

- Close. Bela Lugosi.

Mike laughed despite himself.

- Emily, please tell me you aren't buying this bullshit.

- You were there Mike, are you really telling me none of this strikes a chord?

- No, no it doesn't. Look – I'm happy to have the extra pairs of hands but can you all tone down this crap just a little bit around the guys? I need them focused right now.

- Sure Mike, whatever you say. But you're beginning to believe just a little bit right?

- Not even close.

- All we're suggesting is that we need to look a little further back, look at the history of the mill, and what links the sites and the current attacks.

- You mean see if the mill was built on an Indian burial ground?

- I'm not ruling that out…

- Of course not. Well I am ruling that out. I need you guys taking calls. Lewis, stick to the facts. Look further afield, pull the news reports from the time. Seek out any relatives, I want to know everything I can about this man. I'll be back by eight.

- Yes sir.

But the idea stayed with Lewis. Later that evening when Mike was out on patrol and Potemko was assisting with a hospital supply run he took his chance; Bobby was sitting by the phone and Emily and Rosanna were in the coffee room going through photographs. Lewis refilled his cup and took a look at the photo in Emily's hand. It was the Fairwater mill, before the accident. It was bustling, alive with activity, and someone seemed to be guiding a party around the site.

- What did you both mean earlier – what kind of connection with the mill are you thinking about?

- Rosie, I think you'd better field this one…

- In the past I've found that it is important to look for unfinished business. It is only what is unresolved that keeps something alive after it should be long dead.

- And you think that something is unresolved from the fire?

- It makes sense to me. The mill owner here in Ashenbrooke, the severity of the deaths. You saw him too, you must have seen there was something unusual about him. I think you are very right to have been following this angle.

- I, actually…I've been having these visions.

- Yes?

- Of the mill. I think…I think I might have an idea of what the connection could be.

- These visions – where are you?

- I'm always in the forest, near the mill. The night that it burned down.

- And do you see what happens?

- Yes. And no. I see flashes, scenes. The fight between the foreman and his wife, the party, the fire. But it doesn't all tie together.

- And these visions come to you? In your dreams?

-Not exactly. It's the medication I've been taking, since the attack. It puts me into a sort of trance.

- Aha, Astral projection. Medical experimentation. Timothy Leary would be proud. You know, I can help. I could guide you.

- How?

- Are you familiar with post-hypnotic suggestion? I can guide you in a trancelike state.

- How would it work?

- Why don't you let me show you?

Lewis sat in the back with Bobby as Emily drove the four of them back to her apartment. Once inside she helped to prepare the room, lighting candles on the dark wooden coffee table, throwing a cushion on to the sofa as a makeshift pillow, and dimming the light.

- Okay, so you've done this before?

- Yes. I have a friend, he's in Germany now, but we've done this a few times before. Please, lie down on the sofa. I'll get you some water – you have the pills with you?

- Yes. I do.

Lewis tentatively lay down on the sofa and Emily brought him some water and a hot tea, before taking a seat on the opposite sofa, next to Bobby who watched transfixed. Rosanna turned out the lights and sat immediately behind Lewis.

- Please, drink this too. It will relax you. Now close your eyes and focus on the sound of my voice.

Lewis felt the medication kick in and he began to dissolve from the world, feeling the tension leave his shoulders and spine, sinking in to the sofa *and then through it. The translucent sky held a myriad of stars as Lewis walked through the forests. Time seemed* to overlay itself; he could see the ruins of the mill superimposed on their standing structure, a collage of the passing monstrousness of time. He walked through the woods, the trees floating past him, and the voice guided him. Pale blue lights seemed to guide the path through the woodland. Fireflies floated and alighted on trees. He watched them fly, and followed them into the darkness. Tiny birds chirruped and alighted on branches next to his face. Their eyes flicked fast, watching him as he meandered through the woodlands. Where was he going? What was he doing? The fireflies floated in front of his face, their buzzing blue light the colour of bar signs or deep sea fish. He felt like an explorer, like a deep sea diver, tethered to the world by a fragile cord, exploring the hidden depths of Ashenbrooke. And there were real secrets hidden under the shadowy rocks on the outskirts of town. He moved slowly, as if walking along the bottom of the sea bed, the weight of the atmosphere pressing against his body, impeding his progress. Rosanna's voice guided him through the forests, hypnotising him, its gentle melodic sway leading him through the forests.

Suddenly the bright light of the mill appeared in the distance and sounds came to him, distorted by time as they arrived, elongated cheers, and sharpened talk. People seemed to sway slowly to the music and then swiftly catch up with themselves, speeding off and picking up another beer. The fireflies led the path through the guests and round the corner. The fireflies alighted on a large wooden clock at the base of the stairs and slowly the hands moved backwards, circling, spinning, the rotation spilling out into the room, and the partygoers began to step backwards, putting their drinks down, placing canapes back on trays, returning to their positions on the factory floor.

This time Lewis didn't take the stairs up to the office but instead walked around the mill, following the fireflies to a storeroom on the north side of the factory floor. What is in the storeroom? Indecorous secrets behind sealed doors. The fireflies seemed to hover in front of the door and Lewis could hear movement inside. He hadn't managed to interact with the environment before but this time he wrapped his hand around the door handle and it was solid, he gripped it and pulled the door open. Memories of opening other doors at the mill flooded through his mind and he was nervous; if he could now touch objects in this world could they touch him too? He was unprepared for the scene that met him; there was a man, in his early forties, his pants around his ankles, jackhammering away. The lady had her dress pulled up around her waist and was lying over a pile of cotton sacks stacked up in the middle of the room. They didn't react to Lewis's arrival, but merely continued to pant and thrust. He watched them, hypnotised by the rhythm of it.

All at once there was a loud crash in the hallway and the figures turned round staring at Lewis and he recognised them both; Clarence Durkin, and the foreman's wife. They stopped for a second looking straight through him, and then carried on as if nothing had happened. Lewis watched them in the storeroom, watching them go at it, the man's plump and stolid frame bouncing and hammering away, but they were oblivious to his presence in the room. She screamed, he panted, his chubby fingers clawing at her flowing flesh. The fireflies were alighting on sacks in the storeroom, settling in. But Lewis became aware of another flicker, a shadow fluttering in the room, falling on sacks and boxes, unable to settle. He realised it was coming from the keyhole in the door.

He mustered his strength and stepped through the steel door; the leaden form dissolved in the air. He passed through it, and then something boney, for a second he felt the incandescent coals of rage, jealousy burning in the hearth, and then his vision returned. The foreman was crouched, watching the dirty scene, hunched over on his splayed legs, his erection pushing against his tight pants.

Past and present overlapped and Lewis became aware in an instant. The foreman had known for weeks, had plotted the whole thing. Lewis turned back to the storeroom and time flew forwards; he saw Clarence, gagged and tied up in the storeroom as the fire raged outside. He yelled and screamed but there was no chance he'd be heard above the din of the party. And so Lewis watched him burn, in the room that he would find him in twenty years from then. He *saw the man tied up in the past and saw his wild eyes when he opened the door a few months ago. It had been the mill owner, burnt and disfigured in the storeroom, waiting, tormented, driven mad by years of pain and the desire for revenge and something had used him, snuck in in the darkness where the door had been left open, had inhabited him and turned his rage into something more awesome, more awful and ferocious. Pure anger and hate and darkness, enough to sustain it for the long haul. It had channelled that rage and pain to create more, to visit that pain on the world. And now it had moved on to the next figure in the story; the foreman. It was no accident at all, during the party the mill owner was locked up in the storeroom the whole time. Any element of doubt dissolved; the speed with which the flames took hold, igniting the office, and the lady. The office had been lined with something, so that when he threw the drink it ignited the shrift and the whole place went up in flames. And the foreman was the only one to escape. What had Emily said before? There is no such thing as coincidence. The foreman had known for weeks but waited until his revenge was most visible.*

Lewis rose slowly from the unconscious world, and found himself sitting up on the sofa facing Emily.

- Relax, Relax. I heard it all.

- I'm sure, if I wasn't before I am now. It's him.

Once the tale had been told the four of them sat around Emily's kitchen table, coffee in hand. Bobby was pacing around the kitchen, Lewis looked at them unsure of his next move.

- I have to tell Mike.

- You really think he would listen?

- I don't have to tell him how I worked it out.

- Okay, but where does it get us?

- He'll have a plan.

Emily put her cup down and looked at them all.

- I have a plan. Lewis, you think he's drawn to the fire don't you?

- Yes, the mill, the bonfire. Something in him seeks it.

- I agree. But it's not the only thing that it's drawn to.

- What else?

She looked at Bobby.

- Us. There was no fire when it attacked us. It's drawn to us too.

Bobby looked up from the table, the resolve etched into his face. Lewis looked at them, unsure.

- What do you mean?

- The answer is easy. We don't need to find it. It will find us.

They were silent for a second, not quite sure what to say. Bobby spoke next.

- It's true. It attacked Emily on Halloween, and it was drawn to our house. We can bring it to us.

- Do you both realise how dangerous it would be?

- Yes, but what other choice do we have? We don't know when and where it will attack so we sit around here and wait whilst the bodies stack up or we can do something about it. We can wish that it will all go away, but we are just sitting here waiting for it to end, one way or the other. Charlie's in the hospital and who know if he'll wake up? We can end this – we start a bonfire outside the house and we'll be inside – there is no chance it would resist it.

Lewis put his coffee down on the table.

-You know what? It's the best chance we've got here. But we're taking this to Mike. If we are all in this together we might just beat it.

Later that evening Bobby and Emily sat in her living room, the candlelight flickering off the ceiling. Snow fell swiftly past the windows and the silence of the town set in. They had made the preparations with Lewis. They'd approach Mike tomorrow. The plan was simple. The three of them would go with Lewis and make preparations at the house. Mike and Potemko would stake out the house from either end. One in a car across the street, the other keeping watch in the garden. Then they could trap it, and kill it, once and for all. It was their best shot at coming out of this alive. Or getting themselves killed. Emily knocked back her whiskey.

- There's one more thing Bobby. When we were in the house I felt our father. The patterns of blood on the wall, the anger in his eyes. That's who I saw on Halloween when you rescued me in the alley. Something in this spirit is attached to him and it's drawn to me, to all of us. I know I can do this. We can draw him to us and the house and then we can finish this. This will be the end.

- What do you mean the blood? What about our father?

THE WHITENESS OF
THE WORLD

Bobby walked down the hospital corridors, his feet falling in the path of his old footsteps. They had lived here at times, drinking bad coffee from the café, falling asleep in waiting rooms, running up and down the corridors at night. He waited for Charlie to wake, and sat there in the room with him, his textbooks sitting in a heap on the floor. The world continued, always did. There were books to read, assignments due in, time never seemed to stop even at times like these. But he wanted it to. He sat here, the books slumped on the floor, listening to the frenzy outside. But in here, in this room, the steady beeps beeped, his brother's chest rose and fell, and he wanted to keep it like this. It was funny, what you'd learn to accept. Your world got taken away a piece at a time, and rather than rage at it you would just hope, just wish that nothing more would be taken. You clung to the fragments that you had, clung tighter, hoping through force of will that you wouldn't lose any more. But you couldn't stop the time from pressing on. One not so special day it would all just end. Hospitals were buildings suffused with hope. Hope upon hope against the truth that existed right in front of your eyes. Today they were sitting here, tubes entering and exiting their bodies. Lying unconscious, or pumped full of poison. But tomorrow, tomorrow they would wake up a little brighter. The pain would hurt a little less. Step by step they would return to their old lives and this place would be forgotten, the missing hours spent in brightly lit hallways. The bad coffee drunk from hospital cafeterias, the way that the hours were frozen here. You'd forget it all day by day and then soon the old world would return. That hope suffused the building but it wasn't the truth. The truth of what had happened to them. She hadn't gotten better day by day. We thought that was happening but it wasn't. She was just trying as hard as possible to cling on, to spend another day with us, one more movie, one more conversation. If she could hang on just a little longer it would be okay when she left. But it wasn't. It just happened, one day, like any other. You adjusted your expectation. At first she'd return to normal. Then, she would be bedbound but she'd be there. She'd always be ill, under the surface of it. But we could carry on like that, making food, sitting in that endless room with her, that wonderful place filled with pictures, old schoolwork, piles of magazines, stuffed toys, an old black and white television. Her world, and all the lightblue wonder that it contained. We'd accept that, if things could stay like that forever. And then she couldn't eat, or keep things down. She lost her energy, and couldn't make it through whole movies anymore. But we'd accept that. If we could sit with her. Watch her smile as she slept when the nausea subsided. We'd take it. For a little more time.

And now it was happening again. Bobby held Charlie's hand and watched his chest rise and fall. They'd sit here together, until one day there were more machines, and then less. Until his breathing became erratic, his colour left. One day he would disappear too. And this thing preying on the town would take them all one by one. What kind of world was this that we lost everything in pieces until we were scrambling around just trying to keep hold of the last shreds of our tattered lives? Well, fuck that. There would be no more waiting. He leaned over and kissed Charlie on the forehead. There'd been enough deal making, it was time to stand up and go out with a bang.

She was sitting in the kitchen when we got home, plane tickets and itineraries spread out on the table before her. I'd picked up Bobby on the way home from school and we found her there smiling to herself and drinking herbal tea. Straight from the kettle! That's what she always used to say when someone asked her how she took it. Maybe your tolerance for heat increased when you got older but it was freakish, that was for sure. But she couldn't get enough of it. We walked into the kitchen and there she was.

- What is this? You planning your big get away?

- I'm planning our big get away. You and me boys, we are headed to San Francisco!

She'd booked it all; two weeks away in the best hotels, travelling around the city. She told us that our father had sent her some much overdue child support. It was only later that we realised it was health insurance money; the premium paid out $80,000 upon a terminal diagnosis.

I remember almost everything about that week; hotels that served afternoon tea with port (we weren't complaining), visiting the Japanese gardens together, and SFMoma. But most of all it was the Haight, we stayed in The Red Victorian, right next to a small picture house. I think it gave her a chance to relive some of her hedonistic years at the end of the sixties; she went to college in 68 and jumped in with both feet (there were some of her diaries I had thought it best not to read). I remember on the last night we went to the picture house to watch the reissue of her favourite film: Easy Rider Rides Again! was lit up outside the theatre. Bobby and I sat with her as the lights went down and the screen rolled. She held our hands (we allowed her these few indulgences since she'd been ill) and she smiled as the first chords kicked in.

Bobby made his preparations. If they were all going to die spectacularly he at least wanted to leave something for Charlie in case he woke up. He sat by his bedside, writing letters about their last big trip together. At least if he died in that house he might see her one last time.

Emily sat in the room at Charlie's bedside, holding his hand and watching his face. It moved now whilst he slept, the hint of expression behind it, as if he were sunk deep within himself at the bottom of a deep dark cave and only the quietened echoes of his thoughts could reach the surface and find expression in his face. She couldn't believe she'd found him, and lost him too so quickly. It was odd, how similar, and how different he was. There were echoes of him in Bobby too, in all of them really. The delivery of a sentence, the way he brushed his chin when he felt uncomfortable. This would work, it had to. And then there would be time to know everything, to move forwards. She watched him sleep.

I placed two pieces of ice in the glass and poured whisky, savouring the sympathetic crack of the ice as the whisky warmed it, fissures snaking rapidly, whole ice sheets collapsing. Shhnrack. I felt the whisky cool and burn my lips, the aroma filling my nose. A toast. To the end. I have never felt relief like this. It has been one of the finest evenings of my life. Poetry. Wine. And now it is time for music. The music will carry on, just as the world will. It doesn't end, not really. The key to a great party is to know when to go. I take the pistol from its case, smell the barrel, and feel the cool metallic tang against the roof of my mouth. The pistol, such an ornate item, such a real purpose. Death dealt swiftly and surely. There was a poetry to this too. I listen to the crescendo of viola and nestle the barrel against my heart. The trigger is squeezed and the percussive boom bounces from the walls of the room. The pain is warm and heavy but I already feel its urgency leaving, seeping from me. And then I sit still, listening to the quivering strings, and staring out of my own dead eyes.

The endless night decayed, and my body went with it. Freshly dead, warm but fading, blood permeating the mottled fabric of the chair. I slump, a hole in my chest where my heart was, my vision fixed and glassy, staring at the patterned rug. Those endless stitches, red lines that wander forever down paths of woven cotton. The path had been corrupted, ligaments and tacky red blood spewed across the surface of the rug. Endless and beautiful. I sit and stare out of my own dead eyes for days, I'm in here. In my body still, but without movement there is no fear, no clawing pain in my chest, just the still afternoon air and the smell of gunpowder hanging softly in the afternoon. It was as swift and wonderful as I'd hoped, the train tracks switched, the path altered. This life was over and now something else began. I felt peace, like I hadn't in years. The peace of certain change. They would think it was violent, that I was angry, destroying the place, destroying the world, destroying my body, but more than anything I just wanted to be sure. This clawing depression eats you in pieces, in fragments, in days, and now I'd killed it, killed both of us. Our endless numbered days. Death was not terrible, since anguish can only exist in time, connected to the past and future. Death revealed the absence of time, that the causes of pain no longer had any power over the continually still and newly welcomed present. Quiet, and still, and endless. And wonderful.

I sat in the chair watching the shadow of the sash fall across the carpet and creep quietly across the room. Hours passed, days perhaps, and I felt my sense of time leave me completely. The room grew dark, and then light, and a peace descended that didn't leave. Until at some point light fell from the hallway and I heard steps entering the room. I had begun to fade, my vision was getting misty and I felt like I was preparing for something, some next step, but the sounds brought me back into focus. Shuffling along the carpet. I could feel the air move as someone entered the room. I saw her face, watched her tiptoe across the carpet and saw the tears well and fall down her cheeks. She sat in the corner crying and looking at me and for the first time in what seemed like an age I wanted to stand up, to cross the floor and put my arm around her and tell her that it was okay. But I couldn't. This body wasn't mine anymore and so I sat immobile, fixed in my own old bones, watching her cry and shake in the corner, unable to help in any way.

Death just feels like the emptying out of life. It is as if the clock which has been constantly ticking finally stops and the minute hand hangs there, dead. The sounds that were so unnoticeable in their daily repetition suddenly became stark in their absence. This must be what it felt like to be deaf, or to be a Buddhist monk; an ocean of deafening silence. How beautiful and odd it was. Only in time can the music play, can the drafty church at smokefall be felt, only through time is time conquered. And now it was time for someone else to take up the lance, for my fight was over. Eliot's words wandered round in my head. Time is very long. And this life had ended with a whimper and a bang.

How to disappear in life; to disappear from the warm hubbub, the sounds of chatter, to dissolve steadily into the background music, a wave of sound, bobbing, silent, forever on a dark black sea. To leave the talk, of this, of that, of you, of me, to just evaporate into the sound, to disappear in a sine wave, to be still. Still. Still. He pulled the trigger and the waves of sounds cascaded through his body, the rhythm jarred, erratic, frantic, crescendo of sound and pain, the strings of his heart torn awkwardly, the bow frantic, an atonal fugue of pain and vibration, and then out of the madness sense, a crescendo, and fall, as the instruments relaxed and stilled. The sound dying on the wind. The vibrations sucked into the armchair and cushioned, and stilled.

Charlie wandered freely around the house. It was strange how he now sat in the house of his imagining. He wondered what it meant that location and time had become fluid. He could leave the hospital freely now, could jump into the words of the people nearest him and float through them to their locations around town. But more than that, he could go back, experience the memory or some version of it. Now when he crept around the corridors of their home he could see the endless world behind the present moment. He could smell the popcorn in the kitchen, see Bobby sleeping in his bunk bed. And he felt her here. Not like the others, but just like she had always felt. The safe presence of his mother in the house made him feel calm, at peace. He hadn't seen her. Not yet. But perhaps it was just a matter of time. The fixity of places and times was loosening. He didn't know what it meant for him, but he imagined it probably wasn't a good sign that he would be returning to the world very soon.

He heard movement downstairs and half crept, half floated down the stairs to meet it. Rosanna had let herself in and was moving swiftly through the house. "where are you kid? I can feel you in the walls of this place." "I need you to concentrate, try to move this totem if you can."

She had set up in the kitchen, and unrolled a purple mat laced with mandala designs. She lit candles that blew erratically in the wind. Snow was still scattered across the kitchen floor. Charlie focused all of the energy he could and tried to grasp hold of the small wooden totemic figurine. But his hands passed straight through it. The image wavered and he saw his father standing outside the kitchen window smoking a cigar.

"Come on kid, focus. I know you're here. We're gonna need your help if this is actually gonna work so I need you to do this."

Charlie focussed, watching the figure of his father evaporate in smoke and the solid frame of the kitchen return. He breathed in slowly (did he really still breathe?) and focussed his attention completely on the sensation. He ran his fingers through the figure. It felt rough in texture, the scratch of wood. He pressed into it and his hand went straight through the edge. This is what it feels like to be wood, to be dark wood carved and clear. His hand passed through and rested on the woven fabric of the mandala. He withdrew his hand ready to try once more and the fabric moved with him, toppling the small totem on to the table.

"It's not exactly what I had in mind but it will do."

Charlie sat staring at the door. There were shadows underneath it. Two dark shadows that suggested feet standing there, waiting for him to open the door.

He kept glimpsing something, in the corners of mirrors, at the point where they reflected each other, the reflections barrelling away endlessly. The way you could stare down them at the barber's shop and they would tunnel away forever. You would crane your neck but never quite be able to see around the corner of the mirror. He kept seeing something there, just beyond his vision. Snatches of clothes, of movements, just out of sight. What was there in the mirror world? It went on forever, a vibrant place just beyond. He'd always wanted to see beyond the edges of the frame but no matter how far he moved his head, it was always just out of sight. The clocks had fallen out of step. Second hands meandered around wristwatches, minute hands crept around the face of the town hall clock, stuttering, slowing, and then jerking forwards.

Lewis ran through the forest, his boots slipping on the snow covered ground. Branches whipped past him, clawing at his clothing as he ran. He ran without hesitation, flying through the woods, listening to the tramp and trudge as it pursued him through the darkened woods. He could feel it following him as much as hear it, the dark and rage like a wind whipping through the trees. His footing slipped as his boot fell through light layers of white snow, twisting in something hard and boggy beneath, pulling him down to the floor. Snow glistened on the floor.

[Where am I now? I'm losing it all, losing myself to it. I can feel the strands of the stories weave and I float on it, circling through time and back again. If I can hold still. They need me. Focus. I need me. Where will I go now, lost? Am I?]

I lay in the snow next to her grave and I wondered if this town was damned. I wondered if the weight of every loss we'd suffered has been too much and that the town had cracked in some way and now the pieces would never fit together again. It was in the sound of a maple leaf scraping the bricks as it flew past, it was the sound behind the sound of a tap left dripping into a half filled pail. It was the rhythm of a quiet song underneath these sounds, a melodic quiet full of confusion and grief.

That night Emily and Bobby stayed up talking long into the night.

- Em, what was he like?

- Ha, he was one of a kind, that's for sure. I didn't think guys like him existed outside the pages of books.

- I never really knew him. I have the odd memory of him reading me stories in our bunk beds. But, it's foggy, like I remember his beard maybe but not his face. I remember the bristles rubbing against my face when he'd say goodnight.

- Yeah, I remember that too. It's so strange. When I was in the hospital today with Charlie I had the most vivid memories of him.

- What memories?

She squeezed his hand and tears fell down her cheeks.

- Him dying. I...I can't not see it. He was...I have to tell myself that it was his decision. He was brave, he lived by his principles and I...I remember him telling me, before it happened, that he was happy, that he'd had a great life, and there was no shame in it ending...but, the fucking anger in it. How do you shoot yourself in the heart and not have it mean something? If you'd seen it...it wasn't an act of the mind, it was dark, and it was violent. I, I want to think he was right, but I can't forget the violence of it.

THE END OF ALL OUR WAITING

James Brayman sat at the large oak desk in his study. Shadows from the trees outside crept along the surface, weaving dark patterns on the papers spread across the desk. He would have to leave soon, but the thought wearied him. To return to an empty house, the sofas sitting around aimlessly, the blank face of the television daring him to resist. The house felt heavy, sluggish, and the worst moment was when he first stepped inside and knew there was no-one waiting for him. There was still a memory trapped in his body, when he would walk home, the stillness before opening the door and then noise, the radio blaring, light and sound, she would run up to him and hug him. Or ask him to take the garbage out. She'd hound him, before he properly got in and could put his bag down, and sit and feel the day drain from his limbs. Questions, songs, motion, an onslaught. And now he opened the door to silence, a silence much louder than the cacophony of sound he was hoping for. And it pressed on his body, on his shoulders, and he slumped, felt the energy leaving him. Would sit on the sofa, drop his bags on the floor, and just slump. He'd press the remote and let light flicker over his body, the incessant chatter of the news anchors, the scrolling news, endless, repeated, shocking, but ultimately deadening. Until he felt nothing, just a trance like state. Not peaceful, but not painful either, just an absence as his mind left his body and he drifted towards sleep. But tonight he couldn't face it. The slow accumulation of days had taken its toll and he felt that it was too much, to leave here, to trudge home. How would it feel to get there? And so he stayed. He was much closer to bringing her back now and so he would press on, delving deeper into the book he'd found. Whilst he should have been packing his bags, and closing the library down he stayed, and brewed himself another cup of coffee and looked out the window as the steam rose.

He returned to his desk in the study; the library had recently received a box of Teddy Ashenbrooke's personal correspondence. Jessica Tamby had uncovered a box of artefacts in her mother's attic when they were clearing the house. She was an old friend of Mr B's from their time together at Old Miss, and so she'd thought of him, knew of his interest in the history of the town. Neither of them could yet puzzle out how her mother had come across the letters, whether she had inherited them from generation to generation, or purchased them at an auction. Nevertheless, the letters had arrived here and Mr B had been looking forward to working through them and cataloguing them for his library. It was a project of his that he hoped would take off, an archive of the town down in the catacombs. The endless numbered days of each resident of Ashenbrooke. Births, adventures, deaths, marriages, repeated and endless, a town that always ended, and always continued after it had ended. Life continued, even after death, even after anything that befell it, and here was a record of it all. He watched the snow fall from the last leaves clinging to the trees outside the window. He opened the box and sifted through the papers, letters, scraps of writing paper all bundled together. He unrolled the first one.

Charlie walked the streets of Ashenbrooke at night. He didn't feel the snow as it fell through his body and so he was content to amble, he couldn't really remember where he wanted to be. All urgency had left him now. Perhaps this was forever, walking down paths, feeling the peace of life without time. His feet led him and soon he was at the library. He stepped straight through the window of Teddy Ashenbrooke's study and there was Mr B sitting at the desk. He stood in the corner and watched as Mr B knelt to extract a book from within the desk. He rummaged around and then threw the leather bound book on to the table. Charlie looked around in a daze. There were candles lit around the room and a dark cloth unrolled on the table. He flowed towards the desk and leant over Mr B to read the book's cover. Nothing made any sense to him, just runes scrawled in to the leather bound cover. He couldn't tell if the words were truly illegible or whether this was just another part of the old world he was losing. He let his hand fall onto Mr B's shoulder and it hit him in a rush. Her grave. Time flowing backwards – maggots burrowing their way out of her body, her eyes becoming solid once more. Mr B at night, the candles lit. A shovel. All his will was bent on it. The emptiness of these nights would leave him and she'd once more sleep in his arms. Charlie felt the blue fox coming.

Mike woke with a start to the cacophonous noise of machines. He jumped up and hit the red button above Carter's bedside as she writhed on the bed, pulling at the tubes surrounding her. The doctors ran in and restrained her whilst they settled her down and removed the breathing tube. Mike watched anxiously as the doctors moved, their motions incongruously fast but graceful in their way. They injected her with something and soon the irregular beats returned to normal. Her eyes flickered and then returned to focus. She scanned the room and her eyes fell on Mike. He looked tired but well, the stitches in his jaw pronounced and clear. She relaxed and sank back into the bed; they were alive, they had made it.

Mike stepped outside to speak to the consultant.

- Sir, I need to be straight with you. We are not out of the woods yet but she is reactive and breathing by herself. These are great signs. Her body has taken a great deal of damage and her vocal chords were mostly destroyed by her injuries. We don't know at this stage if she will be able to speak again, but don't misunderstand me; we've come a long way and this is a big step forward. We'll let you sit with her for a while but I'm going to insist on her needing some rest tonight.

- I can't thank you enough. Have you got a pen and pad I can borrow?

- Of course, you go and sit with her and I'll bring you one.

Carter took the pen and scribbled on the pad:

You've been in the wars.

- Ha, yes. They fixed me up pretty good though.

We get him?

Mike squeezed her hand.

- Yes, we got him. That was some impressive shooting.

Still got it. The others?

- They're fine. Potemko is in fine form, terrorising me on all of our supply runs. And Lewis is on the mend, except he's.... Hurry up and get better won't you Carter? I'll be happier once the old team is back together.

I'm trying. What did they say?

- They said you'll be right as rain. Riding horses by the end of the month.

Bad liar. Always were.

Mike drove back to the station house, the white world around him almost complete. For the first time in his life he felt overwhelmed, he was overjoyed that Carter was awake but how in the hell were they gonna get through this without her. Potemko and him were up to their ears trying to keep the town supplied, and respond to the call outs. Lewis and Emily seemed to be spending half of their time chasing ghosts. And they hadn't stopped him, it had almost finished them all last time and it had taken a lot. And now there was something else. Was it something else? Stalking the town. It was a matter of time before the next bodies started piling up. At least Emily and Bobby were at the station house where he could keep an eye on them. But what was the angle? How were they going to come out of this ahead? The roads were almost empty, he could see lights of the homes in the distance. Blues and yellows flickering on the fringes. Where was it? He couldn't see the wood for the trees.

Mike arrived back at the station house to find Lewis, Bobby, Rosanna, and Emily sitting around the kitchen table, photographs of the mill spread out in front of them. There was a fresh pot of coffee on the percolator and a fresh pack of pirate biscuits had been opened.

- Why do I have the feeling I'm walking in to a sales pitch?

Potemko put down the phone and joined them.

- Because you are. I've always thought you were very astute boss.

Lewis poured a coffee and passed it to Mike.

- Boss, just hear us out okay. We know who it is. We can stop this guy.

Mike put his coffee down on the table.

- There is no way. No way. You want me to put everyone in danger for this? For a start it's horseshit. You cannot summon this guy to arrive at that house. The best you can do is put all six of us out in the snow and leave no one to keep watch on this town. It is crazy. Absolute bullshit.

- So, that's a definite no then?

- Yes, no way. We are not going trekking through the snow. We need to keep this town going. We need to keep it supplied and we need to be on hand to help when someone gets in trouble. I can't allow it.

Lewis rubbed his temples and got to his feet. He watched Mike's face.

- Boss, I get where you're coming from, I really do. But how long have we got left here? Most of the supplies are running out. We can barely respond to half the calls. We are on the back foot, with no idea where this guy is gonna strike next. This gives us a chance, a chance to finish it once and for all. I think now is our time to roll the dice.

- This isn't a game of chance. We will make it through this. We are not rolling any dice, because we are not taking the chance of losing. If we can just keep going until the storm breaks, we'll be fine. It'll take the pressure off, and then we can track this guy down but for now we can't, okay? That's an order, and unless I'm very much mistaken I'm still the guy in charge here. Now Lewis, I want you on the phones. Emily and Bobby, you keep running the reports. I need something concrete on likely locations. And Potemko, you're with me, let's refuel and get ready for the next call.

The forests thrashed and dark movement flashed past branches. It felt nothing but anger and speed, the sensation of flowing through trees, tearing their branches off and throwing them arcing into the darkness. Squirrels weren't fast enough, nor spiders, or birds. It grabbed them and stuffed them into its mouth chewing and crunching, the matted dark blood flowing through its beard and down its neck. It twisted necks and discarded them, ate and moved, ploughing forwards. It could taste it, could feel it on the wind. Something ahead, something complete to tear apart, to rip and eat, and pull to pieces. Somewhere, darkness, shadows and light. An instinct, complete, like the rumble of a belly, or the lust for bodies. Pure motion, pure drive. The figure in the woodlands ran rushing from the forest toward the light.

The woods were conspiratorial and shaded under grey skies, threatening snow. Something moved amongst them, winding its way towards the single light shining from the large red brick building. Mr B paced the study, feeling the words take shape in his mind. He heard the still whistling wind outside. It tore at the roof, at the chimney flue. He tried to focus, seeking words and quiet shade in quiet rooms. The candles flickered around the room as he sat and articulated the sounds in his own mind and visualised her coming back to him. He felt leaden weight descend on his body, anchoring him to his chair. He closed his eyes and saw her coffin open, her hand green with gravemold sliding the wooden lid aside. She was coming. Perhaps they all were. Now all he needed was the offering.

Mike and Potemko were out on the other side of town, chasing down spirits in the night. The roads had become almost impassable, and this was perhaps the eighth wild ghost chase of the week. The nights were indistinguishable from the days, the cloud cover had settled in, dropping snow on the town all day and all night. The birds has retreated to their treetop world, roosting in the branches, staying safe from the darkness outside. The town existed in a twilight world, always evening, just too late to step outside. They cruised around the town, the empty streets and gas stations closed up for the winter. The place felt abandoned and forgotten. They had established an emergency radio frequency so that people could get in touch with them if they really needed help. Potemko had gotten into the habit of putting out a nightly bulletin at 7pm every evening.

- Hello all, and welcome to radio Ashenbrooke, your one stop shop for news, and music, to carry you through the long dark night. We may all be going to hell in a handcart but at least we can listen to some good tunes on the way down. Next up is 'The man comes around' by good old Johnny Cash.

They were making their way back to the stationhouse when the radio crackled and Lewis came on the line.

- Sir, I've just had a call from Mr Brayman over at the library. He's reporting strange movement in the forests by the library. You free to get over there?

- We're on it, tell him we're less than 5 minutes out.

Lewis hobbled to the bathroom, the pain dancing in jagged patterns up his lefthand side. He ran his wrists under cold water, feeling his heart slow, and the clarity return to his vision. Fuck, he knew he shouldn't be doing this but how else was he going to get through the night? He took the Percocet from the bottle in his pocket, and swallowed two, washing them down with tap water. He felt a wave of relief course through his body, the tension in his back release, and the pain in his side was turned down from a 9 to a 6. He drank more tap water and faced himself in the mirror, He stared into his dilated pupils, feeling the world soften, and his muscles become loose and pliable. After a few moments he walked back to the squad room, picked up the pile of reports on his desk, and fell into the large sofa. He could concentrate again. His body felt light, his mind relaxed. It was time to work.

Emily shook Lewis to make sure that he was asleep. He sat on the sofa, the pages of reports spread out around him. There was no reaction, he was completely out of it. She gave the signal to the others and they gathered up what they needed from the station house and snuck quietly out of the building. They piled into Emily's car and drove off, ploughing their way through the snow to the fallen house at the peak of Elm Hill.

The last light was falling as Emily drove steadily towards Elm Hill and Bobby stared out the window, watching the snow sweep past the car.

- You think we can actually do this?

She smiled to herself.

- I actually don't know. But I think we have to try.

Charlie was creeping around the old house, looking for her. He saw the light creep down the carpets, watched the snow accumulate on windowpanes, listened to the creaks and sighs, the breath of the house as it slept. She was here. Sleeping upstairs perhaps. He was about to leave and then...orange lights approached the house, the sounds of an engine ceasing.

When they stepped out of the car Bobby was not prepared for the scene that greeted them. There was a 6 foot bonfire standing in the driveway near the kitchen entrance. Rosanna smiled.

- A little of our work. We made sure to incorporate some of the broken wood from the door and walls. Fire and the house combined – how could it resist? Quick, help me brush some of the snow out of the way and let's get inside.

They worked quickly, clearing a path around the bonfire and the entrance to the house, and then Emily swept the remains of the kitchen door aside and they stepped inside. The quiet hallways echoed and enhanced every sound. Bobby felt uneasy returning to the house, the quiet had seeped in and taken over completely. In one night they had lost the fight, the slow steady accumulation of days spent wrestling back control, all lost on that one wild night when it arrived.

- Okay, you remember the plan. Bobby – help me with this and then get to your place in the study. Rosie, you're with me.

Charlie tried to focus, to stay in one place, but he couldn't. He saw tree branches, leaves cloying, whistling past him on either side, and heard the snapping of branches, like broken limbs snapped in two, and then he saw the low light so familiar to him, stretching out to the woods. It was approaching the library.

James Brayman turned off all of the lights except for the desklamp in the study. He could see something rustling in the trees. He'd been drifting in and out of sleep, dreaming about her. Their first date together. A picnic in the woods. The fresh green grass against the gingham fabric. Normally he didn't dream about her here, as if the world of his home and his work were separate, but tonight her ghost was with him, somewhere between the two worlds. They'd been sharing a punnet of strawberries when he'd become aware of the rustling in the trees behind them – and as he turned to look a guttural cry echoed through the night. He snapped awake and realised he was screaming - his throat was raw, his shirt covered in sweat. His heart raced and fell, raced and fell. He tried to stand and couldn't. The noise of rustling trees surrounded him and through the window he could see something dark moving against darkness.

Charlie felt it all. He ran through the woods, devouring creatures, panting and sweating, and rushing towards death in the twilit woods. He ran from the treeline towards the library.

He tried to stand but couldn't. Something was out there and although he wished it was her he couldn't be sure. The flickering flames of the candles appeared to flow sideways in unison. And he panicked. His breath wouldn't come. Had she returned? He watched the woods, wishing her to stumble out of the treeline, and walk towards him through the freshly fallen snow. But instead he saw something else; gnarled and terrible. He tried to scream but no sounds came out.

He'd called the sheriff. He'd be here but when? He ran his

hand down the side of the desk, stretching as far as his body would allow him to move. He fumbled, finding the interlocking wooden latch on the underside of the draw and rearranging the pieces. It was designed as an intricate wooden lock, like the puzzles popular in the last century. He had been reading through the old diaries and he thought he had a handle on it now, the pattern of pieces that needed to be manipulated. He just needed to focus and allow his fingers to move...He slid the final piece across and found the latch. A small compartment opened in the base of the draw and there it was; Teddy Ashenbrooke's antique colt revolver. He felt the cool metal in his hand.

Mike and Potemko arrived at the library, pulling up on the northern side of the building. As the motor died they could hear a shrieking from the forest and could just make out a figure breaking from the treeline towards the library. They both rushed from the vehicle and sprinted around the side of the building.

James Brayman sat at the large oak desk, the colt in his hand, as the bay window shattered into a thousand pieces. A woman leapt through the broken window, shards of glass embedded in her face and arms. She stared at him and howled a deep and broken cry. The stench was overpowering and dark matted blood covered her body, matted in her hair. James sat frozen. It wasn't her (was it her?). She grinned at him, revealing a half filled mouth of black and rotting teeth, drool rolling down her chin. He fired. The gun rang out smoke and fire in the room and the bullet shot straight through her chest and ricocheted off the window frame. She paused for one instant and then charged towards him.

Mike arrived at the destroyed window moments after the shot rang out. He saw it, just like before (was it the same?) a man weathered and strange. There was no time to think, he raised his gun and fired two shots into its back. It turned and stared at him, nothing but death in its swollen black pupils. It was the same and yet wasn't. He planted his feet and aimed. It moved swiftly, taking the desk in one deft motion, and throwing it towards him, knocking him to the floor. Mike felt his ankle snap as the weight of the desk fell on top of him and he watched as the gnarled figure lifted Mr Brayman from the floor and bit straight through the side of his neck. Mike watched in slow motion as blood sprayed across the room and James yelled out in agony as she bathed in his flowing maroon blood. The thing let the crumpled body fall to the floor. As Mike watched it turn and advance toward him he saw something, some colour, flicker across its eyes, something luminous and yellow, glimpsed and then gone. He managed to writhe free from the desk and stood up facing it. He aimed again. Let it come.

Something was being drawn to us through the woods, through the darkened trees, something intent on destroying us for good. It had no sense, no plan, it just fed, consumed what it could of fear and darkness, creating a void that it would fill, and rampage on. Emily and Rosanna finished drawing the pentagonal symbols in the kitchen. Bobby lit the candles and Emily began invoking the chant. The bonfire raged outside the house.

Potemko ran round the corner of the library and saw it again, running towards Mike, its jaw contorted, slather running down its sides. He had no time to think and so he just acted, running towards Mike, matching it for speed. He found something extra from somewhere and he leapt, tackling Mike to the ground. He hit him square in the middle, lifting him out of its path and depositing them both in a heap on the floor. It narrowly missed, barrelling straight past them, out of the destroyed window, and towards the woodland. It slowed and stopped, turning to stare at them, its dark empty pupils endless. And then it turned once more and ran back into the woods.

I am running and I am late. Leaves fly around me, tree branches. A door. A flame. Intent to return, to the start. I will stride to the door and tear it from its hinges. With a force of will Charlie left the snarling mind of the Wildman and flew across town, over hills and down tree lined streets. He was inside the police station. He took a deep breath (did he still breathe?) and stepped inside Lewis's mind. The vision confronted him, complete. Lewis wandered through the mill, the burnt ruins empty and uncared for. There were endless skeletons amongst the ruins and dull fire burned with a luminous blue chill. Charlie ran round and round, through the building, and finally found him standing in the burnt out building staring up at the stars. He seized Lewis and shook him. The stars became fireflies and swept down, bathing Lewis in a halo of light.

Lewis woke with a gasp, sitting up into the florescent flicker of the station house. His body ached, his mind raced, and he knew everything that was happening simultaneously. He rushed to the radio to contact Mike and Potemko.

The radio chattered on Potemko's hip. He rolled off Mike and they both lay on the floor of the study.

- Potemko? Mike? You hear me? It is on the way to Elm Hill, I repeat, it is on the way to Elm Hill.

- Okay. Fuck. Okay. You keep everyone at the station house. We'll follow it there.

- Mike?

- Yes?

- They're already there.

Bobby held the gun that Emily had given him, its cold metal in his palm, this unknown object in his hand. Emily was drawing something on the floor in red paint, a symbol of some sort with intricate lines of geometry. Emily paced, placing lines of salt at the doorways, something to buy them a little extra time.

Charlie was free, and moved swiftly through the house. Rosanna stood beside the cascading fire. Emily was sitting in the kitchen in a circle of red light. The runes glowed softly around her. The fire outside glowed with a blue green flame that whipped up restlessly in the night, melting the snowflakes as they fell. For the first time in a long time he was focussed, alert. He felt so much in the house and knew where to find them. He stepped through the door of his father's study and saw Bobby sitting there, and wished that he would stay out of the fight.

The flames licked high into the night, melting snowflakes as they fell all around it. Rosanna watched it running up the hillside towards the house straight towards the flame and recognised it as it came. She saw her brothers face after the accident. She saw a hundred faces of the town's dead brought back by it, willing and unwilling. She was suddenly frozen in place, unable to do anything but watch and breathe, as it reached the bonfire and stared at her with its cold black eyes. She saw the absence of time in its eyes, the shadows from tree branches rolling endlessly over the quiet graves of the dead.

The front door flew from its hinges and was torn from the face of the house. Emily saw it from her position in the kitchen. It stood at the end of the hallway, naked and tall in the night. Wind and snow gusted around it, lifting pictures from their places on the wall and smashing them carelessly against the floor.

Glass splintered and the wind howled. She acted fast, the chant moving swiftly from her lips. Charlie watched from the ceiling as the glyphs glowed in the darkness, forming a thread in the air. It moved, running towards Emily in the kitchen. It screamed and ran at her, straight across the earthen symbol painted on the floorboards. She leapt gracefully and it stepped directly into the red circle which glowed brightly around it. She chanted one word, *diadavam,* and the glyph glowed with an intense red light. The figure slowed and stopped, quieting in its confusion. Emily advanced chanting, soothing whatever madness lay inside it. Under the matted hair and dirt she could just make out one dark brown eye, which blinked at her.

Emily recited a prayer and raised the shotgun. The thing howled and moved with unnatural speed and grace, its hand taking hold of the shotgun's barrel and twisting it in the same instant that she pulled the trigger. The barrel exploded, shooting fragments of hot metal across the room, and into Emily's arm. The force of the blast knocked her to the floor and the creature howled, turned, and ran back down the hallway. The smell of burnt sage and gunpowder filled the house completely.

Bobby sat in the study listening to the hollow echoes of the stairs and the reverberating sound of gunfire in his ears. Charlie stood beside him, focusing all of his concentration to hold the study door closed. She'd done it for them before and he could do it now. They could both hear it panting on the other side.

Lewis saw the smoke from the fire swirling high into the night, pulled the car up next to the house, and got out. Rosanna was stood motionless beside the fire like a statue and giving up on speaking to her he rushed in through the open door. The smell of burnt blood and gunpowder was overpowering and he could see Emily, blackened and bleeding, trying to stand up.

- Where is he? Emily – where is he!?

- Upstairs...they're upstairs.

Bobby fired the pistol into the door, watching the wood splinter and listening to the howling from outside. The noise was intolerable, awful. Like chalk on chalkboards, like nails bent backwards, the kinds of sounds that made you instinctively writhe and judder. A hand came through the woodwork, tearing wood into splinters and dust. They sat, and watched as it tore the door to pieces. Bobby lowered the gun.

Lewis ran through the hallway to the stairs and saw it. It was raging at the door tearing through the woodwork. He raised his pistol and unloaded the clip into the monstrous form at the top of the staircase. It screamed and tore the door from its hinges, throwing it down the stairs. The door cartwheeled down the stairs, spraying wood and dust into the air. Lewis turned swiftly as the door hit him in the back, knocking him to the ground.

It turned to face the study, searching for them in the room. It walked in, more hesitant than usual, taking in the surroundings, advancing slowly on them both. Bobby moved fast, throwing a container of blessed water into its face. The water burned and rose as steam, the creature howled, and lifted Bobby from the floor, turning to look directly at him, and throwing him against the wall. The gun fell to the floor.

Charlie focused all his will and opened the desk drawer. The figure turned towards him, drawn to the desk. Charlie forced it to focus on him, to ignore Bobby. And he saw Emily on the stairs behind it. He focussed everything he had, put his hand into the draw, and crushed the cigar, its aroma filling the room, a stale time capsule. The thing hesitated for a second. Charlie summoned all of his strength and kicked the fallen pistol across the floor towards her.

Emily saw him, standing there (slumped in his armchair), ligaments and blood strewn from his body, a look of emptiness. He was here for them, as he always had been. Never far from her heart. Sitting, resting in his books, in his poems, his heart continued but it poisoned her. Not the real him but the ghost of him. This figure that stalked his bones like a wraith, this something that was left in the dust of his wake, this shadow of him that still was trapped here, whilst the best part of him was gone. But she was faster than him because she wasn't dead yet. He turned slowly towards her as she swept the pistol up from the floor and fired straight into his chest. The bullets pierced his black heart like a stake. The force left his body and all that was left was a crumpled form where something once was.

*

They sat outside the house together, each watching the dirty black smoke rising high into the night sky. The clouds had cleared and the snow had stopped falling as the first stars came out in the sky. Emily watched the ashes rise and fall as something which had begun in flames had now returned to them and was simply transforming back into the dullness of soot. In time the blue and red lights arrived to take them all away and the fire died down. The house was still again and in a quiet room at the top of the house, a pale nightgown swayed in the breeze of an open window.

EPILOGUE: FROM EACH AND EVERY BRANCH A FRESH BUD BREAKS

The morning had arrived in order and the rhythm could be observed. There was time for percolating, for music, and papers, and when Mike arrived at the station house he already sensed that things were all as they should be. Carter signed good morning to him and he signed back; touching the fingers of his right hand to his left palm, crossing his left arm, and then raising his right. Potemko sat next to her, drawing what appeared to be Garfield cartoons on a sketch pad. Lewis gathered his things and prepared to head out on his first solo patrol since his return. In the three months since that final night his recovery had come along considerably; there was just a slight stiffness to his gait now, a certain asymmetry when he walked.

Bobby sat in the backyard, watching the new blossoms bloom on the trees. The snow had finally thawed and there was a whisper of spring on the breeze. The soft sunlight caressed the branches of the trees and threw a soft warm light on the patchwork quilt of the garden. He nodded to the trees, and then stepped inside. They had accumulated a rather large bookcase in the lounge, and he now found paperbacks tucked in the armrests of chairs. He sat down at the kitchen table and watched as Emily prepared a fresh pot of tea. Charlie came down to join them and they sat eating breakfast in the warm yellow light of the morning. The repairs to the house were going well. Mike would be over that evening to help with the final bannisters on the staircase, and they continued to repair the damage to the walls. The house had begun to take on a new life, the fresh scent of paint mixing with the blossom outside and instilling a sense of peace and hope. Charlie stepped from the house, closed the front door, and made his way down the hill towards the library at a steady pace. The long drawn out chimes of the clock tower boomed out, echoing off the tops of tall buildings. Nine long chimes. It was nine in the morning.

ABOUT THE AUTHOR

Robin Styles

Robin lives in Leeds with his wife and daughter. He teaches modern literature and in the indeterminate hours between midnight and three he drinks coffee and writes fiction in his kitchen. His prose and poetry have appeared in 'Paper Nautilus' and 'The New Luciad.'

To keep in touch, and find out about future projects, you can contact him here:
Twitter @StylesRobin
Email stylesrobin@yahoo.co.uk.

Printed in Great Britain
by Amazon

25108284R00138